The Fifth Queen by Ford Madox Ford

Part One of The Fifth Queen trilogy

Ford Madox Ford was born Ford Hermann Hueffer on 17th December 1873 in Wimbledon, London, England.

Today he is best known for one book, 'The Good Soldier', which is regularly held to be one of the 100 greatest novels of all time. But, rather unfairly, the breadth of his career has been overshadowed. He wrote novels as well as essays, poetry, memoirs and literary criticism. Today he is well-regarded but known only for a few works rather than the grand arc of his career.

Ford collaborated with Joseph Conrad on three novels but would later complain that, as with all his collaborators, and those he so readily championed, his contribution was overshadowed by theirs.

He founded The English Review and The Transatlantic Review which were instrumental in publishing and promoting the works of so many authors and movements.

During WWI he initially worked on propaganda books before enlisting. Ford was invalided back to Britain in 1917, remaining in the army and giving lectures until the War's end. After a spell recuperating in the Sussex countryside he lived mostly in France during the 1920s.

He published the series of four novels known as Parade's End, between 1924 and 1928. These were particularly well-received in America, where Ford spent much of his time from the later 1920s to his death in 1939.

His last years were spent teaching at Olivet College in Olivet, Michigan.

Ford Madox Ford died on 26th June 1939 at Deauville, France at the age of 65.

Index of Contents

PART ONE

THE COMING

I

Magister Nicholas Udal, the Lady Mary's pedagogue, was very hungry and very cold. He stood undecided in the mud of a lane in the Austin Friars. The quickset hedges on either side were only waist high and did not shelter him. The little houses all round him of white daub with grey corner beams had been part of the old friars' stables and offices. All that neighbourhood was a maze of dwellings and gardens, with the hedges dry, the orchard trees bare with frost, the arbours wintry and deserted. This congregation of small cottages was like a patch of common that squatters had taken; the great house of the Lord Privy Seal, who had pulled down the monastery to make room for it, was a central mass. Its gilded vanes were in the shape of men at arms, and tore the ragged clouds with the banners on their lances. Nicholas Udal looked at the roof and cursed the porter of it.

'He could have given me a cup of hypocras,' he said, and muttered, as a man to whom Latin is more familiar than the vulgar tongue, a hexameter about 'pocula plena.'

He had reached London before nine in one of the King's barges that came from Greenwich to take musicians back that night at four. He had breakfasted with the Lady Mary's women at six off warm small beer and fresh meat, but it was eleven already, and he had spent all his money upon good letters.

He muttered: 'Pauper sum, pateor, fateor, quod Di dant fero,' but it did not warm him.

The magister had been put in the Lady Mary's household by the Lord Privy Seal, and he had a piece of news as to the Lady's means of treasonable correspondence with the Emperor her uncle. He had imagined that the news—which would hurt no one because it was imaginary—might be worth some crowns to him. But the Lord Privy Seal and all his secretaries had gone to Greenwich before it was light, and there was nothing there for the magister.

'You might have known as much, a learned man,' the porter had snarled at him. 'Isn't the new Queen at Rochester? Would our lord bide here? Didn't your magistership pass his barge on the river?'

'Nay, it was still dark,' the magister answered. The porter sniffed and slammed to the grating in the wicket. Being of the Old Faith he hated those Lutherans—or those men of the New Learning—that it pleased his master to employ.

Udal hesitated before the closed door; he hesitated in the lane beyond the corner of the house. Perhaps there would be no barges at the steps—no King's barges. The men of the Earl Marshal's service, being Papists, would pelt him with mud if he asked for a passage; even the Protestant lords' men would jeer at him if he had no pence for them—and he had none. He would do best to wait for the musicians' barge at four.

Then he must eat and shelter—and find a wench. He stood in the mud: long, thin, brown in his doctor's gown of fur, with his black flapped cap that buttoned well under his chin and let out his brown, lean, shaven and humorous face like a woodpecker's peering out of a hole in a tree.

The volumes beneath his arms were heavy: they poked out his gown on each side, and the bitter cold pinched his finger ends as if they had been caught in a door. The weight of the books pleased him for there was much good letters there—a book of Tully's epistles for himself and two volumes of Plautus' comedies for the Lady Mary. But what among his day's purchases pleased him most was a medallion in silver he had bought in Cheapside. It showed on the one side Cupid in his sleep and on the other Venus fondling a peacock. It was a heart-compelling gift to any wench or lady of degree.

He puckered up his deprecatory and comical lips as he imagined that that medal would purchase him the right to sigh dolorously in front of whatever stomacher it finally adorned. He could pour out odes in the learned tongue, for the space of a week, a day, or an afternoon according to the rank, the kindness or the patience of the recipient.

Something invisible and harsh touched his cheek. It might have been snow or hail. He turned his thin cunning face to the clouds, and they threatened a downpour. They raced along, like scarves of vapour, so low that you might have thought of touching them if you stood on tiptoe.

If he went to Westminster Hall to find Judge Combers, he would get his belly well filled, but his back wet to the bone. At the corner of the next hedge was the wicket gate of old Master Grocer Badge. There the magister would find at least a piece of bread, some salt and warmed mead. Judge Combers' wife was easy and bounteous: but old John Badge's daughter was a fair and dainty morsel.

He licked his full lips, leered to one side, muttered, 'A curse on all lords' porters,' and made for John Badge's wicket. Badge's dwelling had been part of the monastery's curing house. It had some good rooms and two low storeys—but the tall garden wall of the Lord Privy Seal had been built against its side windows. It had been done without word or warning. Suddenly workmen had pulled down old Badge's pigeon house, set it up twenty yards further in, marked out a line and set up this high wall that pressed so hard against the house end that there was barely room for a man to squeeze between. The wall ran for half a mile, and had swallowed the ground of twenty small householders. But never a word of complaint had reached the ears of the Privy Seal other than through his spies. It was, however, old Badge's ceaseless grief. He had talked of it without interlude for two years.

The Badges' room—their houseplace—was fair sized, but so low ceiled that it appeared long, dark and mysterious in the winter light There was a tall press of dark wood with a face minutely carved and fretted to represent the portal of Amiens Cathedral, and a long black table, littered with large sheets of printed matter in heavy black type, that diffused into the cold room a faint smell of ink. The old man sat quavering in the ingle. The light of the low fire glimmered on his silver hair, on his black square cap two generations old; and, in his old eyes that had seen three generations of changes, it twinkled starrily as if they were spinning round. In the cock forward of his shaven chin, and the settling down of his head into his shoulders, there was a suggestion of sinister and sardonic malice. He was muttering at his son:

'A stiff neck that knows no bending, God shall break one day.'

His son, square, dark, with his sleeves rolled up showing immense muscles developed at the levers of his presses, bent his black beard and frowned his heavy brows above his printings.

'Doubtless God shall break His engine when its work is done,' he muttered.

'You call Privy Seal God's engine?' the old man quavered ironically. 'Thomas Cromwell is a brewer's drunken son. I know them that have seen him in the stocks at Putney not thirty years ago.'

The printer set two proofs side by side on the table and frowningly compared them, shaking his head.

'He is the flail of the monks,' he said abstractedly. 'They would have burned me and thousands more but for him.'

'Aye, and he has put up a fine wall where my arbour stood.'

The printer took a chalk from behind his ear and made a score down his page.

'A wall,' he muttered; 'my Lord Privy Seal hath set up a wall against priestcraft all round these kingdoms—'

'Therefore you would have him welcome to forty feet of my garden?' the old man drawled. 'He pulls down other folks' crucifixes and sets up his own walls with other folks' blood for mortar.'

The printer said darkly:

'Papists' blood.'

The old man pulled his nose and glanced down.

'We were all Papists in my day. I have made the pilgrimage to Compostella, for all you mock me now.'

He turned his head to see Magister Udal entering the door furtively and with eyes that leered round the room. Both the Badges fell into sudden, and as if guilty, silence.

'Domus parva, quies magna,' the magister tittered, and swept across the rushes in his furs to rub his hands before the fire. 'When shall I teach your Margot the learned tongues?'

'When the sun sets in the East,' the printer muttered.

Udal sent to him over his shoulder, as words of consolation:

'The new Queen is come to Rochester.'

The printer heaved an immense sigh:

'God be praised!'

Udal snickered, still over his shoulder:

'You see, neither have the men of the Old Faith put venom in her food, nor have the Emperor's galleys taken her between Calais and Sandwich.'

'Yet she comes ten days late.'

'Oh moody and suspicious artificer. Afflavit deus! The wind hath blown dead against Calais shore this ten days.'

The old man pulled his long white nose:

'In my day we could pray to St Leonard for a fair wind.'

He was too old to care whether the magister reported his words to Thomas Cromwell, the terrible Lord Privy Seal, and too sardonic to keep silence for long about the inferiority of his present day.

'When shall I teach the fair Margot the learned tongue?' Udal asked again.

'When wolves teach conies how to play on pipes,' the master printer snarled from his chest.

'The Lord Privy Seal never stood higher,' Udal said. 'The match with the Cleves Lady hath gained him great honour.'

'God cement it!' the printer said fervently.

The old man pulled at his nose and gazed at nothing.

'I am tired with this chatter of the woman from Cleves,' he croaked, like a malevolent raven. 'An Anne she is, and a Lutheran. I mind we had an Anne and a Lutheran for Queen before. She played the whore and lost her head.'

'Where's your niece Margot?' Udal asked the printer.

'You owe me nine crowns,' the old man said.

'I will give your Margot ten crowns' worth of lessons in Latin.'

'Hold and enough,' the printer muttered heavily. 'Tags from Seneca in a wench's mouth are rose garlands on a cow's horns.'

'The best ladies in the land learn of me,' Udal answered.

'Aye, but my niece shall keep her virtue intact.'

'You defame the Lady Mary of England,' Udal snickered.

The old man said vigorously, 'God save her highness, and send us her for Queen. Have you begged her to get me redress in the matter of that wall?'

'Why, Providence was kind to her when it sent her me for her master,' Udal said. 'I never had apter pupil saving only one.'

'Shall Thomas Cromwell redress?' the old man asked.

'If good learning can make a good queen, trust me to render her one,' Udal avoided the question. 'But alas! being declared bastard—for very excellent reasons—she may not—'

'You owe me nine crowns,' old Badge threatened him. He picked irritably at the fur on his gown and gazed at the carved leg of the table. 'If you will not induce Privy Seal to pull down his wall I will set the tipstaves on you.'

Master Udal laughed. 'I will give thy daughter ten crowns' worth of lessons in the learned tongues.'

'You will receive another broken crown, magister,' the younger John said moodily. 'Have you not scars enow by your wenching?'

Udal pushed back the furs at his collar. 'Master Printer John Badge the Younger,' he flickered, 'if you break my crown I will break your chapel. You shall never have license to print another libel. Give me your niece in wedlock?'

The old man said querulously, 'Here's a wantipole without ten crowns would marry a wench with three beds and seven hundred florins!'

Udal laughed. 'Call her to bring me meat and drink,' he said. 'Large words ill fill an empty stomach.'

The younger John went negligently to the great Flemish press. He opened the face and revealed on its dark shelves a patty of cold fish and a black jack. With heavy movements and a solemn face he moved these things, with a knife and napkins, on to the broad black table.

The old man pulled his nose again and grinned.

'Margot's in her chamber,' he chuckled. 'As you came up the wicket way I sent my John to turn the key upon her. It's there at his girdle.' It clinked indeed among rules, T-squares and callipers at each footstep of the heavy printer between press and table.

Magister Udal stretched his thin hands towards it. 'I will give you the printing of the Lady Mary's commentary of Plautus for that key,' he said.

The printer murmured 'Eat,' and set a great pewter salt-cellar, carved like a Flemish pikeman, a foot high, heavily upon the cloth.

Udal had the appetite of a wolf. He pulled off his cap the better to let his jaws work.

'Here's a letter from the Doctor Wernken of Augsburg,' he said. 'You may see how the Lutherans fare in Germany.'

The printer took the letter and read it, standing, frowning and heavy. Magister Udal ate; the old man fingered his furs and, leaning far back in his mended chair, gazed at nothing.

'Let me have the maid in wedlock,' Udal grunted between two bites. 'Better women have looked favourably upon me. I had a pupil in the North—'

'She was a Howard, and the Howards are all whores,' the printer said, over the letter. 'Your Doctor Wernken writes like an Anabaptist.'

'They are even as the rest of womenkind,' Udal laughed, 'but far quicker with their learning.'

A boy rising twenty, in a grey cloak that showed only his bright red stockings and broad-toed red shoes, rattled the back door and slammed it to. He pulled off his cap and shook it.

'It snows,' he said buoyantly, and then knelt before his grandfather. The old man touched his grandson's cropped fair head.

'Benedicite, grandson Hal Poins,' he muttered, and relapsed into his gaze at the fire.

The young man bent his knee to his uncle and bowed low to the magister. Being about the court, he had for Udal's learning and office a reverence that neither the printer nor his grandfather could share. He unfastened his grey cloak at the neck and cast it into a corner after his hat. His figure flashed out, lithe, young, a blaze of scarlet with a crowned rose embroidered upon a chest rendered enormous by much wadding. He was serving his apprenticeship as ensign in the gentlemen of the King's guard, and because his dead father had been beloved by the Duke of Norfolk it was said that his full ensigncy was near. He begged his grandfather's leave to come near the fire, and stood with his legs apart.

'The new Queen's come to Rochester,' he said; 'I am here with the guard to take the heralds to Greenwich Palace.'

The printer looked at him unfavourably from the corner of his dark and gloomy eyes.

'You come to suck up more money,' he said moodily. 'There is none in this house.'

'As Mary is my protectress!' the boy laughed, 'there is!' He stuck his hands into his breeches pocket and pulled out a big fistful of crowns that he had won over-night at dice, and a long and thin Flemish chain of gold. 'I have enow to last me till the thaw,' he said. 'I came to beg my grandfather's blessing on the first day of the year.'

'Dicing...Wenching...' the printer muttered.

'If I ask thee for no blessing,' the young man said, 'it's because, uncle, thou'rt a Lutheran that can convey none. Where's Margot? This chain's for her.'

'The fair Margot's locked in her chamber,' Udal snickered.

'Why-som-ever then? Hath she stolen a tart?'

'Nay, but I would have her in wedlock.'

'Thou—you—your magistership?' the boy laughed incredulously. The printer caught in his tone his courtier's contempt for the artificer's home, and his courtier's reverence for the magister's learning.

'Keep thy sister from beneath this fox's tooth,' he said. 'The likes of him mate not with the like of us.'

'The like of thee, uncle?' the boy retorted, with a good-humoured insolence. 'My father was a gentleman.'

'Who married my sister for her small money, and died leaving thee and thy sister to starve.'

'Nay, I starve not,' the boy said. 'And Margot's a plump faggot.'

'A very Cynthia among willow-trees,' the magister said.

'Why, your magistership shall have her,' the boy said. 'I am her lawful guardian.'

His grandfather laughed as men laugh to see a colt kick up its heels in a meadow.

But the printer waved his bare arm furiously at the magister.

'Get thee gone out of this decent house.' His eyes rolled, and his clenched fist was as large as a ham. 'Here you come not a-wenching.'

'Moody man,' the magister said, 'your brains are addled with suspicions.'

The young man swelled his scarlet breast still more consequentially. 'This is no house of thine, uncle, but my grandfar's.'

'Young ass's colt!' the printer fulminated. 'Would'st have thy sister undone by this Latin mouth-mincer?'

Udal grinned at him, and licked his lips. The printer snarled:

'Know'st thou not, young ass, that this man was thrown out of his mastership at Eton for his foul living?'

Udal was suddenly on his feet with the long pasty-knife held back among the furs of his gown.

'Ignoble...' he began, but he lost his words in his trembling rage. The printer snatched at his long measuring stick.

'Down knife,' he grunted, for his fury, too, made his throat catch.

'Have a care, nunkey,' the young man laughed at the pair of them. 'They teach knife-thrusts in his Italian books.'

'I will have thy printer's licence revoked, ignoble man,' the magister said, grinning hideously. 'Thou, a Lutheran, to turn upon me who was undone by Papist lies! They said I lived foully; they said I stole the silver cellars...'

He turned upon the old man, stretching out the hand that held the knife in a passionate gesture:

'Your Papists said that,' he appealed. 'But not a one of them believed it, though you dub me Lutheran...See you, do I not govern now the chief Papist of you all? Would that be if they believed me filthy in my living. Have I not governed in the house of the Howards, the lord of it being absent? Would that have been if they had believed it of me?...And then...' He turned again upon the printer. 'For the sake of your men...for the sake of the New Learning, which God prosper, I was cast down.'

The printer grunted surlily:

"Tis known no wench is safe from thy amorousness. How many husbands have broken thy pate?'

The magister threw the knife on to the table and rose, frostily rustling in his gown.

'I shall bring thee down, ignoble man,' he said.

'If thou hast the power to do that,' the old man asked suddenly, 'wherefore canst not get me redress in the matter of my wall?'

The magister answered angrily:

'Privy Seal hath swallowed thy land: he shall not disgorge. But this man he shall swallow. Know you not that you may make a jack swallow, but no man shall make him give back; I, nor thou, nor the devil's self?'

'Oh, a God's name bring not Flail Crummock into this household,' the young man cut in. 'Would you undo us all?'

'Ignoble, ignoble, to twit a man with that Eton villainy,' the magister answered.

'A God's name bring not Privy Seal into the quarrel,' the young man repeated. 'None of us of the Old Faith believe that lie.'

'Keep thy tongue off Cromwell's name, young fool,' his grandfather said. 'We know not what walls have ears.'

The young man went pale: the printer himself went pale, remembering suddenly that the magister was a spy of Cromwell's; all three of them had their eyes upon Udal; only the old man, with his carelessness of his great age, grinned with curiosity as if the matter were a play that did not concern him. The magister was making for the door with the books beneath his arm and a torturing smile round his lips. The boy, with a deep oath, ran out after him, a scarlet flash in the darkening room.

Old Badge pulled at his nose and grinned maliciously at the fire beside him.

'That is thy deliverer: that is thy flail of the monks,' he croaked at his son. The printer gazed moodily at the fire.

'Nay, it is but one of his servants,' he answered mechanically.

'And such servants go up and down this realm of England and ride us with iron bridles.' The old man laughed dryly and bitterly. 'His servant? See how we are held—we dare not shut our doors upon him since he is Cromwell's servant, yet if he come in he shall ruin us, take our money that we dare not refuse, deflower our virgins...What then is left to us between this setter up of walls and his servants?'

The printer, fingering the T-square in his belt, said, slowly, 'I think this man loves too well that books should be printed in the Latin tongue to ruin any printer of them upon a private quarrel. Else I would get me across the seas.'

'He loves any wench much better,' the old man answered maliciously. 'Hearken!'

Through the wall there came a scuffling sound, thumps, and the noise of things falling. The wall there touched on the one that Cromwell had set up, so that there was bare room for a man to creep between.

'Body of God,' the printer said, 'is he eavesdropping now?'

'Nay, this is courtship,' the old man answered. His head leaned forward with a birdlike intentness; he listened with one hand held out as if to still any sound in the room. They heard footsteps from the floor above, a laugh and voices. 'Now Margot talks to him from her window.'

The printer had a motion of convulsed rage:

'I will break that knave's spine across my knee.'

'Nay, let be,' the old man said. 'I command thee, who am thy father, to let the matter be.'

'Would you have him...' the printer began with a snarl.

'I would not have my house burnt down because this Cromwell's spy's body should be found upon our hands...To-morrow the wench shall be sent to her aunt Wardle in Bedfordshire—aye, and she shall be soundly beaten to teach her to love virtue.'

The young man opened the house door and came in, shivering in his scarlet because he had run out without his cloak.

'A pretty medley you have made,' he said to his uncle, 'but I have calmed him. Wherefore should not this magister marry Margot?' He made again for the fire. 'Are we to smell always of ink?' He looked disdainfully at his uncle's proofs, and began to speak with a boy's seriousness and ingenuous confidence. They would tell his uncle at Court that if good print be the body of a book, good learning is even the soul of it. At Court he would learn that it is thought this magister shall rise high. There good learning is much prized. Their Lord the King had been seen to talk and laugh with this magister. 'For our gracious lord loveth good letters. He is in such matters skilled beyond all others in the realm.'

The old man listened to his grandson, smiling maliciously and with pride; the printer shrugged his shoulders bitterly; the muffled sounds and the voices through the house-end continued, and the boy talked on, laying down the law valiantly and with a cheerful voice...He would gain advancement at Court through his sister's marriage with the magister.

Going back to the palace at Greenwich along with the magister, in the barge that was taking the heralds to the King's marriage with Anne of Cleves, the young Poins was importunate with Udal to advance him in his knowledge of the Italian tongue. He thought that in the books of the Sieur Macchiavelli upon armies and the bearing of arms there were unfolded many secret passes with the rapier and the stiletto. But Udal laughed good-humouredly. He had, he said, little skill in the Italian tongue, for it was but a bastard of classical begettings. And for instruction in the books of the Sieur Macchiavelli, let young Poins go to a man who had studied them word by word—to the Lord Privy Seal, Thomas Cromwell.

They both dropped their voices at the name, and, another gentleman of the guard beginning to talk of rich men who had fallen low by the block, the stake, and gaming, Udal mentioned that that day he had seen a strange sight.

'There was in the Northern parts, where I governed in his absence the Lord Edmund Howard's children, a certain Thomas Culpepper. Main rich he was, with many pastures and many thousands of sheep. A cousin of my lady's he was, for ever roaring about the house. A swaggerer he was, that down there went more richly dressed than earls here.'

That day Udal had seen this Culpepper alone, without any servants, dressed in uncostly green, and dragging at the bridle of a mule, on which sat a doxy dressed in ancient and ragged furs. So did men fall in these difficult days.

'How came he in London town?' the Norroy King-at-Arms asked.

'Nay, I stayed not to ask him,' Udal answered. He sighed a little. 'Yet then, in my Lord Edmund's house I had my best pupil of all, and fain was I to have news of her...But he was a braggart; I liked him not, and would not stay to speak with him.'

'I'll warrant you had dealings with some wench he favoured, and you feared a drubbing, magister,' Norroy accused him.

The long cabin of the state barge was ablaze with the scarlet and black of the guards, and with the gold and scarlet of the heralds. Magister Udal sighed.

'You had good, easy days in Lord Edmund's house?' Norroy asked.

II

The Lord Privy Seal was beneath a tall cresset in the stern of his barge, looking across the night and the winter river. They were rowing from Rochester to the palace at Greenwich, where the Court was awaiting Anne of Cleves. The flare of the King's barge a quarter of a mile ahead moved in a glowing patch of lights and their reflections, as though it were some portent creeping in a blaze across the sky. There was nothing else visible in the world but the darkness and a dusky tinge of red where a wave caught the flare of light further out.

He stood invisible behind the lights of his cabin; and the thud of oars, the voluble noises of the water, and the crackling of the cresset overhead had, too, the quality of impersonal and supernatural phenomena. His voice said harshly:

'It is very cold; bring me my greatest cloak.'

Throckmorton, the one of Cromwell's seven hundred spies who at that time was his most constant companion, was hidden in the deep shadow beside the cabin-door. His bearded and heavy form obscured the light for a moment as he hurried to fetch the cloak. But merely to be the Lord Cromwell's gown-bearer was in those days a thing you would run after; and an old man in a flat cap—the Chancellor of the Augmentations, who had been listening intently at the door—was already hurrying out with a heavy cloak of fur. Cromwell let it be hung about his shoulders.

The Chancellor shivered and said, 'We should be within a quarter-hour of Greenwich.'

'Get you in if you be cold,' Cromwell answered. But the Chancellor was quivering with the desire to talk to his master. He had seen the heavy King rush stumbling down the stairs of the Cleves woman's lodging at Rochester, and the sight had been for him terrible and prodigious. It was Cromwell who had made him Chancellor of the Augmentations—who had even invented the office to deal with the land taken from the Abbeys—and he was so much the creature of this Lord Privy Seal that it seemed as if the earth was shivering all the while for the fall of this minister, and that he himself was within an inch of the ruin, execration, and death that would come for them all once Cromwell were down.

Throckmorton, a giant man with an immense golden beard, issued again from the cabin, and the Privy Seal's voice came leisurely and cold:

'What said Lord Cassilis of this? And the fellow Knighton? I saw them at the stairs.'

Privy Seal had such eyes that it was delicate work lying to him. But Throckmorton brought out heavily:

'Cassilis, that this Lady Anne should never be Queen.'

'Aye, but she must,' the Chancellor bleated. He had been bribed by two of the Cleves lords to get them lands in Kent when the Queen should be in power. Cromwell's silence made Throckmorton continue against his will:

'Knighton, that the Queen's breath should turn the King's stomach against you! Dr. Miley, the Lutheran preacher, that by this evening's work the Kingdom of God on earth was set trembling, the King having the nature of a lecher...'

He tried to hold back. After all, it came into his mind, this man was nearly down. Any one of the men upon whom he now spied might come to be his master very soon. But Cromwell's voice said, 'And then?' and he made up his mind to implicate none but the Scotch lord, who was at once harmless and unliable to be harmed.

'Lord Cassilis,' he brought out, 'said again that your lordship's head should fall ere January goes out.'

He seemed to feel the great man's sneer through the darkness, and was coldly angry with himself for having invented no better lie. For if this invisible and threatening phantom that hid itself among these shadows outlasted January he might yet outlast some of them. He wondered which of Cromwell's innumerable ill-wishers it might best serve him to serve. But for the Chancellor of the Augmentations the heavy silence of calamity, like the waiting at a bedside for death to come, seemed to fall upon them. He imagined that the Privy Seal hid himself in that shadow in order to conceal a pale face and shaking knees. But Cromwell's voice came harsh and peremptory to Throckmorton:

'What men be abroad at this night season? Ask my helmsmen.'

Two torchlights, far away to the right, wavered shaking trails in the water that, thus revealed, shewed agitated and chopped by small waves. The Chancellor's white beard shook with the cold, with fear of Cromwell, and with curiosity to know how the man looked and felt. He ventured at last in a faint and bleating voice:

What did his lordship think of this matter? Surely the King should espouse this lady and the Lutheran cause.

Cromwell answered with inscrutable arrogance:

'Why, your cause is valuable. But this is a great matter. Get you in if you be cold.'

Throckmorton appeared noiselessly at his elbow, whilst the Chancellor was mumbling: 'God forbid I should be called Lutheran.'

The torches, Throckmorton said, were those of fishers who caught eels off the mud with worms upon needles.

'Such night work favours treason,' Cromwell muttered. 'Write in my notebook, "The Council to prohibit the fishing of eels by night."'

'What a nose he hath for treasons,' the Chancellor whispered to Throckmorton as they rustled together into the cabin. Throckmorton's face was gloomy and pensive. The Privy Seal had chosen none of his informations for noting down. Assuredly the time was near for him to find another master.

The barge swung round a reach, and the lights of the palace of Greenwich were like a flight of dim or bright squares in mid air, far ahead. The King's barge was already illuminating the crenellated arch at the top of the river steps. A burst of torches flared out to meet it and disappeared. The Court was then at Greenwich, nearly all the lords, the bishops and the several councils lying in the Palace to await the coming of Anne of Cleves on the morrow. She had reached Rochester that evening after some days' delay at Calais, for the winter seas. The King had gone that night to inspect her, having been given to believe that she was soberly fair and of bountiful charms. His courteous visit had been in secret and in disguise; therefore there were no torchmen in the gardens, and darkness lay between the river steps and the great central gateway. But a bonfire, erected by the guards to warm themselves in the courtyard, as it leapt up or subsided before the wind, shewed that tall tower pale and high or vanishing into the night with its carved stone garlands, its stone men at arms, its lions, roses, leopards, and naked boys. The living houses ran away from the foot of the tower, till the wings, coming towards the river, vanished continually into shadows. They were low by comparison, gabled with false fronts over each set of rooms and, in the glass of their small-paned windows, the reflection of the fire gleamed capriciously from unexpected shadows. This palace was called Placentia by the King because it was pleasant to live in.

Cromwell mounted the steps with a slow gait and an arrogant figure. Under the river arch eight of his gentlemen waited upon him, and in the garden the torches of his men shewed black yew trees cut like peacocks, clipped hedges like walls with archways above the broad and tiled paths, and fountains that gleamed and trickled as if secretly in the heavy and bitter night.

A corridor ran from under the great tower right round the palace. It was full of hurrying people and of grooms who stood in knots beside doorways. They flattened themselves against the walls before the Lord Privy Seal's procession of gentlemen in black with white staves, and the ceilings seemed to send down moulded and gilded stalactites to touch his head. The beefeater before the door of the Lady Mary's lodgings spat upon the ground when he had passed. His hard glance travelled along the wall like a palpable ray, about the height of a man's head. It passed over faces and slipped back to the gilded wainscoting; tiring-women upon whom it fell shivered, and the serving men felt their bowels turn within them. His round face was hard and alert, and his lips moved ceaselessly one upon another. All those serving people wondered to see his head so high, for already it was known that the King had turned sick at the sight of his bedfellow that should be. And indeed the palace was only awake at that late hour because of that astounding news, dignitaries lingering in each other's quarters to talk of it, whilst in the passages their waiting men supplied gross commentaries.

He entered his door. In the ante-room two men in his livery removed his outer furs deftly so as not to hinder his walk. Before the fire of his large room a fair boy knelt to pull off his jewelled gloves, and Hanson, one of his secretaries, unclasped from his girdle the corded bag that held the Privy Seal. He laid it on a high stand between two tall candles of wax upon the long table.

The boy went with the gloves and Hanson disappeared silently behind the dark tapestry in the further corner. Cromwell was meditating above a fragment of flaming wood that the fire had spat out far into the tiled fore-hearth. He pressed it with his foot gently towards the blaze of wood in the chimney.

His plump hands were behind his back, his long upper lip ceaselessly caressed its fellow, moving as one line of a snake's coil glides above another. The January wind crept round the shadowy room behind the tapestry, and as it quivered stags seemed to leap over bushes, hounds to spring in pursuit, and a crowned Diana to move her arms, taking an arrow from a quiver behind her shoulder. The tall candles guarded the bag of the Privy Seal, they fluttered and made the gilded heads on the rafters have sudden grins on their faces that represented kings with flowered crowns, queens with their hair combed back on to pillows, and pages with scolloped hats. Cromwell stepped to an aumbry, where there were a glass of wine, a manchet of bread, and a little salt. He began to eat, dipping pieces of bread into the golden salt-cellar. The face of a queen looked down just above his head with her eyes wide open as if she were amazed, thrusting her head from a cloud.

'Why, I have outlived three queens,' he said to himself, and his round face resignedly despised his world and his times. He had forgotten what anxiety felt like because the world was so peopled with blunderers and timid fools full of hatred.

The marriage with Cleves was the deathblow to the power of the Empire. With the Protestant Princes armed behind his back, the imbecile called Charles would never dare to set his troops on board ship in Flanders to aid the continual rebellions, conspiracies and risings in England. He had done it too often, and he had repented as often, at the last moment. It was true that the marriage had thrown Charles into the arms of France: the French King and he were at that very minute supping together in Paris. They would be making treaties that were meant to be broken, and their statesmen were hatching plots that any scullion would reveal. Francis and his men were too mean, too silly, too despicable, and too easily bribed to hold to any union or to carry out any policy...

He sipped his wine slowly. It was a little cold, so he set it down beside the fire. He wanted to go to bed, but the Archbishop was coming to hear how Henry had received his Queen, and to pour out his fears.

Fears! Because the King had been sick at sight of the Cleves woman! He had this King very absolutely in his power; the grey, failing but vindictive and obstinate mass known as Henry was afraid of his contempt, afraid really of a shrug of the shoulder or a small sniff.

With the generosity of his wine and the warmth of his fire, his thoughts went many years ahead. He imagined the King either married to or having repudiated the Lady from Cleves, and then dead. Edward, the Seymour child, was his creature, and would be king or dead. Cleves children would be his creations too. Or if he married the Lady Mary he would still be next the throne.

His mind rested luxuriously and tranquilly on that prospect. He would be perpetually beside the throne, there would be no distraction to maintain a foothold. He would be there by right; he would be able to give all his mind to the directing of this world that he despised for its baseness, its jealousies, its insane brawls, its aimless selfishness, and its blind furies. Then there should be no more war, as there should be no more revolts. There should be no more jealousies; for kingcraft, solid, austere, practical and inspired, should keep down all the peoples, all the priests, and all the nobles of the world. 'Ah,' he thought, 'there would be in France no power to shelter traitors like Brancetor.' His eyes became softer in the contemplation of this Utopia, and he moved his upper lip more slowly.

Now the Archbishop was there. Pale, worn with fears and agitation, he came to say that the King had called to him Bishop Gardiner and the more Catholic lords of the Council. Cranmer's own spy Lascelles had made this new report.

His white sleeves made a shivering sound, the fur that fell round his neck was displaced on one shoulder. His large mouth was open with panic, his lips trembled, and his good-natured and narrow eyes seemed about to drop tears.

'Your Grace knoweth well what passed to-night at Rochester,' Cromwell said. He clapped his hands for a man to snuff the candles. 'You have the common report.'

'Ah, is it even true?' The Archbishop felt a last hope die, and he choked in his throat. Cromwell watched the man at the candles and said:

'Your Grace hath a new riding mule. I pray it may cease to affright you.'

'Why?' he said, as the man went. 'The King's Highness went even to Rochester, disguised, since it was his good pleasure, as a French lord. You have seen the lady. So his Highness was seized with a make of palsy. He cursed to his barge. I know no more than that.'

'And now they sit in the council.'

'It seems,' Cromwell said.

'Ah, dear God have mercy.'

The Archbishop's thin hands wavered before the crucifix on his breast, and made the sign of the cross.

The very faces of his enemies seemed visible to him. He saw Gardiner, of Winchester, with his snake's eyes under the flat cap, and the Duke of Norfolk with his eyes malignant in a long, yellow face. He had a vision of the King, a huge red lump beneath the high dais at the head of the Council table, his face suffused with blood, his cheeks quivering.

He wrung his hands and wondered if at Smithfield the Lutherans would pray for him, or curse him for having been lukewarm.

'Why, goodman gossip,' Cromwell said compassionately, 'we have been nearer death ten times.' He uttered his inmost thoughts out of pity:—All this he had awaited. The King's Highness by the report of his painters, his ambassadors, his spies—they were all in the pay of Cromwell—had awaited a lady of modest demeanour, a coy habit, and a great and placid fairness. 'I had warned the Almains at Rochester to attire her against our coming. But she slobbered with ecstasy and slipped sideways, aiming at a courtesy. Therefore the King was hot with new anger and disgust.'

'You and I are undone.' Cranmer was passive with despair.

'He is very seldom an hour of one mind,' Cromwell answered. 'Unless in that hour those you wot of shall work upon him, it will go well with us.'

'They shall. They shall.'

'I wait to see.'

There seemed to Cranmer something horrible in this impassivity. He wished his leader to go to the King, and he had a frantic moment of imagining himself running to a great distance, hiding his head in darkness.

Cromwell's lips went up in scorn. 'Do you imagine the yellow duke speaking his mind to the King? He is too craven.'

A heavy silence fell between them. The fire rustled, the candles again needed snuffing.

'Best get to bed,' Cromwell said at last.

'Could I sleep?' Cranmer had the irritation of extreme fear. His master seemed to him to have no bowels. But the waiting told at last upon Cromwell himself.

'I could sleep an you would let me,' he said sharply. 'I tell you the King shall be another man in the morning.'

'Ay, but now. But now...' He imagined the pens in that distant room creaking over the paper with their committals, and he wished to upbraid Cromwell. It was his policy of combining with Lutherans that had brought them to this.

Heavy thundering came on the outer door.

'The King comes,' Cromwell cried victoriously. He went swiftly from the room. The Archbishop closed his eyes and suddenly remembered the time when he had been a child.

Privy Seal had an angry and contemptuous frown at his return. 'They have kept him from me.' He threw a little scroll on to the table. Its white silence made Cranmer shudder; it seemed to have something of the heavy threatening of the King's self.

'We may go to bed,' Cromwell said. 'They have devised their shift.'

'You say?'

'They have temporised, they have delayed. I know them.' He quoted contemptuously from the letter: 'We would have you send presently to ask of the Almain Lords with the Lady Anne the papers concerning her pre-contract to the Duke of Lorraine.'

Cranmer was upon the point of going away in the joy of this respite. But his desire to talk delayed him, and he began to talk about the canon law and pre-contracts of marriage. It was a very valid cause of nullity all the doctors held.

'Think you I have not made very certain the pre-contract was nullified? This is no shift,' and Cromwell spoke wearily and angrily. 'Goodman Archbishop, dry your tears. To-night the King is hot with disgust, but I tell you he will not cast away his kingdom upon whether her teeth be white or yellow. This is no woman's man.'

Cranmer came nearer the fire and stretched out his lean hands.

'He hath dandled of late with the Lady Cassilis.'

'Well, he hath been pleasant with her.'

Cranmer urged: 'A full-blown man towards his failing years is more prone to women than before.'

'Then he may go a-wenching.' He began to speak with a weary passion. To cast away the Lady Anne now were a madness. It would be to stand without a friend before all nations armed to their downfall. This King would do no jot to lose a patch upon his sovereignty.

Cranmer sought to speak.

'His Highness is always hot o'nights,' Cromwell kept on. 'It is in his nature so to be. But by morning the German princes shall make him afraid again and the Lutherans of this goodly realm. Those mad swine our friends!'

'He will burn seven of them on to-morrow sennight,' Cranmer said.

'Nay! I shall enlarge them on Wednesday.'

Cranmer shivered. 'They grow very insolent. I am afraid.'

Cromwell answered with a studied nonchalance:

'My bones tell me it shall be an eastward wind. It shall not rain on the new Queen's bridals.' He drank up his warm wine and brushed the crumbs from the furs round his neck.

'You are a very certain man,' the Archbishop said.

Going along the now dark corridors he was afraid that some ruffling boy might spring upon him from the shadows. Norfolk, as the Earl Marshal, had placed his lodgings in a very distant part of the palace to give him long journeys that, telling upon his asthma, made him arrive breathless and convulsed at the King's rooms when he was sent for.

III

The shadow of the King kept hands from throats in the palace, but grooms were breaking each others' heads in the stables till towards morning. They fought about whether it were lawful to eat fish on a Friday, and just after daybreak a gentleman's oarsman from Sittingbourne had all his teeth to swallow for asserting that the sacrament should be administered in the two kinds. The horses were watered by ostlers who hummed the opprobrious song about Privy Seal, called 'Crummock.'

In the hillocks and lawns of the park round the palace Lutherans waited all night to welcome their Queen. They lit small fires on the turf and, standing round them, sang triumphal hymns. A Princess was coming from Cleves, a Lutheran; the day-spring from on high was visiting them; soon, soon now, the axe and the flail should be given into their hands.

In the dawn their boats could be seen pulling like water-beetles all across the pallid river from the Essex shores. They clustered in grey masses round the common steps.

A German horse merchant from the City pulled a putrid cat out of the river mud and held it over his head. He shrieked: 'Hic hocus pocus,' parodying the 'Hoc corpus meum' of the Mass. The soldiers of the Duke of Norfolk were unable to reach him for the crowd. There were but ten of them, under a captain, set to guard the little postern in the side wall of the garden. Towards ten o'clock the Mayor of London came by land. He had with him all his brotherhood with their horses and armed guards in a long train. The mayor and his aldermen had entrance into the palace, but the Duke had given orders that men and horses must bide in the park. There were forty battles of them, each of one hundred men.

The great body came in sight, white, shining even in the grey among the trees along the long garden wall.

'Body of God,' the captain said, 'there shall be broken crowns.' He bade his men hold their pikes across, and paced unconcernedly up and down before the door.

The City men came down in a solid body, and at sight of the red crosses on their white shoulders the Lutherans set up a cry of 'Rome, Rome.' Their stones began to fly at once, and, because they pressed so closely in, the City bowmen had no room to string their bows. The citizens struck out with their silvered staves, but the heavy armour under their white surcoats hindered them. The Lutherans cried out that the Kingdom of God was come on earth because a Queen from Cleves was at hand.

An alderman's charger was struck by a stone. It broke loose and crashed all foaming and furious through a tripe stall on which a preacher was perched to hold forth. The riot began then. All in among the winter trees the City men in their white and silver were fighting with the Lutherans in their grey frieze. The citizens' hearts were enraged because their famous Dominican preacher had been seized by the Archbishop and spirited into Kent. They cried to each other to avenge Dr. Latter on these lowsels.

Men struck out at all and sundry. A woman, covered to the face in a fur hood and riding a grey mule, was hit on the arm by the quarterstaff of a Protestant butcher from the Crays, because she wore a crucifix round her neck. She covered her face and shrieked lamentably. A man in green at the mule's head, on the other side, sprang like a wild cat under the beast's neck. His face blazed white, his teeth shone like a dog's, he screamed and struck his dagger through the butcher's throat.

His motions were those of a mad beast; he stabbed the mule in the shoulder to force it to plunge in the direction of the soldiers who kept the little gate, before in the throng the butcher had reached the ground. The woman was flogging at the mule with her reins. 'I have killed 'un,' he shrieked.

He dived under the pikes of the soldiers and gripped the captain by both shoulders. 'We be the cousins of the Duke of Norfolk,' he cried. His square red beard trembled beneath his pallid face, and suddenly he became speechless with rage.

Hands were already pulling the woman from her saddle, but the guards held their pikes transversely against the faces of the nearest, crushing in noses and sending sudden streaks of blood from jaws. The uproar was like a hurricane and the woman's body, on high, swayed into the little space that the soldiers held. She was crying with the pain of her arm that she held with her other hand. Her cousin ran to her and mumbled words of inarticulate tenderness, ending again in 'I have killed 'un.'

The mob raged round them, but the soldiers stood firm enough. A continual cry of 'Harlot, harlot,' went up. Stones were scarce on the sward of the park, but a case bottle aimed at the woman alighted on the ear of one of the guards. It burst in a foam of red, and he fell beneath the belly of the mule with a dry grunt and the clang of iron. The soldiers put down the points of their pikes and cleared more ground. Men lay wallowing there when they retreated.

The man shouted at the captain: 'Can you clear us a way to yon stairs?' and, at a shake of the head, 'Then let us enter this gate.'

The captain shook his head again.

'I am Thomas Culpepper. This is the Duke's niece, Kat,' the other shouted.

The captain observed him stoically from over his thick and black beard.

'The King's Highness is within this garden,' he said. He spoke to the porter through the little niche at the wicket. A company of the City soldiers, their wands beating like flails, cleared for a moment the space in front of the guards.

Culpepper with the hilt of his sword was hammering at the studded door. The captain caught him by the shoulder and sent him to stagger against the mule's side. He was gasping and snatched at his hilt. His bonnet had fallen off, his yellow hair was like a shock of wheat, and his red beard flecked with foam that spattered from his mouth.

'I have killed one. I will kill thee,' he stuttered at the captain. The woman caught him round the neck.

'Oh, be still,' she shrieked. 'Still. Calm. Y' kill me.' She clutched him so closely that he was half throttled. The captain paced stoically up and down before the gate.

'Madam,' he said, 'I have sent one hastening to his duke-ship. Doubtless you shall enter.' He bent to pull the soldier from beneath the mule's belly by one foot, and picking up his pike, leaned it against the wall.

With his face pressed against his cousin's furred side, Thomas Culpepper swore he would cut the man's throat.

'Aye, come back again,' he answered. 'They call me Sir Christopher Aske.'

The red jerkins of the King's own guards came in a heavy mass round the end of the wall amid shrieks and curses. Their pike-staves rose rhythmically and fell with dull thuds; with their clumsy gloved hands they caught at throats, and they threw dazed men and women into the space that they had cleared before the wall. There armourers were ready, with handcuffs and leg-chains hanging like necklaces round their shoulders.

The door in the wall opened silently, the porter called through his niche: 'These have leave to enter.' Thomas Culpepper shouted 'Coneycatcher' at the captain before he pulled the mule's head round. The beast hung back on his hand, and he struck it on its closed eyes in a tumult of violent rage. It stumbled heavily on the threshold, and then darted forward so swiftly that he did not hear the direction of the porter that they should turn only at the third alley.

Tall and frosted trees reached up into the dim skies, the deserted avenues were shrouded in mist, and there was a dead and dripping silence.

'Seven brawls y' have brought me into,' the woman's voice came from under her hood, 'this weary journey.'

He ran to her stirrup and clutched her glove to his forehead. 'Y'ave calmed me,' he said. 'Your voice shall ever calm me.'

She uttered a hopeless 'Oh, aye,' and then, 'Where be we?'

They had entered a desolate region of clipped yews, frozen fountains, and high, trimmed hedges. He dragged the mule after him. Suddenly there opened up a very broad path, tiled for a width of many feet. On the left it ran to a high tower's gaping arch. On the right it sloped nobly into a grey stretch of water.

'The river is even there,' he muttered. 'We shall find the stairs.'

'I would find my uncle in this palace,' she said. But he muttered, 'Nay, nay,' and began to beat the mule with his fist. It swerved, and she became sick and dizzy with the sudden jar on her hurt arm. She swayed in her saddle and, in a sudden flaw of wind, her old and torn furs ruffled jaggedly all over her body.

IV

The King was pacing the long terrace on the river front. He had been there since very early, for he could not sleep at nights, and had no appetite for his breakfast. When a gentleman from the postern gate asked permission for Culpepper and the mule to pass to the private stairs, he said heavily:

'Let me not be elbowed by cripples,' and then: 'A' God's name let them come,' changing his mind, as was his custom after a bad night, before his first words had left his thick, heavy lips. His great brow was furrowed, his enormous bulk of scarlet, with the great double dog-rose embroidered across the broad chest, limped a little over his right knee and the foot dragged. His eyes were bloodshot and heavy, his head hung forward as though he were about to charge the world with his forehead. From time to time his eyebrows lifted painfully, and he swallowed with an effort as if he were choking.

Behind him the three hundred windows of the palace Placentia seemed to peer at him like eyes, curious, hostile, lugubrious or amazed. He tore violently at his collar and muttered: 'I stifle.' His great hand was swollen by its glove, sewn with pearls, to an immense size.

The gentleman told him of the riot in the park, and narrated the blasphemy of the German Lutheran, who had held up a putrid dog in parody of the Holy Mass.

The face of the King grew suffused with purple blood.

'Let those men be cut down,' he said, and he conceived a sorting out of all heresy, a cleansing of his land with blood. He looked swiftly at the low sky as if a thunderbolt or a leprosy must descend upon his head. He commanded swiftly, 'Let them be taken in scores. Bid the gentlemen of my guard go, and armourers with shackles.'

The sharp pain of the ulcer in his leg gnawed up to his thigh, and he stood, dejected, like a hunted man, with his head hanging on his chest, so that his great bonnet pointed at the ground. He commanded that both Privy Seal and the Duke of Norfolk should come to him there upon the instant.

This grey and heavy King, who had been a great scholar, dreaded to read in Latin now, for it brought the language of the Mass into his mind; he had been a composer of music and a skilful player on the lute, but no music and no voices could any more tickle his ears.

Women he had loved well in his day. Now, when he desired rest, music, good converse and the love of women, he was forced to wed with a creature whose face resembled that of a pig stuck with cloves. He had raged over-night, but, with the morning, he had seen himself growing old, on a tottering throne, assailed by all the forces of the Old Faith in Christendom. Rebellions burst out like fires every day in all the corners of his land. He had no men whom he could trust: if he granted a boon to one party it held them only for a day, and the other side rose up. Now he rested upon the Lutherans, whom he hated, and, standing on that terrace, he had watched gloomily the great State barges of the Ambassadors from the Empire and from France come with majestic ostentation downstream abreast, to moor side by side against the steps of his water-gate.

It was a parade of their new friendship. Six months ago their trains could not have mingled without bloodshed.

At last there stood before him Thomas Cromwell, un-bonneted, smiling, humorous, supple and confident for himself and for his master's cause, a man whom his Prince might trust. And the long melancholy and sinister figure of the Duke of Norfolk stalked stiffly down among the yew trees powdered with frost. The furs from round his neck fluttered about his knees like the wings of a crow, and he dug his Earl Marshal's golden staff viciously into the ground. He waved his jewelled cap and stood still at a little distance. Cromwell regarded him with a sinister and watchful amusement; he looked back at Privy Seal with a black malignancy that hardened his yellow features, his hooked nose and pursed lips into the likeness of a mask representing hatred.

This Norfolk was that Earl of Surrey who had won Flodden Field. They all then esteemed him the greatest captain of his day—in the field a commander sleepless, cunning, cautious, and, in striking, a Hotspur.

A dour and silent man, he was the head of all the Catholics, of all the reaction of that day. But, in the long duel between himself and Cromwell he had seemed fated to be driven from post to post, never daring to proclaim himself openly the foe of the man he dreaded and hated. Cranmer, with his tolerant spirit, he despised. Here was an archbishop who might rack and burn for discipline's sake, and he did nothing...And all these New Learning men with their powers of language, these dark bearded men with twinkling and sagacious eyes, he detested. He went clean shaved, lean and yellow-faced, with a hooked nose that seemed about to dig into his chin. It was he who said first: 'It was merry in England before this New Learning came in.'

The night before, the King had sworn that he would have Privy Seal's head because Anne of Cleves resembled a pig stuck with cloves. And, shaking and shivering with cold that penetrated his very inwards, with a black pain on his brow and sparks dancing before his jaundiced eyes, the Duke cursed himself for not having urged then the immediate arrest of the Privy Seal. For here stood Cromwell, arrogantly by the King's side with the King graciously commanding him to cover his head because it was very cold and Cromwell was known to suffer with the earache.

'You are Earl Marshal,' the King's voice drowned Norfolk's morning greeting. He veered upon the Duke with such violence that his enormous red bulk seemed about to totter over upon the tall and bent figure. A searing pain had shot up his side, and, as he gripped it, he appeared to be furiously plucking at his dagger. He had imagined Chapuys and Marillac, the Ambassadors, coming upon guards with broken heads and sending to Paris letters over which Francis and his nephew should snigger and chuckle.

'You are Earl Marshal. You have the ordering of these ceremonies, and you let rebels and knaves break heads within my very park for all the world to see!'

In his rage Norfolk blurted out:

'Privy Seal hath his friends, too—these Lutherans. What man could have foreseen how insolent they be grown, for joy at welcoming a Queen of their faith,' he repeated hotly. 'No man could have foreseen. My bands are curtailed.'

Cromwell said:

'Aye, men are needed to keep down the Papists of your North parts.'

The two men faced each other. It had been part of the Duke's plan—and Cromwell knew it very well—that the City men should meet with the Lutherans there in the King's own park. It would show the insolence of the heretics upon whom the Privy Seal relied, and it might prove, too, the strength of the Old Faith in the stronghold of the City.

Henry rated violently. It put him to shame, he repeated many times. 'Brawling beneath my face, cries in my ears, and the smell of bloodshed in my nose.'

Norfolk repeated dully that the Protestants were wondrous insolent. But Cromwell pointed out with a genial amusement: 'My Lord Duke should have housed the City men within the palace. Cat will fight with dog the world over if you set them together.'

The Duke answered malignantly:

'It was fitting the citizens should wait to enter. I would not cumber his Highness' courtyards. We know not yet that this Lady cometh to be welcomed Queen.'

'Body of God,' the King said with a new violence: 'do ye prate of these matters?' His heavy jaws threatened like a dog's. 'Hast thou set lousy knaves debating of these?'

Norfolk answered darkly that it had been treated of in the Council last night.

'My Council! My Council!' The King seemed to bay out the words. 'There shall some mothers' sons rue this!'

Norfolk muttered that he had spoken of it with no man not a Councillor. The King's Highness' self had moved first in this.

Henry suddenly waved both hands at the sky.

'Take you good order,' he said heavily into the lean and yellow face of the Duke. 'Marshal these ceremonies fitly from henceforth. Let nothing lack. Get you gone.' An end must be made of talk and gossip. The rumour of last night's Council must appear an idle tale, a falsehood of despairing Papists. 'The Queen cometh,' he said.

With the droop of the Duke's long arms his hat seemed to brush the stones, his head fell on his chest. It was finished.

He had seen so many things go that he loved. And now this old woman with her Germans, her heresies—her children doubtless—meant the final downfall of the Old Order in his day. It would return, but he would never see it. And under Cromwell's sardonic gaze his head hung limply, and his eyes filled with hot and blinding drops. His face trembled like that of a very old man.

The King had thrust his hand through Cromwell's arm, and, with a heavy familiarity as if he would make him forget the Council of last night, he was drawing him away towards the water-gate. He turned his head over his shoulder and repeated balefully:

'The Queen cometh.'

As he did so his eye fell upon a man tugging at the bridle of a mule that had a woman on its back. He passed on with his minister.

V

In turning, Norfolk came against them at the very end of the path. The man's green coat was spotted with filth, one of his sleeves was torn off and dangled about his heel. The mule's knees were cut, and the woman trembled with her hidden face and shrinking figure.

They made him choke with rage and fear. Some other procession might have come against these vagabonds, and the blame would have been his. It disgusted him that they were within a yard of himself.

'Are there no side paths?' he asked harshly.

Culpepper blazed round upon him:

'How might I know? Why sent you no guide?' His vivid red beard was matted into tails, his face pallid and as if blazing with rage. The porter had turned them loose into the empty garden.

'Kat is sore hurt,' he mumbled, half in tears. 'Her arm is welly broken.' He glared at the Duke. 'Care you no more for your own blood and kin?'

Norfolk asked:

'Who is your Kat? Can I know all the Howards?'

Culpepper snarled:

'Aye, we may trust you not to succour your brother's children.'

The Duke said:

'Why, she shall back to the palace. They shall comfort her.'

'That shall she not,' Culpepper flustered. 'Sh'ath her father's commands to hasten to Dover.'

The Duke caught her eyes in the fur hood that hid her face like a Moorish woman's veil. They were large, grey and arresting beneath the pallor of her forehead. They looked at him, questioning and judging.

'Wilt not come to my lodging?' he asked.

'Aye, will I,' came a little muffled by the fur.

'That shall she not,' Culpepper repeated.

The Duke looked at him with gloomy and inquisitive surprise.

'Aye, I am her mother's cousin,' he said. 'I fend for her, which you have never done. Her father's house is burnt by rioters, and her men are joined in the pillaging. But I'll warrant you knew it not.'

Katharine Howard with her sound hand was trying to unfasten her hood, hastily and eagerly.

'Wilt come?' the Duke asked hurriedly. 'This must be determined.'

Culpepper hissed: 'By the bones of St. Nairn she shall not.' She lifted her maimed hand involuntarily, and, at the sear of pain, her eyes closed. Immediately Culpepper was beside her knees, supporting her with his arms and muttering sounds of endearment and despair.

The Duke, hearing behind him the swish pad of heavy soft shoes, as if a bear were coming over the pavement, faced the King.

'This is my brother's child,' he said. 'She is sore hurt. I would not leave her like a dog,' and he asked the King's pardon.

'Why, God forbid,' the King said. 'Your Grace shall succour her.' Culpepper had his back to them, caring nothing for either in his passion. Henry said: 'Aye, take good care for her,' and passed on with Privy Seal on his arm.

The Duke heaved a sigh of relief. But he remembered again that Anne of Cleves was coming, and his black anger that Cromwell should thus once again have the King thrown back to him came out in his haughty and forbidding tone to Culpepper:

'Take thou my niece to the water-gate. I shall send women to her.' He hastened frostily up the path to be gone before Henry should return again.

Culpepper resolved that he would take barge before ever the Duke could send. But the mule slewed right across the terrace; his cousin grasped the brute's neck and her loosened hood began to fall back from her head.

The King, standing twenty yards away, with his hand shaking Cromwell's shoulder, was saying:

'See you how grey I grow.'

The words came hot into a long harangue. He had been urging that he must have more money for his works at Calais. He was agitated because a French chalk pit outside the English lines had been closed to his workmen. They must bring chalk from Dover at a heavy cost for barges and balingers. This was what it was to quarrel with France.

Cromwell had his mind upon widening the breach with France. He said that a poll tax might be levied on the subjects of Charles and Francis then in London. There were goldsmiths, woolstaplers, horse merchants, whore-masters, painters, musicians and vintners...

The King's eyes had wandered to the grey river, and then from a deep and moody abstraction he had blurted out those words.

Henry was very grey, and his face, inanimate and depressed, made him seem worn and old enough. Cromwell was not set to deny it. The King had his glass...

He sighed a little and began:

'The heavy years take their toll.'

Henry caught him up suddenly:

'Why, no. It is the heavy days, the endless nights. You can sleep, you.' But him, the King, incessant work was killing.

'You see, you see, how this world will never let me rest.' In the long, black nights he started from dozing. When he took time to dandle his little son a panic would come over him because he remembered that he lived among traitors and had no God he could pray to. He had no mind to work...

Cromwell said that there was no man in England could outwork his King.

'There is no man in England can love him.' His distracted eyes fell upon the woman on the mule. 'Happy he whom a King never saw and who never saw King,' he muttered.

The beast, inspired with a blind hatred of Culpepper, was jibbing across the terrace, close at hand. Henry became abstractedly interested in the struggle. The woman swayed forward over her knees.

'Your lady faints,' he called to Culpepper.

In his muddled fury the man began once again trying to hold her on the animal. It was backing slowly towards a stone seat in the balustrade, and man and woman swayed and tottered together.

The King said:

'Let her descend and rest upon the seat.'

His mind was swinging back already to his own heavy sorrows. On the stone seat the woman's head lay back upon the balustrade, her eyes were closed and her face livid to the sky. Culpepper, using his teeth to the finger ends, tore the gloves from his hands.

Henry drew Cromwell towards the gatehouse. He had it dimly in his mind to send one of his gentlemen to the assistance of that man and woman.

'Aye, teach me to sleep at night,' he said. 'It is you who make me work.'

'It is for your Highness' dear sake.'

'Aye, for my sake,' the King said angrily. He burst into a sudden invective: 'Thou hast murdered a many men...for my sake. Thou hast found out plots that were no plots: old men hate me, old mothers, wives, maidens, harlots...Why, if I be damned at the end thou shalt escape, for what thou didst thou didst for my sake? Shall it be that?' He breathed heavily. 'My sins are thy glory.'

They reached the long wall of the gatehouse and turned mechanically. A barge at the river steps was disgorging musicians with lutes like half melons set on staves, horns that opened bell mouths to the sky, and cymbals that clanged in the rushing of the river. With his eyes upon them Henry said: 'A common man may commonly choose his bedfellow.' They had reminded him of the Queen for whose welcome they had been commanded.

Cromwell swept his hand composedly round the half horizon that held the palace, the grey river and the inlands.

'Your Highness may choose among ten thousand,' he answered.

The sound of a horn blown faintly to test it within the gatehouse, the tinkle of a lutestring, brought to the King's lips: 'Aye. Bring me music that shall charm my thoughts. You cannot do it.'

'A Queen is in the nature of a defence, a pledge, a cement, the keystone of a bulwark,' Cromwell said. 'We know now our friends and our foes. You may rest from this onwards.'

He spoke earnestly: This was the end of a long struggle. The King should have his rest.

They moved back along the terrace. The woman's head still lay back, her chin showed pointed and her neck, long, thin and supple. Culpepper was bending over her, sprinkling water out of his cap upon her upturned face.

The King said to Cromwell: 'Who is that wench?' and, in the same tone: 'Aye, you are a great comforter. We shall see how the cat jumps,' and then, answering his own question, 'Norfolk's niece?'

His body automatically grew upright, the limp disappeared from his gait and he moved sturdily and gently towards them.

Culpepper faced round like a wild cat from a piece of meat, but seeing the great hulk, the intent and friendly eyes, the gold collar over the chest, the heavy hands, and the great feet that appeared to hold down the very stones of the terrace, he stood rigid in a pose of disturbance.

'Why do ye travel?' the King asked. 'This shall be Katharine Howard?'

Culpepper's hushed but harsh voice answered that they came out of Lincolnshire on the Norfolk border. This was the Lord Edmund's daughter.

'I have never seen her,' the King said.

'Sh'ath never been in this town.'

The King laughed: 'Why, poor wench!'

'Sh'ath been well schooled,' Culpepper answered proudly, 'hath had mastern, hath sung, hath danced, hath your Latin and your Greek... Hath ten daughters, her father.'

The King laughed again: 'Why, poor man!'

'Poorer than ever now,' Culpepper muttered. Katharine Howard stirred uneasily and his face shot round to her. 'Rioters have brent his only house and wasted all his sheep.'

The King frowned heavily: 'Anan? Who rioted?'

'These knaves that love not our giving our ploughlands to sheep,' Culpepper said. 'They say they starved through it. Yet 'tis the only way to wealth. I had all my wealth by it. By now 'tis well gone, but I go to the wars to get me more.'

'Rioters?' the King said again, heavily.

''Twas a small tulzie—a score of starved yeomen here and there. I killed seven. The others were they that were hanged at Norwich...But the barns were brent, the sheep gone, and the house down and the servants fled. I am her cousin of the mother's side. Of as good a strain as Howards be.'

Henry, with his eyes still upon them, beckoned behind his back for Cromwell to come. A score or so of poor yeomen, hinds and women, cast out of their tenancies that wool might be grown for the Netherlands weavers, starving, desperate, and seeing no trace of might and order in their hidden lands, had banded, broken a few hedges and burnt a few barns before the posse of the country could come together and take them.

The King had not heard of it or had forgotten it, because such risings were so frequent. His brows came down into portentous and bulging knots, his eyes were veiled and threatening towards the woman's face. He had conceived that a great rebellion had been hidden from his knowledge.

She raised her head and shrieked at the sight of him, half started to her feet, and once more sank down on the bench, clasping at her cousin's hand. He said:

'Peace, Kate, it is the King.'

She answered: 'No, no,' and covered her face with her hands.

Henry bent a little towards her, indulgent, amused, and gentle as if to a child.

'I am Harry,' he said.

She muttered:

'There was a great crowd, a great cry. One smote me on the arm. And then this quiet here.'

She uncovered her face and sat looking at the ground. Her furs were all grey, she had had none new for four years, and they were tight to her young body that had grown into them. The roses embroidered on her glove had come unstitched, and, against the steely grey of the river, her face in its whiteness had the tint of mother of pearl and an expression of engrossed and grievous absence.

'I have fared on foul ways this journey,' she said.

'Thy father's barns we will build again,' the King answered. 'You shall have twice the sheep to your dower. Show me your eyes.'

'I had not thought to have seen the King so stern,' she answered.

Culpepper caught at the mule's bridle.

'Y' are mad,' he muttered. 'Let us begone.'

'Nay, in my day,' the King answered, 'y'ad found me more than kind.'

She raised her eyes to his face, steadfast, enquiring and unconcerned. He bent his great bulk downwards and kissed her upon the temple.

'Be welcome to this place.' He smiled with a pleasure in his own affability and because, since his beard had pricked her, she rubbed her cheek. Culpepper said:

'Come away. We stay the King's Highness.'

Henry said: 'Bide ye here.' He wished to hear what Cromwell might say of these Howards, and he took him down the terrace.

Culpepper bent over her with his mouth opened to whisper.

'I am weary,' she said. 'Set me a saddle cushion behind my shoulders.'

He whispered hurriedly:

'I do not like this place.'

'I like it well. Shall we not see brave shews?'

'The mule did stumble on the threshold.'

'I marked it not. The King did bid us bide here.'

She had once more laid her head back on the stone balustrade.

'If thou lovest me...' he whispered. It enraged and confused him to have to speak low. He could not think of any words.

She answered unconcernedly:

'If thou lovest my bones...they ache and they ache.'

'I have sold farms to buy thee gowns,' he said desperately.

'I never asked it,' she answered coldly.

Henry was saying:

'Ah, Princes take as is brought them by others. Poor men be commonly at their own choice.' His voice had a sort of patient regret. 'Why brought ye not such a wench?'

Cromwell answered that in Lincoln, they said, she had been a coin that would not bear ringing.

'You do not love her house,' the King said. 'Y' had better have brought me such a one.'

Cromwell answered that his meaning was she had been won by others. The King's Highness should have her for a wink.

Henry raised his shoulders with a haughty and angry shrug. Such a quarry was below his stooping. He craved no light loves.

'I do not miscall the wench,' Cromwell answered. She was as her kind. The King's Highness should find them all of a make in England.

'Y' are foul-mouthed,' Henry said negligently. ''Tis a well-spoken wench. You shall find her a place in the Lady Mary's house.'

Cromwell smiled, and made a note upon a piece of paper that he pulled from his pocket.

Culpepper, his arms jerking angularly, was creaking out:

'Come away, a' God's name. By all our pacts. By all our secret vows.'

'Ay thou didst vow and didst vow,' she said with a bitter weariness. 'What hast to shew? I have slept in filthy beds all this journey. Speak the King well. He shall make thee at a word.'

He spat out at her.

'Is thine eye cocked up to that level?...I am very hot, very choleric. Thou hast seen me. Thou shalt not live. I will slay thee. I shall do such things as make the moon turn bloody red.'

'Aye art thou there?' she answered coldly. 'Ye have me no longer upon lone heaths and moors. Mend thy tongue. Here I have good friends.'

Suddenly he began to entreat:

'Thy mule did stumble—an evil omen. Come away, come away. I know well thou lovest me.'

'I know well I love thee too well,' she answered, as if in scorn of herself.

'Come away to thy father.'

'Why what a bother is this,' she said. 'Thou wouldst to the wars to get thee gold? Thou wouldst trail a pike? Thou canst do little without the ear of some captain. Here is the great captain of them all.'

'I dare not speak here,' he muttered huskily. 'But this King...' He paused and added swiftly: 'He is of an ill omen to all Katharines.'

'Why, he shall give me his old gloves to darn,' she laughed. 'Fond knave, this King standeth on a mountain a league high. A King shall take notice of one for the duration of a raindrop's fall. Then it is done. One may make oneself ere it reach the ground, or never. Besides, 'tis a well-spoken elder. 'Tis the spit of our grandfather Culpepper.'

When Henry came hurrying back, engrossed, to send Culpepper and the mule to the gatehouse for a guide, she laughed gently for pleasure.

Culpepper said tremulously: 'She hath her father's commands to hasten to Dover.'

'Her father taketh and giveth commands from me,' Henry answered, and his glove flicked once more towards the gate. He had turned his face away before Culpepper's hand grasped convulsively at his dagger and he had Katharine Howard at his side sweeping back towards Cromwell.

She asked, confidingly and curiously: 'Who is that lord?' and, after his answer, she mused, 'He is no friend to Howards.'

'Nay, that man taketh his friends among mine,' he answered. He stopped to regard her, his face one heavy and indulgent smile. The garter on his knee, broad and golden, showed her the words: 'Y pense'; the collars moved up and down on his immense chest, the needlework of roses was so fine that she wondered how many women had sat up how many nights to finish it: but the man was grey and homely.

'I know none of your ways here,' she said.

'Never let fear blanch thy cheeks till we are no more thy friend,' he reassured her. He composed one of his gallant speeches:

'Here lives for thee nothing but joy.' Pleasurable hopes should be her comrades while the jolly sun shone, and sweet content at night her bedfellow...

He handed her to the care of the Lord Cromwell to take her to the Lady Mary's lodgings. It was unfitting that she should walk with him, and, with his heavy and bearlike gait, swinging his immense shoulders, he preceded them up the broad path.

Cromwell watched the King's great back with an attentive smile. He said, ironically, that he was her ladyship's servant.

'I would ye were,' she answered. 'They say you love not those that I love.'

'I would have you not heed what men say,' he answered, grimly. 'I am douce to those that be of good-will to his Highness. Those that hate me are his ill-wishers.'

'Then the times are evil,' she said, 'for they are many.'

She added suddenly, as if she could not keep a prudent silence:

'I am for the Old Faith in the Old Way. You have hanged many dear friends of mine whose souls I pray for.'

He looked at her attentively.

She had a supple, long body, a fair-tinted face, fair and reddish hair, and eyes that had a glint of almond green—but her cheeks were flushed and her eyes sparkled. She was so intent upon speaking her mind that she had forgotten the pain of her arm. She thought that she must have said enough to anger this brewer's son. But he answered only:

'I think you have never been in the King's court'—and, from his tranquil manner, she realised very suddenly that this man was not the dirt beneath her feet.

She had never been in the King's court; she had never, indeed, been out of the North parts. Her father had always been a very poor man, with an ancient castle and a small estate that he had nearly always neglected because it had not paid for the farming. Living men she had never respected—for they seemed to her like wild beasts when she compared them with such of the ancients as Brutus or as Seneca. She had been made love to and threatened by such men as her cousin; she had been made love to and taught Latin by her pedagogues. She was more learned than any man she had ever met—and, thinking upon the heroes of Plutarch, she found the present times despicable. She hardly owed allegiance to the King. Now she had seen him and felt his consciousness of his own power, she was less certain. But the King's writs had hardly run in the Northern parts. Her men-folk and her mother's people had hanged their own peasants when they thought fit. She had seen bodies swinging from tree-tops when she rode hawking. All that she had ever known of the King's power was when the convent by their castle gates had been thrown out of doors, and then her men-folk, cursing and raging, had sworn that it was the work of Crummock. 'Knaves ruled about the King.'

If knaves ruled about him, the King was not a man that one need trouble much over. Her own men-folk, she knew, had made and unmade Kings. So that, when she thought of the hosts of saints and of the blessed angels that hovered, wringing their hands and weeping above England, she had wondered a little at times why they had never unmade this King.

But to her all these things had seemed very far away. She had nothing to do but to read books in the learned tongues, to imagine herself holding disquisitions upon the spiritual republic of Plato, to ride, to shoot with the bow, to do needlework, or to chide the maids. Her cousin had loved her passionately; it was true that once, when she had had nothing to her back, he had sold a farm to buy her a gown. But he had menaced her with his knife till she was weary, and the ways of men were troublesome to her; nevertheless she submitted to them with a patient wisdom.

She submitted to the King; she submitted—though she hated him by repute—to Cromwell's catechism as they followed the King at a decent interval.

He walked beside her with his eyes on her face. He spoke of the King's bounty in a voice that implied his own power. She was to be the Lady Mary's woman. He had that lady especially in his good will, he saved for her household ladies of egregious gifts, presence and attainments. They received liberal honorariums, seven dresses by the year, vails, presents, perfumes from the King's own still-rooms, and a parcel-gilt chain at the New Year. The Lady Rochford, who ruled over these ladies, was kind, courteous, free in her graces as in the liberties she allowed the ladies under her easy charge.

He enlarged upon this picture as if it were a bribe that he alone could offer or withhold. And something at once cautious and priestly in his tone let her quick intuition know that he was both warning her and sounding her, to see how far her mutinous spirit would carry her. Once he said, 'There must be tranquillity in the kingdom. The times are very evil!'

She had felt very quickly that insults to this man would be a useless folly. He could not even feel them, and she kept her eyes on the ground and listened to him.

He went on sounding her. It was part of his profession of kingcraft to know the secret hearts of every person with whom he spoke.

'And your goodly cousin?' He paused. The King had commanded that a place should be found for him. 'Should he be best at Calais? There shall be blows struck there.'

She knew very well that he was trying to discover how much she loved her cousin, and she answered in a low voice, 'I would have him stay here. He is the sole friend I have in this place.'

Cromwell said, with a hidden and encouraging meaning, her cousin was not her only friend there.

'Aye, but your lordship is not so old a friend as he.'

'Not me. Call me your good servant.'

'There is even then my uncle.'

'Little good of a friend you will have of Norfolk. 'Tis a bitter apple and a very rotten plank to lean upon.'

She could not any longer miss his meaning. The King's scarlet and immense figure was already in the grey shadow of the arch under the tower. In walking, they had come near him, and while they waited he stood for a minute, gazing back down the path with boding and pathetic eyes; then he disappeared.

She looked at Cromwell and thanked him for the warning, 'quia spicula praevisa minus laedunt.'

'I would have you read it: gaudia plus laetificant,' he answered gravely.

A man with a conch-shaped horn upturned was suddenly blowing beneath the archway seven hollow and reverberating grunts of sound that drowned his voice. A clear answering whistle came from the water-gate. Cromwell stayed, listening attentively; another stood forward to blow four blasts, another six, another three. Each time the whistle answered. They were the great officers' signals for their barges that the men blew, and the whistle signified that these lay at readiness in the tideway. A bustle of men running, calling, and making pennons ready, began beyond the archway in the quadrangle.

Cromwell's face grew calm and contented; the King was sending to meet Anne of Cleves.

'Y' are well read?' he asked her slowly.

'I was brought up in the Latin tongue or ever I had the English,' she answered. 'I had a good master, one that spoke the learned language always.'

'Aye, Nicholas Udal,' Cromwell said.

'You know all men in the land,' she said, with fear and surprise.

'I had him to master for the Lady Mary, since he is well disposed.'

''Tis an arrant knave tho' the best of pedagogues,' she answered. 'He was cast out of his mastership at Eton for being a rogue.'

'For that, the worshipful your father had him to master,' he said ironically.

'No, for that he was a ruined man, and taught for his victuals. We welly starved at home, my sisters and I.'

He said slowly:

'The better need that you should grow beloved here.'

Standing there, before the bushes where no ears could overhear, he put to her more questions. She had some Greek, more than a little French, she could judge a good song, she could turn a verse in Latin or the vulgar tongue. She professed to be able to ride well, to be conversant with the terms of venery, to shoot with the bow, and to have studied the Fathers of the Church.

'These things are well liked in high places,' he said. 'His Highness' self speaks five tongues, loveth a nimble answer, and is a noble huntsman.' He surveyed her as if she were a horse he were pricing. 'But I doubt not you have appraised yourself passing well,' he uttered.

'I have had some to make me pleasant speeches,' she answered, 'but too many cannot be had.'

'See you,' he said slowly, 'these tuckets that they blow from the gate signify that the new Queen cometh with a great state.' He bit his under lip and looked at her meaningly. 'But a great state ensueth a great heaviness to the head of the State. Principis hymen, principium gravitatis...'Tis a small matter to me; you may make it a great one to your ladyship's light fortunes.'

She knew that he awaited her saying:

'I do not take your lordship,' and she pulled the hood further over her face because it was cold, and uttered the words with her eyes on the ground.

'Why,' he said readily, 'you are a lady having gifts that are much in favour in these days. Be careful to use those gifts and no others. Meddle in nothing that does not concern you. So you may make a great marriage with some lord in favour. But meddle in naught else!'

She would find many to set her an evil example. The other ladies amongst whom she was going were a mutinous knot. Let her be careful! If by her good behaviour she earned it, he would put the King in mind to advance her. If by good speeches and good example—since she had great store of learning—she could turn the hearts of these wicked ladies; if she could report to him evil designs or plots, he would speak to the King in such wise that His Highness should give her a great dower and any lord would marry her. Or he would advance her cousin so that he should become marriageable.

She said submissively:

'Your lordship would have me become a spy upon the ladies who shall be my fellows?'

He waved his hand with a large and calming gesture.

'I would have you work for the good of the State as you find it,' he said gravely. 'That, too, is a doctrine of the Ancients.' He cited the case of Seneca, who supported the government of Nero, and she noted that he twisted to suit his purpose Tacitus' account of the soldiers of that same Prince.

Nevertheless, she made no comment. For she knew that it is the nature of men calmly to ask hateful sacrifices of women. But her throat ached with rage. And when she followed him along the corridors of the palace she seemed to feel that each man, each woman that they passed hated that lord with a hatred born of fear.

He walked in front of her arrogantly, as if she were a straw to be drawn along in the wind of his progress. Doors flew open at a flick of his finger.

Suddenly they were in a tall room, long, and dim because it faced the north. It seemed an empty cavern, but there were in it many books upon a long table and at the far end, so that they looked quite small, two figures stood before a reading-pulpit. The voice of the serving man who had thrown open the door made the words 'The Lord Privy Seal of England' echo mournfully along the gilded and dim rafters of the ceiling.

Cromwell hastened over the smooth, cold floor. The woman's figure in black, the long tail of her hood falling almost to her feet like a widow's veil, turned from the pulpit; a man remained bent down at his reading.

'Annuntio vobis gaudium magnum,' Cromwell's voice uttered. The lady stood, rigid and straight, her hands clasped before her. Her face, pale so that not even a touch of red showed above the cheekbones and hardly any in the tightly-pursed lips, was as if framed in her black hood that fastened beneath the chin. The high, narrow forehead had the hair tightly drawn back so that none was visible, and the coif that showed beneath the hood was white, like a nun's; the temples were hollowed so that she looked careworn inexpressibly, and her lips had hard lines around them. Above her head all sounds in that dim room seemed to whisper for a long time among the rafters as if here dwelt something mysterious, sepulchral, a great grief or a great passion.

'I announce to you a master-joy,' Cromwell was saying. 'I bring your La'ship a damsel of great erudition and knowledge of good letters.'

His voice was playful and full; his back was bent supply. His face lit up with a debonnaire and pleasant smile. The lady's eyes turned upon the girl, forbidding and suspicious; she remained motionless, even her lips did not move. Cromwell said that this was a Katharine of the Howards, and one fit to aid her Ladyship and Magister Udal with their erudite commentary of Plautus his works.

The man at the reading desk looked round and then back at his book. His pen scratched upon the margin of a great volume. Katharine Howard was upon her knees grasping at the lady's hand to kiss it. But it was snatched roughly away.

'This is a folly,' the voice came harshly from the pursed lips. 'Get up, wench.' Katharine remained kneeling. For this was the Lady Mary of England—a martyr for whom she had prayed nightly since she could pray.

'Get up, fool,' the voice said above her head. 'It is proclaimed treason to kneel to me. This is to risk your neck to act thus before Privy Seal.'

The hard words were aimed straight at the face of Cromwell.

'Your ladyship knows well I would fain have it otherwise,' he answered softly.

'I do not ask it,' she answered.

He maintained a gentle smile of deprecation, beckoning a little with his head and with his eyes, begging her for private conversation. She lifted Katharine roughly to her feet and followed him to a distant window. She seemed as if she were an automaton without will or independent motions of her own, so small were her steps and her feet so hidden beneath her stiff black skirts. He began talking to her in a voice of which only the persuasive higher notes came into the room.

At that time she was still proclaimed bastard, and her name was erased from the list of those it was lawful to pray for in the churches. At times she endured great hardships, even to going short of food, for she suffered from a wasting complaint that made her a great eater. But starvation could not make her submit to the King, her father, or to the Lord Cromwell who was ruler in the land. Sometimes they gave her a great train, strove to make her dress herself richly, and dragged her to such festivals as this of the marriage with Anne of Cleves. This was done when the Lord Privy Seal dangled her before the eyes of the Emperor of France as a match; then it was necessary to increase the appearance of her worth in England. But sometimes the King, out of a warm and generous feeling of satisfaction with his young son, was moved to behave bountifully to his daughter, and, seeking to dazzle her with his munificence, gave her golden crosses and learned books annotated with his own hand, richly jewelled and with embroidered covers. Or when the Emperor, her cousin, interceded that she should be treated more kindly, she was threatened with the block. Of late Cromwell had set himself to gain her heart with his intrigue that he could make so smooth and with his air that could be so gentle—that the King found so lovable. But nothing moved her to set her hand to a deed countenancing her dead mother's disgrace; to smile upon her father and his minister, who had devised the means for casting down her mother; or to consent to relinquish her right to the throne. So that at times, when the cloud of the Church abroad, and of the rebellions all over the extremities of the kingdoms, threatened very greatly, the King was driven to agonies of fear and rage lest his enemies or his subjects should displace him who was excommunicated and set her, whom all Catholics regarded as undergoing a martyrdom, on his throne. He feared her sometimes so much that it was only Cromwell that saved her from death. Cromwell would spend hours of his busy days in the long window of her work room, urging her to submission, dilating upon the powers that might be hers, studying her tastes to devise bribes for her. It was with that aim, because her whole days in her solitude were given to the learned writers, that he had sought out for her Magister Udal as a companion and preceptor who might both please her with his erudition and induce her to look kindly upon the New Learning and a more lax habit of mind. But she never thanked Cromwell. Whilst he talked she remained frozen and silent. At times, under the spur of a cold rage, she said harsh things of himself and her father, calling upon the memory of her mother and the wrongs her Church had suffered—and, on his departing, before he had even left the room she would return, frigidly and without change of face, to the book upon her desk.

So the Privy Seal talked to her by the window for the fiftieth time. Katharine Howard saw, before the high reading pulpit, the back of a man in the long robes of a Master of Arts. He held a pen in his hand and turned over his shoulder at her a face thin, brown, humorous and deprecatory, as if he were used to bearing chiding with philosophy.

'Magister Udal!' she uttered.

He motioned with his mouth for her to be silent, but pointed with the feather of his quill to a line of a little book that lay upon the pulpit near his elbow. She came closer to read:

'Circumspectatrix cum oculis emisitiis!' and written above it in a minute hand: 'A spie with eyes that peer about and stick out.'

He pointed over his shoulder at the Lord Privy Seal.

'How poor this room is, for a King's daughter!' she said, without much dropping her voice.

He hissed: 'Hush! hush!' with an appearance of terror, and whispered, forming the words with his lips rather than uttering them: 'How fared you and your house in the nonce?'

'I have read in many texts,' she answered, 'to pass the heavy hours.'

He spoke then, aloud and with an admonitory air:

'Never say the heavy hours—for what hours are heavy that can be spent with the ancient writers for companions?'

She avoided his reproachful eyes with:

'My father's house was burnt last month; my cousin Culpepper is in the courts below. Dear Nick Ardham, with his lute, is dead an outlaw beyond sea, and Sir Ferris was hanged at Doncaster—both after last year's rising, pray all good men that God assail them!'

Udal muttered:

'Hush, for God's dear sake. That is treason here. There is a listener behind the hangings.'

He began to scrawl hastily with a dry pen that he had not time to dip in the well of ink. The shadow of the Lord Cromwell's silent return was cast upon them both, and Katharine shivered.

He said harshly to the magister:

'I will that you write me an interlude in the vulgar tongue in three days' time. Such a piece as being spoken by skilful players may make a sad man laugh.'

Udal said: 'Well-a-day!'

'It shall get you advancement. I am minded the piece shall be given at my house before his Highness and the new Queen in a week.'

Udal remained silent, dejected, his head resting upon his breast.

'For,' Cromwell spoke with a raised voice, 'it is well that the King be distracted of his griefs.' He went on as if he were uttering an admonition that he meant should be heeded and repeated. The times were very evil with risings, mutinies in close fortresses, schism, and the bad hearts of men. Here, therefore, he would that the King should find distraction. Such of them as had gifts should display those talents for his beguiling; such of them as had beauty should make valuable that beauty; others whose wealth could provide them with rich garments and pleasant displays should work, each man and each woman, after his sort or hers. 'And I will that you report my words where either of you have resort. Who loves me shall hear it; who fears me shall take warning.'

He surveyed both Katharine and the master with a heavy and encouraging glance, having the air of offering great things if they aided him and avoided dealing with his enemies.

The Lady Mary was gliding towards them like a cold shadow casting itself upon his warm words; she would have ignored him altogether, knowing that contempt is harder to bear than bitter speeches. But the fascination of hatred made it hard to keep aloof from her father's instrument. He looked negligently over his shoulder and was gone before she could speak. He did not care to hear more bitter words that could make the breach between them only wider, since words once spoken are so hard to wash away, and the bringing of this bitter woman back to obedience to her father was so great a part of his religion of kingcraft. In that, when it came, there should be nothing but concord and oblivion of bitter speeches, silent loyalty, and a throne upheld, revered, and unassailable.

Udal groaned lamentably when the door closed upon him:

'I shall write to make men laugh! In the vulgar tongue! I! To gain advancement!'

The Lady Mary's face hardly relaxed:

'Others of us take harder usage from my lord,' she said. She addressed Katharine: 'You are named after my mother. I wish you a better fate than your namesake had.' Her harsh voice dismayed Katharine, who had been prepared to worship her. She had eaten nothing since dawn, she had travelled very far and with this discouragement the pain in her arm came back. She could find no words to say, and the Lady Mary continued bitterly: 'But if you love that dear name and would sojourn near me I would have you hide it. For—though I care little—I would yet have women about me that believe my mother to have been foully murdered.'

'I cannot easily dissemble.' Katharine found her tongue. 'Where I hate I speak things disparaging.'

'That I attest to of old,' Udal commented. 'But I shall be shamed before all learned doctors, if I write in the vulgar tongue.'

'Silence is ever best for me!' the Lady Mary answered her deadly. 'I live in the shadows that I love.'

'That, full surely, shall be reversed,' Katharine said loyally.

'I do not ask it,' Mary said.

'Wherefore must I write in the vulgar tongue?' Udal asked again, 'Oh, Mistress of my actions and my heart, what whim is this? The King is an excellent good Latinist!'

'Too good!' the Lady Mary said bitterly. 'With his learning he hath overset the Church of Christ.'

She spoke harshly to Katharine: 'What reversal should give my mother her life again? Wench! Wench!...' Then she turned upon Udal indifferently:

'God knows why this man would have you write in the vulgar tongue. But so he wills it.'

Udal groaned.

'My dinner hour is here,' the Lady Mary said. 'I am very hungry. Get you to your writing and take this lady to my women.'

VII

The Lady Mary's rooms were seventeen in number; they ran the one into the other, but they could each be reached by the public corridor alongside. It was Magister Udal's privilege, his condition being above that of serving man, to make his way through the rooms if he knew that the Lady Mary was not in one of them. These chambers were tall and gloomy; the light fell into them bluish and dismal; in one a pane was lacking in a window; in another a stool was upset before a fire that had gone out.

To traverse this cold wilderness Udal had set on his cap. He stood in front of Katharine Howard in the third room and asked:

'You are ever of the same mind towards your magister?'

'I was never of any mind towards you,' she answered. Her eyes went round the room to see how Princes were housed. The arras pictured the story of the nymph Galatea; the windows bore intertwined in red glass the cyphers H and K that stood for Katharine of Aragon. 'Your broken fortunes are mended?' she asked indifferently.

He pulled a small book out of his pocket, ferreted among the leaves and then setting his eye near the page pointed out his beloved line:

'Pauper sum, pateor, fateor, quod Di dant fero.' Which had been translated: 'I am poor, I confess; I bear it, and what the gods vouchsafe that I take'—and on the broad margin of the book had written: 'Cicero sayeth: That one cannot sufficiently praise them that be patient having little: And Seneca: The first measure of riches is to have things necessary—and, as ensueth therefrom, to be therewith content!'

'I will give you a text from Juvenal,' she said, 'to add to these: Who writes that no man is poor unless he be worthy of ridicule.'

He winced a little.

'Nay, you are hard! The text should be read: Nothing else maketh poverty so hard to bear as that it forceth men to ridiculous shifts...Quam quod ridiculos esse...'

'Aye, magister, you are more learned even yet than I,' she said indifferently. She made a step towards the next door but he stood in front of her holding up his thin hands.

'You were my best pupil,' he said, with a hungry humility as if he mocked himself. 'Poor I am, but mated to me you should live as do the Hyperboreans, in a calm and voluptuous air.'

'Aye, to hang myself of weariness, as they do,' she answered.

He corrected her with the version of Pliny, but she answered only: 'I have a great thirst upon me.'

His eyes were humorous, despairing and excited.

'Why should a lady not love her master?' he asked. 'There are examples. Know you not the old rhyme:

'Ah, unspeakable!' she said. 'You bring me examples in the vulgar tongue!'

'I babble for joy at seeing you and for grief at your harsh words,' he answered.

She stood waiting with a sort of haughty submissiveness.

'I would you would delay your wooing. I have been on the road since dawn with neither bit nor sup.'

He protested that he had starved more hideously than Tantalus since he had seen her last.

She gave him indifferently her cheek to kiss.

'For pity's sake take me where I may rest,' she said, 'I have a maimed arm.'

He uttered her panegyric, after a model of Tibullus, to the Lady Rochford and the seven maids of honour under that lady's charge. He was set upon Katharine's enjoyment, and he invented a lie that the King had commanded a dress to be found for her to attend at the revels that night. The maids were already dressing themselves. Two of them were fairheaded, and four neither fair nor dark; but one was dark as night, and dressed all in black with a white coif, so that she resembled a magpie. Some were curling each other's hair and others tightening stay-laces with little wheels set in their companions' backs. Their bare shoulders were blue with the cold of the great room, and their dresses lay in heaps upon sheets that were spread about the clean floor—brocades sewn with pearls, velvets that were inlaid with filagree work, indoor furs and coifs of fine lawn that were delicately edged with black thread.

The high sounds of their laughter had reached through the door, but a dead silence fell. The dark girl with a very long bust that raked back like a pigeon's, and with dark and sparkling eyes, tittered derisively at the magister and went on slowly rubbing a perfumed ointment into the skin of her throat and shoulders.

'Shall he bring his ragged doxies here too?' she laughed. 'What a taradiddle is this of Cophetua and a beggar wench.' The other maids all tittered derisively at Udal.

The Lady Rochford, warming her back close before the fire, said helplessly, 'I have no dresses beyond what you see.' She was already attired in a bountiful wine-coloured velvet that was embroidered with silver wire into entwined monograms of the initials of her name. Her hood of purple made, above her ample brows, a castellated pattern resembling the gate of a drawbridge. She, being the mistress of that household, and compassionately loved by the ladies because she was so helpless, timorous, and unable to control them, they had combined to comb and perfume her and to lace her stomacher before setting about their own clothing. White-haired and with a wrinkled face, she appeared, under her rich clothes, like some will-less and pallid captive that had been gorgeously bedizened to grace a conqueror's triumph. She was cousin to the late Queen Anne Boleyn, and the terror of her own escape, when the Queen and so many of her house had been swept away, seemed still to remain in the drawing-in of her eyes. In the mien of the youngest girls there, there could be seen a strained tenseness of lids and lips as though, in the midst of laughter, they were hearkening for distant sounds or the rustle of listeners behind the tapestry. And where a small door came into one wall they had pulled down the arras from in front of it, so that no one should enter unobserved. Lady Rochford addressed herself to Katharine with limp gestures of protest:

'God knows I would help you to a gown, but we have no more than we are granted; here are seven ladies and seven dresses. Where can another be got? The King's Highness knoweth little of ladies' gowns or he had never ordered one against to-night. Each of those hath taken the women seven weeks to sew.'

Udal said with a touch of anger, since it enraged him to have to invent further, as if the one lie about the King were not enough: 'The Lord Privy Seal commanded very strictly this thing to be done. He is this lady's very diligent protector. Have a care how you disoblige her.'

The ladies rustled their slight clothing at that name, turned their backs, and looked at Katharine above their shoulders. The Lady Rochford recoiled so far that her skirts were in danger from the fire in the great hearth; her woebegone, flaccid face was suddenly drawn at the mention of Cromwell, and she appeared about to kneel at Katharine's feet. She looked round at the figures of the girls.

'One of these can stay if your ladyship will wear her dress,' she flustered. 'But who is tall enow? Cicely is too long in the shank. Bess's shoulders are too broad. Alack! God help me! I will do what I can'—and she waved her hands disconsolately.

Cold, fatigue, and her maimed arm made Katharine waver on her feet. This white-haired woman's panic seemed to her grotesque and disgusting.

'Why, the magister lies,' she said. 'I am no such friend of Privy Seal's.'

Swift and wicked glances passed among the girls; the dark one threw back her head and laughed discordantly, like a magpie. She came with a deft and hopping step and gazed at Katharine with her head on one side.

'Old Crummock will want our teeth next to make him a new set. He may have my head, tell him. I have no need for it, it aches so since he killed my men-folk.'

Lady Rochford shuddered as if she had been struck.

'Beseech you,' she said weakly to Katharine. 'Cicely Elliott is sometimes distraught. Believe not that we speak like this among ourselves.' Her eyes wandered in a flustered and piteous way over her girls and she whimpered, 'Jane Gaskell, stand back to back with this lady.'

Katharine Howard cried out, 'Keep your gowns for your backs and your tongues still. Woe betide the girl who calls me a gossip of Privy Seal.'

Cicely Elliott cast her dark head back and uttered one of her discordant laughs at the ceiling, and a girl, hiding behind the others, called out, 'What a fine —!'

Katharine cried, 'It is all lies that this fool magister utters. I will go to no masques nor revels.' She turned upon Lady Rochford, her face pallid, her lips open: 'Give me water,' she said harshly. 'I will get me back to my pig-sties.'

Lady Rochford wrung her hands and protested that her ladyship should not repeat that they were always thus. Privy Seal should not visit it upon them.

The magister blinked upon the riot that his muddling had raised. He called out, 'Be quiet. Be quiet. This lady is sick!' and stretched out his hands to hold Katharine on her feet.

Cicely Elliott cried, 'God send all Crummock's informers always sick.'

'Thou dastard!' Katharine screamed aloud. She tried to speak but she choked; she grasped Udal's hand as if to wring from him the denial of his foolish lies, but a sharp and numbing pain shot up her maimed wrist to her shoulders and leaped across her forehead.

'Thou filthy spy,' the dark girl laughed wildly into her agonised face. 'If there had never been any like thee all the dear men of my house had still breathed.'

Katharine sprang wildly towards her tormentor, but a black sheet seemed to drop across her eyes. She fell right down and screamed as her elbow struck the floor.

PART TWO

THE HOUSE OF EYES

I

A grave and bearded man was found to cup her. He gave her a potion composed of the juice of nightshade and an infusion of churchyard moss. Her eyes grew dilated and she had evil dreams. She lay in a small chamber that was quite bare and had a broken window, and the magister ran from room to room begging for quilts to cover her.

It was nobody's affair. The Lord Privy Seal, her uncle, the Catholics, and the King were still perturbed about Anne of Cleves, and there were no warrants signed for Katharine's housing or food. All the palace was trembling with confusion, for, when the Queen had been upon the point of setting out from Rochester, the King was said to have been overcome by a new spasm of disgust: she was put by again.

The young Earl of Surrey, a cousin of Katharine's, gave Udal contemptuously a couple of crowns towards her nourishment. Udal applied them to bribing Throckmorton, the spy who had been with Privy Seal upon the barge, to inscribe on his lord's tablets the words: 'Katharine Howard to be provided for.' Udal made up his courage sufficiently to speak to the Duke, whom he met in a corridor. The Duke was jaundiced against his niece, because her cousin Culpepper had fallen upon Sir Christopher Aske, the Duke's captain who had kept the postern. It had needed seven men to master him, and this great tumult had arisen in the King's own courtyard. Nevertheless, the Duke sent his astrologer to cast Katharine's horoscope. He signed, too, an order that some girl be found to attend on her.

Udal filled in the girl's name as Margot Poins, the granddaughter of old Badge, of Austin Friars. Even among these clamours his tooth watered for her, and he gave the order to young Poins to execute. The young man rode off into Bedfordshire, where his sister had been sent out of the way to the house of their aunt. He presented the order as in the nature of a writ from the Duke, and amongst Lutherans in London a heavy growl of rage went up—against Norfolk, against the Papists of the Privy Council, and, above all, against Katharine Howard, whom they called the New Harlot.

Katharine, having taken much nightshade juice, was raving upon her bed. The leech became convinced that she was possessed by a demon, because the pupils of her eyes were as large as silver groats, and her hands picked at the coverlets. He ordered that thirteen priests should say an exorcism at the door of her room, and that the potion of nightshade—since it might inconvenience without dislodging the fiend inhabiting her slender body—should be discontinued.

Udal sought for priests, but having no money, he was disregarded by them. He ran to the chaplain of the Bishop of Winchester. For the clergy upheld or ordained by Archbishop Cranmer were held to be less efficacious in matters of witchcraft and possession. Just then Cromwell had triumphed, and Anne of Cleves was upon the water coming to the palace.

Bishop Gardiner's chaplain, a fat man, with beady and guileless eyes sunk in under an immense forehead, imagined that Udal's visit was a pretext for overhearing the words of rage and discomfiture that in that Papist centre might be let drop about the new Queen. For Udal, because Privy Seal had set him with the Lady Mary, passed amongst the Papists for one of Cromwell's informants, and it amused his sardonic and fantastic nature to affect mysterious denials, which made the fiction the more firmly believed and gave to Udal himself a certain hated prestige. The chaplain answered that in the present turmoil no such body as thirteen clergymen could be found.

'But the lady shall be torn in pieces,' Udal shrieked. Panic had overcome him. Who knew that the fiend, having torn his Katharine asunder, might not enter into the body of his Margot, who was already at her bedside? His lips quivered with terror, his eyes smiled furiously, he wrung his hands. He swore he would penetrate to the King's Highness' self. Udal was a man who stuck at nothing to gain a point. He had heard from Katharine that the King had spoken graciously to her, and he swore once more that she was the apple of the King's eye, as well as a beloved disciple of Privy Seal's.

'Be sure,' he foamed, 'they shall be avenged on a Gardiner and his crew if you let her die.'

The chaplain said impassively: 'God forbid that we, who are loyal to his Highness, should listen to these tales you bring us of his lechery!' They had there a new Queen, their duty was to her, and to no Katharine Howard. The bishop's clergy were all joyfully setting to welcome the lady from Cleves, they had no time to waste over a leman's demons. It overjoyed him to refuse Privy Seal's man a boon on the plea of loyalty to the new Queen. Nevertheless, he went straight to the presence of the bishop, and told him the marvels that Udal had reported.

'The man is incontinent and a babbler,' the chaplain said. 'We may believe one tenth.'

'Well, you shall find for once how this wench is housed and where,' his master answered moodily. 'God knows what we may believe in these days. Doubtless the Nuntio of Satan hath a new plot in the hatching.' Making these enquiries, the chaplain came upon the backwash of Udal's reports that the King loved some leman. Some lady, somewhere—some said a Howard, some a Rochford, some would have it a Spanish woman—was being hidden up, either by the King, by the Duke of Norfolk, or by Privy Seal. God knew the truth of these things: but similar had happened before; and it was certain that the Cleves woman had been for long kept dangling at Rochester. Perhaps that was the reason. His Highness had his own ways in these matters: but where there was smoke, generally fire was to be found. The chaplain brought this budget back to Bishop Gardiner. Gardiner swore a wild oath that, by the bones of the Confessor, they had unmasked a new plot of Satan's Legate, the Privy Seal. But, by the grace of God, he would counter-plot him.

Udal, who had started all these rumours, had run to get the help of a Dean of Durham, with whom formerly he had had much converse as to the position of the Islands of the Blest. He never found him; the palace was in confusion, with the doors all open and men running from room to room to ask each other how far it might be safe to be extravagant in their demonstrations of joy at the coming of the new Queen.

All night long, from about dusk, the palace rang with salvos of artillery, loud shouts and the blowing of horns: the windows glowed duskily now and again with the light of bonfires that leapt up and subsided. Margot Poins, who was used to rejoicings in the City, set the heavy wooden bar across the door in Katharine Howard's room, turned the immense key in the rusty lock, and opened to no knocking until the day broke. There were shouts and stumblings in the corridor outside and the magister himself, very intoxicated and shrieking, came hammering at the door with several others towards one in the morning.

Katharine could walk by noon to the lodging that had at last been assigned to her by Privy Seal's warrant. The magister, having got himself soundly beaten the night before, was still sleeping away the effects of it, so she and Margot stayed for an hour in solitude. Voices passed the door many times, and at last a Master Viridus entered stealthily. He was one of the Lord Cromwell's secretaries, and he bore a purse. His name had been Greene but he had translated it to give a more worshipful sound. His eyes were furtive and he moved his lips perpetually in imitation of his master; wore a hooded cap, and made much use of the Italian language.

'Bounty is the sign of the great, and honourable service ensureth its continuance,' he said in a dry and arrogant voice. 'This is my Lord Privy Seal's vails. My lord hath gone to his own house.'

He presented the purse of gold, and peered round at the room which, following the warrant, had been assigned by a clerk from the Earl Marshal's office.

'I thank your lord, and shall endeavour to deserve his good bounty,' Katharine said. The nightshade juice being left two days behind she had the use of her eyes and much of the stiffness had gone out of her wrist.

'Your ladyship had much the wiser,' he answered. He lifted the hangings and, under pretence of examining into her comfort, peered into the great Flemish press and felt under the heavy black table to see if it had a drawer for papers. Cromwell had been forced, following the King's command, to give Katharine her place. But he had no love for Howards, and already the maids of the Lady Mary were a mutinous knot. Viridus was instructed to keep an attentive eye upon this girl—for they might hang her very easily since she was outspoken; or, having got her neck into a noose, they could work upon her terror and make her spy upon the Lady Mary herself. None of the Lady Mary's women were housed very sumptuously, but in this room there were at least an old tapestry, a large Flemish chair, a feather bed in a niche like an arched cell over which the hangings could be drawn, and a cord of wood for the fire. He hummed and hawed that workmen must come to bring her better hangings, and a servitor be found to keep her door. A watch was to be set on her; the women who measured her for clothes would try to discover whom she loved and hated, and the serving man at her door would report her visitors.

'My lord hath you very present in his mind,' Viridus said.

She was commanded to go on the Saturday to the house in Austin Friars, where my lord was preparing a great feast in the honour of the Queen.

Katharine said that she had no dress to go in.

'A seemly decent habit shall be got ready,' he answered. 'You shall sit in a gallery in private, and it shall be pointed out to you what lords you shall speak with and whom avoid.' For 'com' è bella giovinezza'...How beautiful is youth, what a pleasant season! And since it lasted but a short space it behoved us all—and her as much as any—to make as much as might be whilst it endured. The regard of a great lord such as Privy Seal brought present favours and future honours in the land, honours being pleasant in their turn, when youth is passed, like the mellow suns of autumn. 'Thereby indeed,' he apostrophised her, 'the savour of youth reneweth itself again and again..."Anzi rinuova come fa la luna," in the words of Boccace.'

Her fair and upright beauty made Viridus acknowledge how excellent a spy upon the Lady Mary she might make. Papistry and a loyal love for the Old Faith seemed to be as strong in her candid eyes as it was implicit in her name. The Lady Mary might trust her for that and talk with her because of her skill in the learned tongues. Then, if they held her in their hands, how splendid a spy she might make, being so trusted! She might well be won for their cause by the offer of liberal rewards, though Privy Seal's hand had been heavy upon all her kinsfolk. These men of Privy Seal's get from him a maxim which he got in turn from his master Macchiavelli: 'Advance therefore those whom it shall profit thee to make thy servants: for men forget sooner the death of a father than the loss of a patrimony'—and either by threats or by rewards they might make her very useful.

She had been minded to mock him in the beginning of his speech, but his dangerous pale-blue eyes made her feel that if he were ridiculous he was also very powerful, and that she was in the hands of these men.

Therefore she answered that youth indeed was a pleasant season when health, good victuals and the love of God sustained it.

He surveyed her out of the corners of his eyes.

'Seek, then, to deserve these good things,' he said. He stayed some time longer directing her how she should wear her clothes, and then in the gathering dusk he dwindled stealthily through the door.

'It is to make you like a chained-up beast or slave,' Margot said to her mistress.

'Why, hold your tongue, coney, after to-day,' Katharine answered, 'the walls shall hear. I am a very poor man's daughter and must even earn my bread if I would stay here.'

'They could never tie me so,' Margot retorted.

Her mistress laughed:

'Why, you may set nets for the wind, but what a man will catch is still uncertain.'

It was cold, and they piled up the fire, waiting for some one to bring them candles.

A tall and bulky figure, with a heavy cloak cast over one shoulder in the Spanish fashion, but with a priest's cap, was suddenly in the doorway.

'Ha, magister,' Katharine said, knowing no other man that could visit her. But the firelight shone upon a heavy, firm jaw that was never the magister's, on white hands and in threatening, steadfast eyes.

'I am the unworthy Bishop Gardiner, of Winchester,' a harsh voice said. 'I seek one Katharine Howard. Peace be with you in these evil days.'

Katharine fell upon her knees before this holy man. He gave her his blessing perfunctorily, and muttered some words of the exorcism against demons.

'I am even cured,' Katharine said.

He sent Margot Poins from the room, and stood in the firelight that threw his great shadow to shake upon the hangings, towering above Katharine Howard upon her knees. He was silent, as if he would threaten her, and his brooding eyes glowed and devoured her face. Here then, she thought, was the man from the other camp descending secretly upon her. He had no need to threaten, for she was of his side.

He said that a Magister Udal had reported that she stood in need of Christian aid, and, speaking Latin with a heavy voice, he interrogated her as to her faith. The times were evil: many and various heresies stalked about the land: let her beware of trafficking with them.

Kneeling still in the firelight, she answered that, so far as was lawful, she was a daughter of the Church.

He muttered: 'Lawful!' and looked at her for a long time with brooding and fanatical eyes. 'I hear you have read many heathen books under a strange master.'

She answered: 'Most Reverend, I am for the Old Faith in the old way.'

'A prudent tongue is also a Christian possession,' he muttered.

'Nay there is no one to hear in this room,' she said.

He bent over her to raise her to her feet and holding before her eyes his missal, he indicated to her certain prayers that she should recite in order to prevent the fiend's coming to her again. Suddenly he commanded her to tell him how often she had conversed with the King's Highness.

Gardiner was the bitterest of all whom Cromwell had to hate him. He had been of the King's Council, and a secretary before Cromwell had reached the Court, and, but for Cromwell, he might well have been the King's best minister. But Cromwell had even taken his secretaryship; and he was set upon having Privy Seal down all through those ten years. He had been bishop before any of these changes had been thought of, and by such Papists as Katharine Howard he was esteemed the most holy man in the land.

She told him that she had seen the King but once for a little time.

'They told me it was many times,' he answered fiercely. 'Should I have come here merely to chatter with you?'

There was something sinister and harsh even in the bluish tinge of his shaven jaws, and his agate-blue eyes were sombre, threatening and suspicious.

She answered: 'But once,' and related the story very soberly.

He threatened her with his finger.

'Have a care that you speak truth. Things will not always remain in this guise. I come to warn you that you speak the King with a loyal purpose. His Highness listens sometimes to the promptings of his women.'

'You might have saved your journey,' she answered. 'I could speak no otherwise if he loved me.'

He gazed involuntarily round at the hangings as if he suspected a listener.

'Your Most Reverence does ill to doubt me,' Katharine said submissively. 'I am of a true house.'

'No house is true save where it finds its account,' he answered moodily. He could not believe that she spoke the truth—for he was unable to believe that any man could speak the truth—but it was true she was poorly housed, raggedly dressed and hidden up in a corner. Nevertheless, these might be artifices. He made ostentatiously and disdainfully towards the door.

'Why, God keep you,'—he moved his fingers in a negligent blessing—'I believe you are true, though you are of little use.' Suddenly he shot out:

'If you would stay here in peace your cousin Culpepper must begone.'

Katharine put her hand to her heart in sudden fear of these men who surrounded her and knew everything.

'What hath Tom done?' she asked.

'He hath put a shame upon thee,' the bishop answered. He had fallen upon Sir Christopher Aske: he had been set in chains for it, in the Duke's ward room. But upon the coming of the Queen the night before, all misdemeanants had been cast loose again. Culpepper had been kept by the guards from entering the palace, where he had no place. But he had fallen in with the Magister Udal in the courtyard. Being maudlin and friendly at the time, he had cast his arms round the magister's neck claiming him for a loved acquaintance. They had drunk together and had started, towards midnight, to find the chamber of Katharine Howard, Culpepper seeking his cousin, and the magister, Margot Poins. On the way they had enlisted other jovial souls, and the tumult in the corridor had arisen. 'These scandals are best avoided,' the bishop finished. 'I have known women lose their lives through them when they came to have husbands.'

'I could have calmed him,' Katharine said. 'He is always silent at a word from me.'

Gardiner stood pondering, his head hanging down. His eyes, hard and blue, flashed at her and then down again at the floor.

'They told me you were the King's good friend,' he said, resentfully. 'Your gossip Udal told my chaplain, and it hath been repeated.'

'They will talk where there are a many together,' Katharine answered; 'the magister is a notorious babbler and will have told many lies.'

'He is a spy of Privy Seal's and deep in his councils,' Gardiner answered gloomily.

A heavy wind that had arisen hurled itself against the dark casement. Little flaws of cold air penetrated the room, and the bishop pulled his cap further down over his ears.

'My Lord Privy Seal would send my cousin to Calais where there is fighting to come,' Katharine said.

Gardiner raised his head sharply at Cromwell's name.

'You speak sense at the end,' he muttered. To him too it had occurred that if she was to be the King's peaceably, this madman must begone. If Cromwell wished this lover of this girl out of the way, the reason was not obscure.

'A man of his hath been here this very day,' Katharine said.

'Privy Seal learned whoremastering in Italy,' Gardiner cried triumphantly. 'He saw signs that his Highness inclined to you. Have a care for your little soul.'

'Why, I think Privy Seal had no such vain imagination,' Katharine answered submissively. She would have laughed that the magister's insane babblings should have raised such a coil; but Gardiner was a man esteemed very saintly, and she kept her eyes on the floor.

'Give thou ear to no doctrines of Privy Seal's,' he answered swiftly. 'Thy soul should burn: I will curse thee. If the King shall offer thee favours for thy friends come thou to me for spiritual guidance.'

She opened amazed and candid eyes upon him.

'But this is a folly,' she said. 'A King may regard one for a minute, then it is past. Privy Seal would not bring me up against the King.'

He flashed his gloomy blue eyes at her, suspecting her, and still threatening.

'I know how Privy Seal will plot,' he said passionately. 'Having failed with one woman he will bring another.'

He clenched his hands angrily and unclenched them: the wind moaned for a moment among the chimney stacks.

'So it is!' he cried, from deep down in his chest. 'If it were not so, how is there all this clamour about his Highness and a woman?'

'Most Reverend,' she said, 'there is no end to the inventions of Magister Udal.'

'There is none to the machinations of the fiend, and Udal is of his councils,' he said. 'Be careful, I tell you, for your soul's sake. Cromwell shall come to you offering you great bribes. Have a care I say!'

She attempted to say that Udal had no voice at all in Privy Seal's councils, being a garrulous magpie that no sane man would trust. But Gardiner had crossed his arms and stood, immense and shadowy, in the firelight. He hissed irritably between his teeth when she spoke, as if she interrupted his meditation.

'All the world knows Udal for his spy,' he said, sombrely. 'If Udal hath babbled, God be thanked. I say again: if Privy Seal bring thee to the King, come thou to me. But, by the Grace of Heaven, I will forestall Privy Seal with thee and the King!'

She forbore to contradict him any more; he had this maggot in his head, and was so wild to defeat Privy Seal with his own tool.

He muttered: 'Think you Privy Seal knoweth not the King's taste? I tell you he hath seen an inclination in him towards you. This is a plot, but I have sounded it!'

She let him talk, and asked, with a malice too fine for him to discern:

'I should not shun the King's presence for my soul's sake?'

'God forbid,' he answered. 'I may use thee to bring down Privy Seal.'

He picked up a piece of bark from a faggot beside the fire and rolled it between his fingers. She stood looking at him intently, her lips a little parted, tall, graceful and submissive.

'You are more fair-skinned than any his Highness has favoured before,' he said in a meditative voice. 'Yet Cromwell knows the King's tastes better than any man.' He sank down into her tall-backed chair and suddenly tossed the piece of bark into the fire. 'I would have you walk across the floor, elevating your arms as you were the goddess Flora.'

She tripped towards the door, held her arms above her head, turned her long body to right and left, bent very low in a courtesy to him, and let her hands fall restfully into her lap. The firelight shone upon the folds of her dress and in the white lining of her hood. He looked at her, leaning over the arm of the chair, his blue eyes hard with the strenuous rage of his new project.

'You could take a part in an Italian interlude? A masque?'

'I have a better memory of the French or Latin,' she answered.

'You do not turn pale? Your knees knock not together?'

'I think I blush most,' she said seriously.

He answered, 'You will be the better of a little colour,' and began muffling his face with his cloak.

'See you, then,' his harsh voice commanded. 'You shall see their Highnesses at Privy Seal's house on the Saturday; but they shall see you at mine on the Tuesday. If you are good enough to serve the turn of Privy Seal, you may be good enough to serve mine. The King listens sometimes to the promptings of his women. I will teach you how you may bring this man down and set me in his place.'

She reflected for a moment. 'I would well serve you,' she said. 'But I do not believe this fable of the King, and I have no memory of Italian.' She talked of being the Lady Mary's servant, or that she must get her lady's leave.

His brows grew heavy, his eyes threatening and alarming beneath their heavy lids.

'Be you faithful to me,' he thundered. Even his thin and delicate hands seemed to menace her. 'Retain your obedience to your Faith. Your duty is to that, and to no earthly lady before that.'

Her eyes were cast down, her lips did not move. He said, harshly, 'It will go ill with you if it become known to Cromwell I have visited you. Keep this matter secret as you love your liberty. I will send you the words you shall say by a private bearer. After, maybe, his Highness shall safeguard you, I admonishing him. But the Lady Mary shall bid you obey me in all things.'

He opened the door and put his head out cautiously. Suddenly he drew it back and said in Latin, 'Here is a spy.' He did not flinch, but advanced into the corridor, keeping his back to the servitor whom already Master Viridus had sent to keep her door. Gardiner fumbled in his robes and pulled out his missal. He turned the pages over, and, speaking in a feigned and squeaky voice, once more indicated to her prayers against the visitations of fiends. Reading them aloud, he interspersed the Latin of the missal with the phrases, 'You may pray to God he have not seen my face. Be you very silent and secret, or you are undone. I could in no wise save you from Cromwell unless the King becomes your protector.' He finished in the vulgar tongue. 'I pray my prayers with you may have availed to give you relief. But a simple priest as myself is of small skill in these visitations. You should have sent to some great Churchman or one of the worshipful bishops.'

'Good Father Henry, I thank you,' she answered, having entered into his artifice. He went away, feigning to limp on his right knee, and keeping his face from the spy.

At the corner of the corridor Margot Poins, an immense blonde and gentle figure in Lutheran grey, stood back in the hangings. The Magister Udal leant over her, supporting himself with one hand against the wall above her head and one leg crossed beneath his gown.

'Come you into my room,' Katharine said to the girl; and to the magister, 'Avoid, man of books. I will have no maid of mine undone by thee.'

'Venio honoris causa,' he said pertly, and Margot uttered, 'He seeks me in wedlock,' in a gruff, uncontrolled voice of a great young girl's confusion, and immense blushes covered her large cheeks.

Katharine laughed; she was sorely afraid of the serving man behind her, for that he was a spy set there by Viridus she was very sure, and she was casting about in her mind for a device that should let her tell whether or no he had known the bishop. The squeaky voice and the feigned limp seemed to her stratagems ignoble and futile on the part of a great Churchman, and his mania of plots and counter-plottings had depressed and wearied her, for she expected the great to be wise. But she played her part for him as it was her duty. She spoke to the girl with her scarlet cheeks.

'Believe thou the magister after he hath ta'en thee afore a priest. He hath sought me and two score others in the cause of honour. Get you in, sweetheart.'

She pushed the girl in at the door. The serving man sat on his stool; his shock of yellow hair had never known a comb, but he had a decent suit of a purplish wool-cloth. He had his eyes dully on the ground.

'As you value your servitorship, let no man come into my room when I be out,' Katharine said to him. 'Saving only the Father Henry that was here now.'

The man raised expressionless blue eyes to her face.

'I know not his favours,' he said in a peasant's mutter. 'Maybe I should know him if I saw him again. I am main good at knowing people.'

'Why, he is from the Sheeres,' Katharine added, still playing, though she was certain that the man knew Gardiner. 'You shall know him by his voice and his limp.'

He answered, 'Maybe,' and dropped his eyes to the ground. She sent him to fetch her some candles, and shut the door upon him.

II

The Queen came to the revels given in her honour by the Lord Privy Seal. Cromwell had three hundred servants dressed in new liveries: pikemen with their staves held transversely, like a barrier, kept the road all the way from the Tower Steps to Austin Friars, and in that Lutheran quarter of the town there was a great crowding together. Caps were pitched high and lost for ever, and loud shouts of praise to God went up when the Queen and her Germans passed, with boys casting branches of holm, holly, bay and yew, the only plants that were green in the winter season, before the feet of her mule. But the King did not come. It was reported to the crowd that he was ill at Greenwich.

It was known very well by those that sat at dinner with her that, after three days, he had abandoned his Queen and kept his separate room. She sat eating alone, on high beneath the dais, heavy, silent, placid and so fair that her eyebrows appeared to be white upon her red forehead. She did not speak a word, having no English, and it was considered disgusting that she wiped her fingers upon pieces of bread.

Hostile lords remarked upon all her physical imperfections, which the King, it was known, had reported to his physicians in a writing of many pages. Besides, she had no English, no French, no Italian; she could not even play cards with his Highness. It was true that they had squeezed her into English stays, but she was reported to have wept at having to mount a horse. So she could not go a-hawking, neither could she shoot with the bow, and her attendants—the women, bound about the middle and spreading out above and below like bolsters, and the men, who wore their immense scolloped hats falling over their ears even at meal-times—excited disgust and derision by the noises they made when they ate.

The Master Viridus had Katharine Howard in his keeping. He took her up into a small gallery near the gilded roof of the long hall and pointed out to her, far below, the courtiers that it was safe for her to consort with, because they were friends of Privy Seal. His manner was more sinister and more meaning.

'You would do well to have to do with no others,' he said.

'I am like to have to do with none at all,' Katharine answered, 'for no mother's son cometh anigh me.'

He looked away from her. Down below she made out her cousin Surrey, sitting with his back ostentatiously turned to a Lord Roydon, of Cromwell's following; her uncle, plunged in his silent and malignant gloom; and Cromwell, his face lit up and smiling, talking earnestly with Chapuys, the Ambassador from the Emperor.

'Eleven hundred dishes shall be served this day,' Viridus proclaimed, seeming to warn her. 'There can no other lord find so many plates of parcel gilt.' His level and cold voice penetrated through all the ascending din of voices, of knives, of tuckets of trumpets that announced the courses of meat and of the three men's songs that introduced the sweet jellies which only Privy Seal, it was said, could direct to be prepared.

'Other lordings all,' Viridus continued with his sermon, 'ha' ruined themselves seeking in vain to vie with my lord. Most of those you see are broken men, whose favour would be worth naught to you.'

Tables were ranged down each side of the great hall, the men sitting on the right, each wearing upon his shoulder a red rose made of silk since no flowers were to be had. The women, sitting upon the left, had white favours in their caps. In the wide space between these tables were two bears; chained to tall gilt posts, they rolled on their hams and growled at each other. From time to time the serving men who went up and down in the middle let fall great dishes containing craspisces, cranes, swans or boars. These meats were kicked contemptuously aside for the bears to fight over, and their places supplied immediately with new. Other serving men broke priceless bottles of Venetian glass against the corners of tables, and let the costly Rhenish wines run about their feet.

This, the Master Viridus said, was intended to point out the wealth of their lord and his zealousness to entertain his Sovereigns.

'It would serve the purpose as well to give them twice as much fare,' Katharine said.

'They could never contain it,' Viridus answered gravely, 'so great is the bounty of my lord.'

Throckmorton, the spy, enormous, bearded and with the half-lion badge of the Privy Seal hanging round his neck from a gilt chain, walked up and down behind the guests, bearing the wand of a major-domo, affecting to direct the servers when to fill goblets and listening at tables where much wine had been served. Once he looked up at the gallery, and his scrutinising and defiant brown eyes remained for a long time upon Katharine's face, as if he too were appraising her beauty.

'I would not drink much wine with that man listening at my back. He came from my country, and was such a foul villain that mothers fright their children with his name,' Katharine said.

Viridus moved his lips quickly one upon another, and suddenly directed her to observe the new Queen's head-dress, broad and stiffened with a wire of gold, upon which large pearls had been sewn.

'Many ladies will now get themselves such headdresses,' he said.

'That will I never,' she answered. It appeared atrocious and Flemish-clumsy, spreading out and overshadowing the Queen's heavy face. Their English hoods with the tails down made the head sleek and comely; or, with the tails folded up and pinned square like flat caps they could give to the face a gallant or a pensive expression.

'Why, I could never get me in at the door of the confessional with such a spreading cloth.'

Viridus had his chin on the rail of the gallery; he gazed down below with his snaky eyes. She could not tell whether he were old or young.

'You would more prudently abandon the confessing,' he said, without looking at her. 'My lord is minded that ladies who look to him should wear such.'

'That is to be a bond-slave,' Katharine cried indignantly. He looked round.

'Here is a great magnificence,' he uttered, moving his hand towards the hall. 'My Lord Privy Seal hath a mighty power.'

'Not power enow to make me a laughing-stock for the men.'

'Why, this is a free land,' he answered. 'You may rot in a ditch if you will, or worse if treasonable actions be brought home to you.'

Down below, wild men dressed in the skins of wolves, hares and stags ran round the tethered bears bearing torches of sweet wood, and a heavy and languorous smoke, like incense, mounted up to the gallery. Viridus' unveiled threat made the necessity for submission come once more into her mind. Other wild men were leading in a lion, immense and lean as if it were a fawn-coloured ass. It roared and pulled at the golden chains by which the knot of men held it. Many ladies shrieked out, but the men dragged the lion into the open space before the dais where the Queen sat unmoved and stolid.

'Would your master have me dip my fingers in the dish and wipe them on bread-manchets as the Queen does?' Katharine asked in a serious expostulation.

'It were an excellent action,' Viridus answered.

There was a brazen flare of trumpets so that the smoke swirled among the rafters. Men with brass helmets and shields of brass were below in the hall.

'They are costumed as the ancient Romans,' Katharine said, lost in other thoughts.

Suddenly she saw that whilst all the other eyes were upon the lion, Throckmorton's glare was again upon her face. He appeared to shake his head and to bow his immense and bearded form. It brought into her mind the dangerous visit of Bishop Gardiner. Suddenly he dropped his eyes.

'You see some friends,' Viridus' voice asked beside her.

'Nay, I have no friends here,' Katharine answered.

She could not tell that the bearded spy's eyes were not merely amorous in their intention, for such looks she was used to, and he was a very vile man.

'In short,' Viridus spoke, 'it were an excellent action to act in all things as the Queen does. For fashions are a matter of fashion. It is all one whether you wipe your fingers on bread-manchets or on napkins. But when a fashion becometh general its strangeness departeth and it is esteemed fit for a King's Court. Thus you may earn your bread: this is your duteous work. Observe the king of the beasts. See how it shall do its duty before the Queen, and mark the lesson.' His voice penetrated, low and level, through all the din from below. Yet the men dressed like gladiators advanced towards the dais where the Queen sat eating unmoved. The lion before her growled frightfully, and dragged its keepers towards the men in brass. They drew their short swords and beat upon their shields crying: 'We be Roman traitors that war upon this land.' Then it appeared that among them in their crowd they had a large mannikin, dressed like themselves in brass and running upon wheels.

The ladies pressed the tables with their hands, making as if to rise in terror. But the mannikin toppling forward fell before the lion with a hollow sound of brass. The lean beast, springing at its throat, tore it to reach the highly smelling flesh that was concealed within the tunic, and the Romans fled, casting away their shields and swords. One of them had a red forked beard and wide-open blue eyes. He brought into Katharine's mind the remembrance of her cousin. She wondered where he could be, and imagined him with that short sword, cutting his way to her side.

'That sight is allegorically to show,' Viridus was commenting beside her, 'how the high valour of Britain shall defend from all foes this noble Queen.'

The lion having reached its meat lay down upon it.

Katharine remembered that Bishop Gardiner said that her cousin must be begone. She tried to say to Viridus: 'Sir, I would fain obey you in these things, but I have a cousin that shall much hinder me.'

But the applause of the people below drowned her voice and Viridus continued talking.

Let it be true that the Queen, being alone, showed amongst their English fineries and nicenesses a gross and repulsive strangeness. But if their ladies put on her manners she should no longer be alone, and it would appear to the King and to all men that her example was both commended and emulated. It was a matter of kingcraft, and so the Lord Privy Seal was minded and determined.

'Then I will even get myself such a hat and tear my capons apart with my fingers,' Katharine said.

'You had much the wiser,' he answered.

The hall was now full of wild men, nymphs in white gowns, men bearing aspergers with which to scatter perfumes, and merry andrews, so that the floor could no longer be seen. A party of lords had overset a table in their efforts to get to the nymphs. The Queen was schooled to go out behind the arras, and the ladies, laughing, calling to each other and to the men at the other tables, and pinning up their hoods, filed out after her.

'I shall do my best to please your master and mine,' Katharine said. 'But he must even help me, or I can be no example to emulate, but one at whom the finger of scorn is likely to be pointed.'

Viridus paused before he led his charge from the gallery. His pale-blue eyes were more placable.

'You shall be well seconded. But have a care. Dally with no traitors. Speak fairly of your master's friends.' He touched her above the left breast with a claw-like finger. 'The Italian writes: "Whoso mocketh my love mocketh also mine own self."'

'I mock none,' Katharine said. 'But I have a cousin to be provided for that neither you nor I shall mock with much safety if he be sober enough to stand.'

He listened to her with his hand upon the door of the gallery: his air was attentive and aroused. She related very simply how Culpepper had besieged her door—'He came to London to help me on my way and to seek fortune in some war. I would that a place might be found for him, for here he is like to ruin both himself and me.'

'We have need of good swordsmen for an errand,' he said, in an absorbed voice.

'There was never a better than Tom,' Katharine said. 'He hath cut a score of throats. Your lord would have sent him to Calais.'

He muttered:

'Why, there are places other than Calais where a man may make a fortune.'

Something sinister in his brooding voice made her say:

'I would not have him killed. He hath made me many presents.'

He looked at her expressionlessly:

'It is very certain that you can not serve my lord with such a firebrand to your tail,' he said. 'I will find him an errand.'

'But not where he shall be killed,' she said again.

'Why,' he said slowly, 'I will send him where he will make a great fortune.'

'A great fortune would help him little,' she answered. 'I would have him sent where he may fight evenly matched.'

He laid his hand upon her wrist.

'He is in as much danger here as anywhere. This is not Lincolnshire, but an ordered Court.'—A man drew his sword with some peril there, for there were laws against it. If men came brawling in the maids' quarters at nights there were penalties of losing fingers, hands, or even heads. And the maids themselves were liable to be whipped.—He shook his head at her:

'If your cousin hath so violent an inclination to you I were your best friend to send him far away.'

It was in his mind that if they were to breed this girl to be a spy they must keep her protected from madmen. Something of mystery in his manner penetrated to her quick senses.

'God help me, what a dangerous place this is!' she said. 'I would I had never spoken to you of my cousin.'

He eyed her solemnly and said that if she were minded to wed this roaring boy they might both, and soon, earn fortunes to buy them land in a distant shire.

III

The young Poins, in his scarlet and black, drew his sister into a corner of the hall in which the gentry of the Lords that were there had already dined. It was a vast place, used as a rule for hearing suitors to the Lord Privy Seal and for the audit dinners of his tenantry in London. On its whitened walls there were trophies of arms, and between the wall and the platform at the end of the hall was a small space convenient for private talk. The rest of the people there were playing round games for kissing forfeits or clustered round a magician who had brought a large ape to tell fortunes by the Sortes Virgilianæ. It fumbled about in the pages of a black-letter Æneid, and scratched its side voluptuously: taking its own time it looked at the pages attentively with a mournful parody of an aged sage, and set its finger upon a line that the fates directed.

'Here's a great ado about thee,' Poins said, laughing at his sister. 'Thy name is up in this town of London.'

He had come in the bodyguard of the Queen, and had made time to slip round to old Badge's low house behind the wall in order to beg from his grandfather ten crowns to pay for a cloak he had lost at cards.

'Such a cackle among these Lutherans,' he mocked at Margot. 'Heard you no hootings as your lady rode here behind us of the guard?'

'I heard none, nor she deserveth none,' Margot answered. 'For I love her most well.'

'Aye, she hath done a rape on thee,' he laughed. 'Aye, our good uncle hath printed a very secret libel upon her.' He began to whisper: Let it not be known or a sudden vengeance might fall upon their house. It was no small matter to print unlicensed broadsides. But their moody uncle was out of all fear of consequences, so mad with rage. 'He would have broken my back, because I tore thee from his tender keeping.'

'Sure it was never so tender,' Margot said. 'When was there a day that he did not beat me?' But he would have married her to his apprentice, a young fellow with a golden tongue, that preached every night to a secret congregation in a Cripplegate cellar.

'Why, an thou observest my maxims,' the boy said, sententiously, 'I will have thee a great lady. But uncle hath printed this libel, and tongues are at work in Austin Friars.' It was said that this was a new Papist plot. Margot was but the first that they should carry off. The Duke and Bishop Gardiner were reported to have signed papers for abducting all the Lutheran virgins in London. They were to be led from the paths of virtue into Catholic lewdnesses, and all their boys were to be abducted and sent into monasteries across the seas.

'Thus the race of Lutherans should die out,' he laughed. 'Why they are hiding their maidens in pigeon-houses in Holborn. A boy called Hugh hath gone out and never come home, and it is said that masked men in black stuff gowns were seen to put him into a sack in Moorfields.'

'Well, here be great marvels,' Margot laughed.

He shook his red sides, and his blue eyes grew malicious and teasing:

'Such a strumpet as thy lady,' he uttered. 'A Papist Howard that is known to have been loved by twenty men in Lincoln.'

Margot passed from laughter into hot anger:

'It is a marvel God strikes not their tongues with palsy that said that,' she said swiftly. 'Why do you not kill some of them if you be a man?'

'Why, be calmed,' he said. 'You have heard such tales before now. It is no more than saying that a woman goes not to their churches to pray.'

A young Marten Pewtress, half page, half familiar to the Earl of Surrey, came towards them calling, 'Hal Poins.' He had black down upon his chin and a roving eye. He wore a purple coat like a tabard, and a cap with his master's arms upon a jewelled brooch.

'They say there's a Howard wench come to Court,' he cried from a distance, 'and thy sister in her service.'

'We talk of her,' Poins answered. 'Here is my sister.'

The young Pewtress kissed the girl upon the cheek.

'Pray, you, sweetheart, unfold,' he said. 'You are a pretty piece, and have a good brother that's my friend.'

He asked all of a breath whether this lady had yet had the small-pox? whether her hair were her own? how tall she stood without high heels to her shoon? whether her breath were sweet or her language unpleasing in the Lincolnshire jargon? whether the King had sent her many presents?

Margaret Poins was a very large, fair, and credulous creature, rising twenty. Florid and slow-speaking, she had impulses of daring that covered her broad face with immense blushes. She was dressed in grey linsey-woolsey, and wore a black hood after the manner of the stricter Protestants, but she had round her neck a gilt medallion on a gold chain that Katharine Howard had given her already. She was, it was true, the daughter of a gentleman courtier, but he had been knocked on the head by rebels near Exeter just before her birth, and her mother had died soon after. She had been treated with gloomy austerity by her uncle and with sinister kindness by her grandfather, whom she dreaded. So that, coming from her Bedfordshire aunt, who had a hard cane, to this palace, where she had seen fine dresses and had already been kissed by two lords in the corridors, she was ready to aver that the Lady Katharine had a breath as sweet as the kine, a white skin which the small-pox had left unscarred, hair that reached to her ankles, and a learning and a wit unimaginable. Her own fortune was made, she believed, in serving her. Both the magister and her brother had sworn it, and, living in an age of marvels—dragons, portents from the heavens, and the romances of knight errantry—she was ready to believe it. It was true that the lady's room had proved a cell more bare and darker than her own at home, but Katharine's bright and careless laughter, her fair and radiant height, and her ready kisses and pleasant words, made the girl say with hot loyalty:

'She is more fair than any in the land, and, indeed, she is the apple of the King's eye.' Her voice was gruff with emotion, but, suddenly becoming very aware that she was talking to a strange young gentleman who might scoff, she seemed to choke and put her hand over her mouth.

Brocades for dresses, perfumes, gloves, oranges, and even another netted purse of green silk holding gold had continued to be brought to their chamber ever since Privy Seal had signed the warrant, and, it being about the new year, these ordinary vails and perquisites of a Maid of Honour made a show. Margot believed very sincerely that these things came direct from the King's hands, since they were formally announced as coming of his Highness' great bounty.

She reported to young Pewtress, 'And even now she is with the Lord Privy Seal, who brought her to Court.'

'He will go poaching among our Howards now,' Pewtress said. He stood considering with an air of gloom that the Norfolk servants imitated from their master, along with such sayings as that the times were very evil, and that no true man's neck was safe on his shoulders. 'Pray you, Sweetlips, tell no one this for a day until I have told my master. It may get me some crowns.' He pinched her chin between his thumb and forefinger. 'I will be your sweetheart, pretty.'

'Nay, I am provided with a good one,' Margot said seriously.

'You cannot have too many in this place. Take me for when the other's in gaol and another for when I am hung, as all good men are like to be.' He turned away lightly and loosened one of his jewelled garters, so that his stockings should hang in slovenly folds to prove that he was a man and despised niceness in his dress.

'I would that you be not too cheap to these gentry,' her brother said, with his eyes on Pewtress.

'I did naught,' she answered. 'If a gentleman will kiss one, it is uncourtly to turn away the cheek.'

'There is a way of not lending the lip,' he lectured her. 'I shall school you. A kiss here, a kiss there, I grant you. But consider that you be a gentleman's child, and ask who a man is.'

'He was well enough favoured,' she remonstrated.

'In these changing days many upstarts are come about the Court,' he went on with his lesson. 'Such were not here in the old days. Crummock hath wrought this. Seek advancement; pleasure your mistress, who can advance you; smile upon the magister, who, being advanced, can advance you. Speak courteous and fair words to any great lords that shall observe you. So we can rise in the world.'

'I will observe thy words,' she said submissively, for he seemed to her great and learned; 'but I like not that thou call'st me "you."'

'Why, these be grave matters,' he replied, 'and "you" is graver than "thou." But I love thee well. I will take thee a walk if the sun shine to-morrow.' He tightened his belt and took his pike from the corner. 'As for your lady; those that made these lies are lowsels. I could slay a score of them if they pressed upon you two.'

'I would not be so spoken of,' Margot answered.

'Then you must never rise in the world, as I am minded you shall,' he retorted, 'for, you being in a high place, eyes will be upon you.'

Nevertheless, Katharine Howard heard no evil words shouted after her that day. Pikemen and servitors of Cromwell were too thick upon all the road to the Tower, where the courtiers took barge again. Cromwell made very good order that no insults should reach the ears of such of the Papist nobles as came to his feast; they would make use with the King of evil words if any such were shouted. Thus the more dangerous and the most foul-mouthed of that neighbourhood, when the Court went by, found hands pressed over their mouths or scarves suddenly tightened round their throats by stalwart men that squeezed behind them in the narrow ways, so that not many more than twenty heads on both sides were broken that day; and Margot Poins kept her mouth closed tight with a sort of rustic caution—a shyness of her mistress and a desire to spare her any pain. Thus it was not until long after that Katharine heard of these rumours.

Katharine was in high good spirits. She had no great reason, for Viridus had threatened her; the Queen had rolled her large eyes round when Katharine had made her courtesy, but no words intelligible to a Christian had come from the thick lips; and no lord or lady had noticed her with a word except that, late in the afternoon, her cousin Surrey, a young man with a sleepily insolent air and front teeth that resembled a rabbit's, had suddenly planted himself in front of her as she sat on a stool against the hangings. He had begun to ask her where she was housed, when another young man caught him by the shoulder and pulled him away before he could do more than bid her sit there till he came again. She had been in no mood to do that for her cousin Surrey; besides, she would not be seen to speak much with a Papist henchman in that house. He could seek her if he wanted her company, so she went into another part of the hall, where they were all strangers.

Except for the mere prudence of pretending to obey Viridus until it should be safe to defy him and his master, she troubled little about what was going to happen to her. It was enough that she was away from the home where she had pined and been lonely. She sat on her stool, watched the many figures that passed her, marked fashions of embroidery, and thought that such speeches as she chanced to hear were ill-turned. Her sister Maids of Honour turned their backs upon her. Only the dark girl, Cicely Elliott, who had gibed at her a week ago, helped her to pin her sleeve that had been torn by a sword-hilt of some man who had turned suddenly in a crowd. But Katharine had learnt, as well as the magister, that when one is poor one must accept what the gods send. Besides, she knew that in the Lady Mary's household she was certain to be avoided, for she was regarded still as a spy of old Crummock's. That, most likely, would end some day, and she had no love for women's chatter.

She sat late at night correcting the embroidery of some true-love-knots that Margot had been making for her. A huckster had been there selling ribands from France, and showing a doll dressed as the ladies of the French King's Court were dressing that new year. He had been talking of a monster that had been born to a pig-sty on Cornhill, and lamenting that travel was become a grievous costly thing since the monasteries, with their free hostel, had been done away with. The monster had been much pondered in the city; certainly it portended wars or strange public happenings, since it had the face of a child, greyhound's ears, a sow's forelegs, and a dragon's tail. But the huckster had gone to another room, and Margot was getting her supper with the Lady Mary's serving-maids.

'Save us!' Katharine said to herself over her embroidery-frame, 'here be more drunkards. If I were a Queen I would make a law that any man should be burnt on the tongue that was drunk more than seven times in the week.' But she was already on her feet, making for the door, her frame dropped to the ground. There had been a murmur of voices through the thick oak, and then shouts and objurgations.

Thomas Culpepper stood in the doorway, his sword drawn, his left hand clutching the throat of the serving man who was guarding her room.

'God help us!' Katharine said angrily; 'will you ruin me?'

'Cut throats?' he muttered. 'Aye, I can cut a throat with any man in Christendom or out.' He shook the man backwards and forwards to support himself. 'Kat, this offal would have kept me from thee.'

Katharine said, 'Hush! it is very late.'

At the sound of her voice his face began to smile.

'Oh, Kat,' he stuttered jovially, 'what law should keep me from thee? Thou'rt better than my wife. Heathen to keep man and wife apart, I say, I.'

'Be still. It is very late. You will shame me,' she answered.

'Why, I would not have thee shamed, Kat of the world,' he said. He shook the man again and threw him good humouredly against the wall. 'Bide thou there until I come out,' he muttered, and sought to replace his sword in the scabbard. He missed the hole and scratched his left wrist with the point. 'Well, 'tis good to let blood at times,' he laughed. He wiped his hand upon his breeches.

'God help thee, thou'rt very drunk,' Katharine laughed at him. 'Let me put up thy sword.'

'Nay, no woman's hand shall touch this blade. It was my father's.'

An old knight with a fat belly, a clipped grey beard and roguish, tranquil eyes was ambling along the gallery, swinging a small pair of cheverel gloves. Culpepper made a jovial lunge at the old man's chest and suddenly the sword was whistling through the shadows.

The old fellow planted himself on his sturdy legs. He laughed pleasantly at the pair of them.

'An' you had not been very drunk I could never have done that,' he said to Culpepper, 'for I am passed of sixty, God help me.'

'God help thee for a gay old cock,' Culpepper said. 'You could not have done it without these gloves in your fist.'

'See you, but the gloves are not cut,' the knight answered. He held them flat in his fat hands. 'I learnt that twist forty years ago.'

'Well, get you to the wench the gloves are for,' Culpepper retorted. 'I am not long together of this pleasant mind.' He went into Katharine's room and propped himself against the door post.

The old man winked at Katharine.

'Bid that gallant not draw his sword in these galleries,' he said. 'There is a penalty of losing an eye. I am Rochford of Bosworth Hedge.'

'Get thee to thy wench, for a Rochford,' Culpepper snarled over his shoulder. 'I will have no man speak with my coz. You struck a good blow at Bosworth Hedge. But I go to Paris to cut a better throat than thine ever was, Rochford or no Rochford.'

The old man surveyed him sturdily from his head to his heels and winked once more at Katharine.

'I would I had had such manners as a stripling,' he uttered in a round and friendly voice. 'I might have prospered better in love.' Going sturdily along the corridor he picked up Culpepper's sword and set it against the wall.

Culpepper, leaning against the doorpost, was gazing with ferocious solemnity at the open clothes-press in which some hanging dresses appeared like women standing. He smoothed his red beard and thrust his cap far back on his thatch of yellow hair.

'Mark you,' he addressed the clothes-press harshly, 'that is Rochford of Bosworth Hedge. At the end of that day they found him with seventeen body wounds and the corpses of seventeen Scotsmen round him. He is famous throughout Christendom. Yet in me you see a greater than he. I am sent to cut such a throat. But that's a secret. Only I am a made man.'

Katharine had closed her door. She knew it would take her twenty minutes to get him into the frame of mind that he would go peaceably away.

'Thou art very pleasant to-night,' she said. 'I have seldom seen thee so pleasant.'

'For joy of seeing thee, Kat. I have not seen thee this six days.' He made a hideous grinding sound with his teeth. 'But I have broken some heads that kept me from thee.'

'Be calm,' Katharine answered; 'thou seest me now.'

He passed his hand over his eyes.

'I'll be calm to pleasure thee,' he muttered apologetically. 'You said I was very pleasant, Kat.' He puffed out his chest and strutted to the middle of the room. 'Behold a made man. I could tell you such secrets. I am sent to slay a traitor at Rome, at Ravenna, at Ratisbon—wherever I find him. But he's in Paris, I'll tell thee that.'

Katharine's knees trembled; she sank down into her tall chair.

'Whom shalt thou slay?'

'Aye, and that's a secret. It's all secrets. I have sworn upon the hilt of my knife. But I am bidden to go by an old-young man, a make of no man at all, with lips that minced and mowed. It was he bade the guards pass me to thee this night.'

'I would know whom thou shalt slay,' she asked harshly.

'Nay, I tell no secrets. My soul would burn. But I am sent to slay this traitor—a great enemy to the King's Highness, from the Bishop of Rome. Thus I shall slay him as he comes from a Mass.'

He squatted about the room, stabbing at shadows.

'It is a man with a red hat,' he grunted. 'Filthy for an Englishman to wear a red hat these days!'

'Put up your knife,' Katharine cried, 'I have seen too much of it.'

'Aye, I am a good man,' he boasted, 'but when I come back you shall see me a great one. There shall be patents for farms given me. There shall be gold. There shall be never such another as I. I will give thee such gowns, Kat.'

She sat still, but smoothed back a lock of her fair hair that glowed in the firelight.

'When I am a great man,' he babbled on, 'I will not wed thee, for who art thou to wed with a great man? Thou art more cheaply won. But I will give thee...'

'Thou fool,' she shrieked suddenly at him. 'These men shall slay thee. Get thee to Paris to murder as thou wilt. Thou shalt never come back and I shall be well rid of thee.'

He gave her a snarling laugh:

'Toy thou with no man when I am gone,' he said with sudden ferocity, so that his blue eyes appeared to start from his head.

'Poor fool, thou shalt never come back,' she answered.

He had an air of cunning and triumph.

'I have settled all this with that man that's no man, Viridus; thou art here as in a cloister amongst the maids of the Court. No man shall see thee; thou shalt speak with none that wears not a petticoat. I have so contracted with that man.'

'I tell thee they have contrived this to be rid of thee,' she said.

His tone became patronising.

'Wherefore should they?' he asked. When there came no answer from her he boasted, 'Aye, thou wouldst not have me go because thou lovest me too well.'

'Stay here,' she said. 'I will give thee money.' He stood gazing at her with his jaw fallen. 'Thou art a drunkard and a foul tongue,' she said, 'but if thou goest to Paris to murder a cardinal thou shalt never come out of that town alive. Be sure thou shalt be rendered up to death.'

He staggered towards her and caught one of her hands.

'Why, it is but cutting of a man's throat,' he said. 'I have cut many throats and have taken no harm. Be not sad! This man is a cardinal. But 'tis all one. It shall make me a great man.'

She muttered, 'Poor fool.'

'I have sworn to go,' he said. 'I am to have great farms and a great man shall watch over thee to keep thee virtuous. They have promised it or I had not gone.'

'Do you believe their promises?' she asked derisively.

'Why, 'tis a good knave, yon Viridus. He promised or ever I asked it.'

He was on his knees before her as she sat, with his arms about her waist.

'Sha't not cry, dear dove,' he mumbled. 'Sha't go with me to Paris.'

She sighed:

'No, no. Bide here,' and passed her hand through his ruffled hair.

'I would slay thee an thou were false to me,' he whispered over her hand. 'Get thee with me.'

She said, 'No, no,' again in a stifled voice.

He cried urgently:

'Come! Come! By all our pacts. By all our secret vows.'

She shook her head, sobbing:

'Poor fool. Poor fool. I am very lonely.'

He clutched her tightly and whispered in a hoarse voice:

'It were merrier at home now. Thou didst vow. At home now. Of a summer's night...'

She whispered: 'Peace. Peace.'

'At home now. In June, thou didst...'

She said urgently: 'Be still. Wouldst thou woo me again to the grunting of hogs?'

'Aye, would I,' he answered. 'Thou didst...'

She moved convulsively in her chair. He grasped her more tightly.

'Thou yieldest, I know thee!' he cried triumphantly. He staggered to his feet, still holding her hand.

'Thou shalt come to Paris. Sha't be lodged like a Princess. Sha't see great sights.'

She sprang up, tearing herself from him.

'Get thee gone from here,' she shivered. 'I am done with starving with thee. I know thy apple orchard wooings. Get thee gone from here. It is late. I shall be shamed if a man be seen to leave my room so late.'

'Why, I would not have thee shamed, Kat,' he muttered, her strenuous tone making him docile as a child.

'Get thee gone,' she answered, panting. 'I will not starve.'

'Wilt not come with me?' he asked ruefully. 'Thou didst yield in my arms.'

'I do bid thee begone,' she answered imperiously. 'Get thee gold if thou would'st have me. I have starved too much with thee.'

'Why, I will go,' he muttered. 'Buss me. For I depart towards Dover to-night, else this springald cardinal will be gone from Paris ere I come.'

IV

'Men shall make us cry, in the end, steel our hearts how we will,' she said to Margot Poins, who found her weeping with her head down upon the table above a piece of paper.

'I would weep for no man,' Margot answered.

Large, florid, fair, and slow speaking, she gave way to one of her impulses of daring that covered her afterwards with immense blushes and left her buried in speechless confusion. 'I could never weep for such an oaf as your cousin. He beats good men.'

'Once he sold a farm to buy me a gown,' Katharine said, 'and he goes to a sure death if I may not stay him.'

'It is even the province of men—to die,' Margot answered. Her voice, gruff with emotion, astonished herself. She covered her mouth with the back of her great white hand as if she wished to wipe the word away.

'Beseech you, spoil not your eyes with sitting to write at this hour for the sake of this roaring boy.'

Katharine sat to the table: a gentle knocking came at the door. 'Let no one come, I have told the serving knave as much.' She sank into a pondering over the wording of her letter to Bishop Gardiner. It was not to be thought of that her cousin should murder a Prince of the Church; therefore the bishop must warn the Catholics in Paris that Cromwell had this in mind. And Bishop Gardiner must stay her cousin on his journey: by a false message if needs were. It would be an easy matter to send him such a message as that she lay dying and must see him, or anything that should delay him until this cardinal had left Paris.

The great maid behind her back was fetching from the clothes-prop a waterglobe upon its stand; she set it down on the table before the rush-light, moving on tiptoe, for to her the writing of a letter was a sort of necromancy, and she was distressed for Katharine's sake. She had heard that to write at night would make a woman blind before thirty. The light grew immense behind the globe; watery rays flickered broad upon the ceiling and on the hangings, and the paper shone with a mellow radiance. The gentle knocking was repeated, and Katharine frowned. For before she was half way through with the humble words of greeting to the bishop it had come to her that this was a very dangerous matter to meddle in, and she had no one by whom to send the letter. Margot could not go, for it was perilous for her maid to be seen near the bishop's quarters with all Cromwell's men spying about.

Behind her was the pleasant and authoritative voice of old Sir Nicholas Rochford talking to Margot Poins. Katharine caught the name of Cicely Elliott, the dark maid of honour who had flouted her a week ago, and had pinned up her sleeve that day in Privy Seal's house.

The old man stood, grey and sturdy, his hand upon her doorpost. His pleasant keen eyes blinked upon her in the strong light from her globe as if he were before a good fire.

'Why, you are as fair as a saint with a halo, in front of that jigamaree,' he said. 'I am sent to offer you the friendship of Cicely Elliott.' When he moved, the golden collar of his knighthood shone upon his chest; his cropped grey beard glistened on his chin, and he shaded his eyes with his hand.

'I was writing of a letter,' Katharine said. She turned her face towards him: the stray rays from the globe outlined her red curved lips, her swelling chest, her low forehead; and it shone like the moon rising over a hill, yellow and fiery in the hair above her brow. The lines of her face drooped with her perplexities, and her eyes were large and shadowed, because she had been shedding many tears.

'Cicely Elliott shall make you a good friend,' he said, with a modest pride of his property; 'she shall marry me, therefore I do her such services.'

'You are old for her,' Katharine said.

He laughed.

'Since I have neither chick nor child and am main rich for a subject.'

'Why, she is happy in her servant,' Katharine said abstractedly. 'You are a very famous knight.'

'There are ballads of me,' he answered complacently. 'I pray to die in a good tulzie yet.'

'If Cicely Elliott have her scarf in your helmet,' Katharine said, 'I may not give you mine.' She was considering of her messenger to the bishop. 'Will you do me a service?'

'Why,' he answered, with a gentle mockery, 'you have one tricksy swordsman to bear your goodly colours.'

Katharine turned clean about to him and looked at him with attention, to make out whether he might be such a man as would carry her letter for her.

He returned her gaze directly, for he was proud of himself and of his fame. He had fought in all the wars that a man might fight in since he had been eighteen, and for fifteen years he had been captain of a troop employed by the Council in keeping back the Scots of the Borders. It was before Flodden Field that he had done his most famous deed, about which there were many ballads. Being fallen upon by a bevy of Scotsmen near a tall hedge, after he had been unhorsed, he had set his back into a thorn bush, and had fought for many hours in the rear of the Scottish troop, alone and with only his sword. The ballad that had been made about him said that seventeen corpses lay in front of the bush after the English won through to him. But since Cromwell had broken up the Northern Councils, and filled them again with his own men of no birth, the old man had come away from the Borders, disdaining to serve at the orders of knaves that had been butchers' sons and worse. He owned much land and was very wealthy, and, having been very abstemious, because he came of an old time when knighthood had still some of the sacredness and austerity of a religion, he was a man very sound in limb and peaceable of disposition. In his day he had been esteemed the most graceful whiffler in the world: now he used only the heavy sword, because he was himself grown heavy.

Katharine answered his gentle sneer at her cousin:

'It is true that I have a servant, but he is gone and may not serve me.' Yet the knight would find it in the books of chivalry that certain occasions or great quests allowed of a knight's doing the errands of more than one lady: but one lady, as for instance the celebrated Dorinda, might have her claims asserted by an illimitable number of knights, and she begged him to do her a service.

'I have heard of these Errantry books,' he said. 'In my day there were none such, and now I have no letters.'

'How, then, do you pass the long days of peace,' Katharine asked, 'if you neither drink nor dice?'

He answered: 'In telling of old tales and teaching their paces to the King's horses.'

He drew himself up a little. He would have her understand that he was not a horse leech: but there was in these four-footed beasts a certain love for him, so that Richmond, the King's favourite gelding, would stand still to be bled if he but laid his hand on the great creature's withers to calm him. These animals he loved, since he grew old and might not follow arguments and disputations of hic and hoc. 'There were none such in my day. But a good horse is the same from year's end to year's end...'

'Will you carry a letter for me?' Katharine asked.

'I would have you let me show you some of his Highness' beasts,' he added. 'I breed them to the manage myself. You shall find none that step more proudly in Christendom or Heathenasse.'

'Why, I believe you,' she answered. Suddenly she asked: 'You have ridden as knight errant?'

He said: 'For three weeks only. Then the Scots came on too thick and fast to waste time.' His dark eyes blinked and his broad lips moved humorously with his beard. 'I swore to do service to any lady; pray you let me serve you.'

'You can do me a service,' she said.

He moved his hand to silence her.

'Pray you take it not amiss. But there is one that hates you.'

She said:

'Perhaps there are a many; but do me a service if you will.'

'Look you,' he said, 'these times are no times of mine. But I know it is prudent to have servitors that love one. I saw yours shake a fist at your door.'

Katharine said:

'A man?' She looked at Margot, who, big, silent and flushed, was devouring the celebrated hero of ballads with adoring eyes. He laughed.

'That maid would kiss your feet. But, in these days, it is well to make friends with them that keep doors. The fellow at yours would spit upon you if he dared.'

Katharine said carelessly:

'Let him even spit in his imagination, and I shall whip him.'

The old knight looked out of the door. He left it wide open, so that no man might listen.

'Why, he is still gone,' he said. He cleared his throat. 'See you,' he began. 'So I should have said in the old days. These fellows then we could slush open to bathe our feet in their warm blood when we came tired-foot from hunting. Now it is otherwise. Such a loon may be a spy set upon one.'

He turned stiffly and majestically to move back her new hangings that only that day, in her absence at Privy Seal's, had been set in place. He tapped spots in the wall with his broad and gentle fingers, talking all the time with his broad back to her.

'See you, you have had here workmen to hang you a new arras. There be tricks of boring ear-holes through walls in hanging these things. So that if you have a cousin who shall catch a scullion by the throat...'

Katharine said hastily:

'He hath heard little to harm me.'

'It is what a man swears he hath heard that shall harm one,' the old knight answered. 'I meddle in no matters of statecraft, but I am sent to you by certain ladies; one shall wed me and I am her servant; one bears my name and wedded a good cousin of mine, now dead for his treasons.'

Katharine said:

'I am beholden to Cicely Elliott and the Lady Rochford...'

He silenced her with one of his small gestures of old-fashioned dignity and distinction.

'I meddle in none of these matters,' he said again. 'But these ladies know that you hate one they hate.'

He said suddenly, 'Ah!' a little grunt of satisfaction. His fingers tapping gently made what seemed a stone of the wall quiver and let drop small flakes of plaster. He turned gravely upon Katharine:

'I do not ask what you spoke of with that worshipful swordsman,' he said. 'But your servitor is gone to tell upon you. A stone is gone from here and there is his ear-hole, like a drum of canvas.'

Katharine said swiftly:

'Take, then, a letter for me—to the Bishop of Winchester!'

He started back with a little exaggerated pantomime of horror.

'Must I go into your plots?' he asked, blinking and amused, as if he had expected the errand.

She said urgently:

'I would have you tell me what Englishman now wears a red hat and is like to be in Paris. I am very ignorant in these matters.'

'Then meddle not in them,' he said, 'for that man is even Cardinal Pole; one that the King's Highness would very willingly know to be dead.'

'God forbid that my cousin should murder a Prince of the Church, and be slain in that quarrel,' she answered.

He started back and held his hands over his head.

'Why, God help you, child! Is that your errand?' he said, deep from his chest. 'I meddle not in this matter.'

She answered obstinately:

'Pray you—by your early vows—consent to carry me my letter.'

He shook his head bodingly.

'I thought it had been a matter of a masque at the Bishop of Winchester's; or I had never come nigh you. Cicely Elliott hath copied out the part you should speak. Pray you ask me no more of the other errand.'

She said:

'For a great knight you are a friend only in little matters!'

He uttered reproachfully:

'Child: it is no little matter to act as go-between for the Bishop of Winchester, even if it be for no more than a masque. How otherwise does he not send to you direct? So much I was ready to do for you, a stranger, who am a man that has no party.'

She uttered maliciously:

'Well, well. I thought you came of the better times before our day.'

'I have shewn myself a good enough man,' he said composedly. He pointed one of his fingers at her.

'Pole is not one that shall be easily slain. He is like to have in his pay the defter spadassins of the two. I have known him since he was a child till when he fled abroad.'

'But my cousin!' Katharine pleaded.

'For the sake of your own little neck, let that gallant be hanged,' he said smartly. 'You have need of many friends; I can see it in your complexion, which is of a hasty loyalty. But I tell you, I had never come near you, so your cousin miscalled me, a man of worth and credit, had these ladies not prayed me to come to you.'

She raised herself to her full height.

'It is not in the books of your knight-errantry,' she cried, 'that one should leave one's friends to the hangman of Paris.'

The large figure of Margot Poins thrust itself upon them.

'A' God's name,' said her gruff voice of great emotion, 'hear the words of this valiant soldier. Your cousin shall ruin you. It is true that he will drive from you all your good friends...' She faltered, and her impulse carried her no further. Rochford tapped her flushed cheek gently with his glove, but a light and hushing step in the corridor made them all silent.

The Magister Udal stood before the door blinking his eyes at the light; Katharine addressed him imperiously—

'You will carry a letter for me to save my cousin from death.'

He started, and leered at Margot, who was ready to sink into the ground.

'Why, I had rather carry a bull to the temple of Jupiter, as Macrobius has it,' he said, 'meaning that...'

'Yet you have drunk with him,' Katharine interrupted him hotly, 'you have gone hurling through the night with him. You have shamed me together.'

'Yet I cannot forget Tully,' he answered sardonically, 'who warns me that a prudent man should be able to moderate the course of his friendship, even as he reins his horse. Est prudentis sustinere ut cursum...'

'Mark you that!' the old knight said to Katharine. 'I will get my boy to read to me out of Tully, for that is excellent wisdom.'

'God help me, this is Christendom!' Katharine said, bitterly. 'Shall one abandon one that lay in the same cradle with one?'

'Your ladyship hath borne with him a day too long,' Udal said. 'He beat me like a dog five days since. Have you heard of the city called Ponceropolis, founded by the King Philip? Your good cousin should be ruler of that city, for the Great King peopled it with all the brawlers, cut-throats, and roaring boys of his dominions, to be rid of them.' She became aware that he was very angry, for his whisper shook like the neigh of a horse.

The old knight winked at Margot.

'Why this is a monstrous wise man,' he said, 'who yet speaks some sense.'

'In short,' the magister said, 'If you will stick to this man, you shall lose me. For I have taken beatings and borne no malice—as in the case of men with whose loves or wives I have prospered better than themselves. But that this man should miscall me and beat me for the pure frenzy of his mind, causelessly, and for the love of blows! That is unbearable. To-night I walk for the first time after five days since he did beat me. And I ask you whom you shall here find the better servant?'

His thin figure was suddenly shaking with rage.

'Why, this is conspiracy!' Katharine cried.

'A conspiracy!' Udal's voice rose up into a shriek. 'If your ladyship were a Queen I would not be a Queen's cousin's whipping post.' His arms jerked with the spasms of his rage like those of a marionette.

'A shame that learned men should be so beaten!' Margot's gruff voice uttered.

Katharine turned upon her.

'That is what made you speak e'ennow. You have been with this flibbertigibbet.'

'This is a free land,' the girl mumbled, her mild eyes sparkling with the contagious anger of her lover.

The old knight stood blinking upon Katharine.

'You are like to lose all your servants in this quarrel,' he said.

Katharine wrung her hands, and then turned her back upon them and drummed upon the table with her fingers. Udal caught Margot's large hand and fumbled it beneath the furs of his robe: the old knight kept his smiling eyes upon Katharine's back. Her voice came at last:

'Why, I will not have Tom killed upon this occasion into which I brought him.'

Rochford shrugged his shoulders up to his ears.

'Oh marvellous infatuation,' he said.

Katharine spoke, still with her back turned and her shoulders heaving:

'A marvellous infatuation!' she said, her voice coming softly and deeply in her chest. 'Why, after his fashion this man loved me. God help us, what other men have I seen here that would strike a straight blow? Here it is moving in the dark, listening at pierced walls, swearing of false treasons—'

She swept round upon the old man, her face moved, her eyes tender and angry. She stretched out her hand, and her voice was pitiful and urgent.

'Sir! Sir! What counsel do you give me, who are a knight of honour? Would you let a man who lay in the cradle with you go to a shameful death in an errand you had made for him?'

She leaned back upon the table with her eyes upon his face. 'No you would not. How then could you give me such counsel?'

He said: 'Well, well. You are in the right.'

'Nearly I went with him to another place,' she answered, 'but half an hour ago. Would to God I had! for here it is all treacheries.'

'Write your letter, child,' he answered. 'You shall give it to Cicely Elliott to-morrow in the morning. I will have it conveyed, but I will not be seen to handle it, for I am too young to be hanged.'

'Why, God help you, knight,' Udal whispered urgently from the doorway, 'carry no letter in this affair—if you escape, assuredly this mad pupil of mine shall die. For the King—?' Suddenly he raised his voice to a high nasal drawl that rang out like a jackdaw's: 'That is very true; and, in this matter of Death you may read in Socrates' Apology. Nevertheless we may believe that if Death be a transmigration from one place into another, there is certainly amendment in going whither so many great men have already passed, and to be subtracted from the way of so many judges that be iniquitous and corrupt.'

'Why, what a plague...' Katharine began.

He interrupted her quickly.

'Here is your serving man back at last if you would rate him for leaving your door unkept.'

The man stood in the doorway, his lanthorn dangling in his hand, his cudgel stuck through his belt, his shock of hair rough like an old thatch, and his eyes upon the ground. He mumbled, feeling at his throat:

'A man must eat. I was gone to my supper.'

'You are like to have the nightmare, friend,' the old knight said pleasantly. 'It is ill to eat when most of the world sleeps.'

V

Cicely Elliott had indeed sent her old knight to Katharine with those overtures of friendship. Careless, dark, and a madcap, she had flown at Katharine because she had believed her a creature of Cromwell's, set to spy upon the Lady Mary's maids. They formed, the seven of them, a little, mutinous, babbling circle. Their lady's cause they adored, for it was that of an Old Faith, such as women will not let die. The Lady Mary treated them with a hard indifference: it was all one to her whether they loved her or not; so they babbled, and told evil tales of the other side. The Lady Rochford could do little to hold them, for, having come very near death when the Queen Anne fell, she had been timid ever since, and Cicely Elliott was their ringleader.

Thus it was to her that one of Gardiner's priests had come begging her to deliver to Katharine a copy of the words she was to speak in the masque, and from the priest Cicely had learnt that Katharine loved the Old Faith and hated Privy Seal as much as any of them. She had been struck with a quick remorse, and had suddenly seen Katharine as one that must be helped and made amends to. Thus she had pinned up her sleeve at Privy Seal's. There, however, it had not been safe to speak with her.

'Dear child,' she said to Katharine next morning, 'we may well be foils one to another, for I am dark and pert, like a pynot. They call me Mag Pie here. You shall be Jenny Dove of the Sun. But I am not afraid of your looks. Men that like the touch of the sloe in me shall never be drawn away by your sweet lips.'

She was, indeed, like a magpie, never still for a minute, fingering Katharine's hair, lifting the medallion upon her chest, poking her dark eyes close to the embroidery on her stomacher. She had a trick of standing with her side face to you, so that her body seemed very long to her hips, and her dark eyes looked at you askance and roguish, whilst her lips puckered to a smile, a little on one side.

'It was not your old knight called me Sweetlips,' Katharine said. 'I miscalled him foully last night.'

Cicely Elliott threw back her head and laughed.

'Why, he is worshipful heavy to send on a message; but you may trust his advice when he gives it.'

'I am come to think the same,' Katharine said; 'yet in this one matter I cannot take it.'

Cicely Elliott had taken to herself the largest and highest of the rooms set apart for these maids. The tapestries, which were her own, were worked in fair reds and greens, like flowers. She had a great silver mirror and many glass vases, in which were set flowers worked in silver and enamel, and a large, thin box carved out of an elephant's tusk, to hold her pins; and all these were presents from the old knight.

'Why,' she said, 'sometimes his advice shall fit a woman's mood; sometimes he goes astray, as in the case of these gloves. Cheverel is a skin that will stretch so that after one wearing you may not tell the thumbs from stocking-feet. Nevertheless, I would be rid of your cousin.'

'Not in this quarrel,' Katharine answered. 'Find him an honourable errand, and he shall go to Kathay.'

Cicely threw the stretched cheverel glove into the fire.

'My knight shall give me a dozen pairs of silk, stitched with gold to stiffen them,' she said. 'You shall have six; but send your cousin in quest of the Islands of the Blest. They lie well out in the Western Ocean. If you can make him mislay his compass he will never come back to you.'

Katharine laughed.

'I think he would come without compass or chart. Nevertheless, I will send me my letter by means of your knight to Bishop Gardiner.'

Cicely Elliott hung her head on her chest.

'I do not ask its contents, but you may give it me.'

Katharine brought it out from the bosom of her dress, and the dark girl passed it up her sleeve.

'This shall no doubt ruin you,' she said. 'But get you to our mistress. I will carry your letter.'

Katharine started back.

'You!' she said. 'It was Sir Nicholas should have it conveyed.'

'That poor, silly old man shall not be hanged in this matter,' Cicely answered. 'It is all one to me. If Crummock would have had my head he could have shortened me by that much a year ago.'

Katharine's eyes dilated proudly.

'Give me my letter,' she said; 'I will have no woman in trouble for me.'

The dark girl laughed at her.

'Your letter is in my sleeve. No hands shall touch it before mine deliver it to him it is written to. Get you to our mistress. I thank you for an errand I may laugh over; laughter here is not over mirthful.'

She stood side face to Katharine, her mouth puckered up into her smile, her eyes roguish, her hands clasped behind her back.

'Why, you see Cicely Elliott,' she said, 'whose folk all died after the Marquis of Exeter's rising, who has neither kith nor kin, nor house nor home. I had a man loved me passing well. He is dead with the rest; so I pass my time in pranks because the hours are heavy. To-day the prank is on thy side; take it as a gift the gods send, for to-morrow I may play thee one, since thou art soft, and fair, and tender. That is why they call me here the Magpie. My old knight will tell you I have tweaked his nose now and again, but I will not have him shortened by the head for thy sake.'

'Why, you are very bitter,' Katharine said.

The girl answered, 'If your head ached as mine does now and again when I remember my men who are dead; if your head ached as mine does...' She stopped and gave a peal of laughter. 'Why, child, your face is like a startled moon. You have not stayed days enough here to have met many like me; but if you tarry here for long you will laugh much as I laugh, or you will have grown blind long since with weeping.'

Katharine said, 'Poor child, poor child!'

But the girl cried out, 'Get you gone, I say! In the Lady Mary's room you shall find my old knight babbling with the maidens. Send him to me, for my head aches scurvily, and he shall dip his handkerchief in vinegar and set it upon my forehead.'

'Let me comb thy hair,' Katharine said; 'my hand is sovereign against a headache.'

'No, get you gone,' the girl said harshly; 'I will have men of war to do these errands for me.'

Katharine answered, 'Sit thee down. Thou wilt take my letter; I must ease thy pains.'

'As like as not I shall scratch thy pink face,' Cicely said. 'At these times I cannot bear the touch of a woman. It was a woman made my father run with the Marquis of Exeter.'

'Sweetheart,' Katharine said softly, 'I could hold both thy wrists with my two fingers. I am stronger than most men.'

'Why, no!' the girl cried; 'I may not sit still. Get you gone. I will run upon your errand. If you had knelt to as many men as I have you could not sit still either. And not one of my men was pardoned.'

She ran from the room with a sidelong step like a magpie's, and her laugh rang out discordantly from the corridor.

The Lady Mary sat reading her Plautus in her large painted gallery, with all her maids about her sewing, some at a dress for her, some winding silk for their own uses. The old knight stood holding his sturdy hands apart between a rope of wool that his namesake Lady Rochford was making into balls. Other gentlemen were beside some of the maids, toying with their silks or whispering in their ears. No one much marked Katharine Howard.

She glided to her lady and kissed the dry hand that lay in the lap motionless. Mary raised her eyes from her book, looked for a leisurely time at the girl's face, and then began again to read. Old Rochford winked pleasantly at her, and, after she had saluted his cousin, he begged her to hold the wool in his stead, for his hands, which were used to sword and shield, were very cold, and his legs, inured to the saddle, brooked standing very ill.

'Cicely Elliott hath a headache,' Katharine said; 'she bade me send you to her.'

He waited before her, helping her to adjust the wool on to her white hands, and she uttered, in a low voice:

'She hath taken my letter for me.'

He said, 'Why, what a' the plague's name...' and stood fingering his peaked little beard in a gentle perplexity.

Lady Rochford pulled at her wool and gave a hissing sigh of pain, for the joint of her wrist was swollen.

'It has always been easterly winds in January since the Holy Blood of Hailes was lost,' she sighed. 'In its day I could get me some ease in the wrist by touching the phial that held it.' She shivered with discomfort, and smiled distractedly upon Katharine. Her large and buxom face was mild, and she seemed upon the point of shedding tears.

'Why, if you will put your wool round a stool, I will wind it for you,' Katharine said, because the gentle helplessness of the large woman filled her with compassion, as if this were her old, mild mother.

Lady Rochford shook her head disconsolately.

'Then I must do something else, and my bones would ache more. But I would you would make my cousin Rochford ask the Archbishop where they have hidden the Sacred Blood of Hailes, that I may touch it and be cured.'

The old knight frowned very slightly.

'I have told thee to wrap thy fist in lamb's-wool,' he said. 'A hundred times I have told thee. It is very dangerous to meddle with these old saints and phials that are done away with.'

Lady Rochford sighed gently and hung her head.

'My cousin Anne, that was a sinful Queen, God rest her soul...' she began.

Sir Nicholas listened to her no more.

'See you,' he whispered to Katharine. 'Peradventure it is best that Cicely have gone. Being a madcap, her comings and goings are heeded by no man, and it is true that she resorteth daily to the Bishop of Winchester, to plague his priests.'

'I would not speak so, being a man,' Katharine said.

He smiled at her and patted her shoulder.

'Why, I have struck good blows in my time,' he said.

'And have learned worldly wisdom,' Katharine retorted.

'I would not risk my neck on grounds where I am but ill acquainted,' he answered soberly. He was all will to please her. The King, he said, was coming on the Wednesday, after the Bishop of Winchester's, to see three new stallions walk in their manage-steps. 'I pray that you will come with Cicely Elliott to watch from the little window in the stables. These great creatures are a noble sight. I bred them myself to it.' His mild brown eyes were bright with enthusiasm and cordiality.

Suddenly there was a great silence in the room, and the Lady Mary raised her head. The burly figure of Throckmorton, the spy, was in the doorway. Katharine shuddered at the sight of him, for, in her Lincolnshire house, where he was accounted more hateful than Judas who betrayed the Lord, she had seen him beat the nuns when the convents had been turned out of doors, and he had brought to death his own brother, who had had a small estate near her father's house. The smile upon his face made her feel sick. He stroked his long, golden-brown beard, glanced swiftly round the room, and advanced to the mistress's chair, swinging his great shoulders. He made a leg and pulled off his cap, and at that there was a rustle of astonishment, for it had been held treasonable to cap the Lady Mary. Her eyes regarded him fixedly, with a granite cold and hardness, and he seemed to have at once a grin of power and a shrinking motion of currying favour. He said that Privy Seal begged her leave that her maid Katharine Howard might go to him soon after one o'clock. The Lady Mary neither spoke nor moved, but the old knight shrank away from Katharine, and affected to be talking in the ear of Lady Rochford, who went on winding her wool. Throckmorton turned on his heels and swung away, his eyes on the floor, but with a grin on his evil face.

He left a sudden whisper behind him, and then the silence fell once more. Katharine stood, a tall figure, holding out the hands on which the wool was as if she were praying to some invisible deity or welcoming some invisible lover. Some heads were raised to look at her, but they fell again; the old knight shuffled nearer her to whisper hoarsely from his moustachioed lips:

'Your serving man hath reported. Pray God we come safe out of this!' Then he went out of the room. Lady Rochford sighed deeply, for no apparent reason.

After a time the Lady Mary raised her head and made a minute, cold beckoning to Katharine. Her dry finger pointed to a word in her book of Plautus.

'Tell me what you know of this,' she commanded.

The play was the Menechmi, and the phrase ran, 'Nimis autem bene ora commetavi...' It was difficult for Katharine to bring her mind down to this text, for she had been wondering if indeed her time were at an end before it had begun. She said:

'I have never loved this play very well,' to excuse herself.

'Then you are out of the fashion,' Mary said coldly, 'for this Menechmi is prized here above all the rest, and shall be played at Winchester's before his Highness.'

Katharine bowed her head submissively, and read the words again.

'I remember me,' she said, 'I had this play in a manuscript where your commetavi read commentavi.'

Mary kept her eyes upon the girl's face, and said:

'Signifying?'

'Why, it signifies,' Katharine said, 'that Messenio did well mark a face. If you read commetavi it should mean that he scratched it with his nails so that it resembled a harrowed field; if commentavi, that he bethumped it with his fist so that bruises came out like the stops on a fair writing.'

'It is true that you are a good Latinist,' Mary said expressionlessly. 'Bring me my inkhorn to that window. I will write down your commentavi.'

Katharine lifted the inkhorn from its hole in the arm of the chair and gracefully followed the stiff and rigid figure into the embrasure of a distant window.

Mary bent her head over the book that she held in her hand, and writing in the margin, she uttered:

'Pity that such an excellent Latinist should meddle in matters that nothing concern her.'

Katharine held the inkhorn carefully, as if it had been a precious vase.

'If you will bid me do naught but serve you, I will do naught else,' she said.

'I will neither bid thee nor aid thee,' Mary answered. 'The Bishop of Winchester claims thy service. Serve him as thou wilt.'

'I would serve my mistress in serving him,' Katharine said. 'He is a man I love little.'

Mary pulled suddenly from her bodice a piece of crumpled parchment that had been torn across. She thrust it into Katharine's free hand.

'Such letters I have had written me by my father's men,' she said. 'If this bishop should come to be my father's man I would take no service from him.'

Katharine read on the crumpled parchment such words as:

'It was Thomas Cromwell wrote that,' the Lady Mary cried. 'My father's man!'

'But if this brewer's son be brought down?' Katharine pleaded.

'Why, I tore his letter across for it is filthy,' Mary said, 'and I keep the halves of his letter that I may remember. If he be brought down, who shall bring his master down that let him write so?'

Katharine said:

'If this tempter of the Devil's brood were brought down there should ensue so great an atonement from his sorrowful master whom he deludes...'

Mary uttered a 'Tush!' of scorn and impatience. 'This is the babbling of a child. My father is no holy innocent as you and your like feign to believe.'

'Nevertheless I love you most well,' Katharine pleaded.

Mary snapped her book to. Her cold tone came back over her heat as the grey clouds of a bitter day shut down again upon a dangerous flicker of lightning.

'Do as you will,' she said, 'only if your head fall I will stir no finger to aid you. Or, if by these plottings my father could be got to send me his men upon their knees and bearing crowns, I would turn my back upon them and say no word.'

'Well, my plottings are like to end full soon,' Katharine said. 'Privy Seal hath sent for me upon no pleasant errand.'

Mary said: 'God help you!' with a frigid unconcern, and walked back to her chair.

VI

Cromwell kept as a rule his private courts either in his house at Austin Friars, or in a larger one that he had near the Rolls. But, when the King was as far away from London as Greenwich, or when such ill-wishers as the Duke of Norfolk were in the King's neighbourhood, Cromwell never slept far out of earshot from the King's rooms. It was said indeed that never once since he had become the King's man had he passed a day without seeing his Highness once at least, or writing him a great letter. But he contrived continually to send the nobles that were against him upon errands at a distance—as when Bishop Gardiner was made Ambassador to Paris, or Norfolk sent to put down the North after the Pilgrimage of Grace. Such errands served a double purpose: Gardiner, acting under the pressure of the King, was in Paris forced to make enemies of many of his foreign friends; and the Duke, in his panic-stricken desire to curry favour with Henry, had done more harrying, hanging and burning among the Papists than ever Henry or his minister would have dared to command, for in those northern parts the King's writ did not run freely. Thus, in spite of himself the Duke at York had been forced to hold the country whilst creatures of Privy Seal, men of the lowest birth and of the highest arrogance, had been made Wardens of the Marches and filled the Councils of the Borders. Such men, with others, like the judges and proctors of the Court of Augmentations, which Cromwell had invented to administer the estates of the monasteries and escheated lords' lands, with a burgess or two from the shires in Parliament, many lawyers and some suppliants of rank, filled the anterooms of Privy Seal. There was a matter of two hundred of them, mostly coming not upon any particular business so much as that any enemies they had who should hear of their having been there might tremble the more.

Cromwell himself was in the room that had the King's and Queen's heads on the ceiling and the tapestry of Diana hunting. He was speaking with a great violence to Sir Leonard Ughtred, whose sister-in-law, the widow of Sir Anthony Ughtred, and sister of the Queen Jane, his son Gregory had married two years before. It was a good match, for it made Cromwell's son the uncle of the Prince of Wales, but there had been a trouble about their estates ever since.

'Sir,' Cromwell threatened the knight, 'Gregory my son was ever a fool. If he be content that you have Hyde Farm that am not I. His wife may twist him to consent, but I will not suffer it.'

Ughtred hung his head, which was closely shaved, and fingered his jewelled belt.

'It is plain justice,' he muttered. 'The farm was ceded to my brother after Hyde Monastery was torn down. It was to my brother, not to my brother's wife, who is now your son's.'

Cromwell turned upon the Chancellor of the Augmentations who stood in the shadow of the tall mantelpiece. He was twisting his fingers in his thin grey beard that wagged tremulously when he spoke.

'Truly,' he bleated piteously, 'it stands in the register of the Augmentations as the worshipful knight says.'

Cromwell cried out, in a studied rage: 'I made thee and I made thy office: I will unmake the one and the other if it and thou know no better law.'

'God help me,' the Chancellor gasped. He shrank again into the shadow of the chimney, and his blinking eyes fell upon Cromwell's back with a look of dread and the hatred of a beast that is threatened at the end of its hole.

'Sir,' Cromwell frowned darkly upon Ughtred, 'the law stands thus if the Augmentation people know it not. This farm and others were given to your late brother upon his marriage, that the sister of the Queen might have a proper state. The Statute of Uses hath here no say. Understand me: It was the King's to give; it is the King's still.' He opened his mouth so wide that he appeared to bellow. 'That farm falleth to the survivor of those two, who is now my son's wife. What judge shall gainsay that?' He swayed his body round on his motionless and sturdily planted legs, veering upon the Chancellor and the knight in turn, as if he challenged them to gainsay him who had been an attorney for ten years after he had been a wool merchant.

Ughtred shrugged his shoulders heavily, and the Chancellor hastened to bleat:

'No judge shall gainsay your lordship. Your lordship hath an excellent knowledge of the law.'

'Why hast thou not as good a one?' Cromwell rated him. 'I made thee since I thought thou hadst.' The Chancellor choked in his throat and waved his hands.

'Thus the law is,' Cromwell said to Ughtred. 'And if it were not so Parliament should pass an Act so to make it. For it is a scandal that a Queen's sister, an aunt of the Prince that shall be King, should lose her lands upon the death of her husband. It savours of treason that you should ask it. I have known men go to the Tower upon less occasion.'

'Well, I am a broken man,' Sir Leonard muttered.

'Why, God help you,' Cromwell said. 'Get you gone. The law takes no account of whether a man be broken, but seeketh to do honour to the King's Highness and to render justice.'

Viridus and Sadler, who was another of Cromwell's secretaries, had come in whilst Privy Seal had been speaking, and Cromwell turned upon them laughing as the knight went out, his head hanging.

'Here is another broken man,' he said, and they all laughed together.

'Well, he is another very notable swordsman,' Viridus said. 'We might well post him at Milan, lest Pole flee back to Rome that way.'

Cromwell turned upon the Chancellor with a bitter contempt.

'Find thou for this knight some monk's lands in Kent. He shall to Milan with them for a price.'

Viridus laughed.

'Now we shall soon have these broken swordsmen in every town of Italy between France and Rome. Such a net Pole shall not easily break through.'

'It were well he were done with soon,' Cromwell said.

'The King shall love us much the more; and it is time.'

'Why, there will in two days be such a clamour of assassins in Paris that he shall soon bolt from there towards Rome,' Viridus answered. 'It will go hard if he escape all our Italy men. I hold it for certain that Winchester shall have reported to him in Paris that this Culpepper is on the road. Will you speak with this Howard wench?'

Cromwell knitted his brows in uncertainty.

'It was her cousin that should clamour about this murder in Paris,' Viridus reminded him.

'Is she without?' Cromwell asked. 'Have you it for certain that she hath reported to my lord of Winchester?'

'Winchester's priest of the bedchamber hath shewn me a copy of the letter she wrote. I would have your lordship send some reward to that Father Michael. He hath served us in many other matters.'

Cromwell motioned with his hand that Sadler should note down this Father Michael's name.

'Are there many men in my antechambers?' he asked Viridus, and hearing that there were more than one hundred and fifty: 'Why, let this wench stay there a half-hour. It humbles a woman to be alone among so many men, and she shall come here without a sound clout to her back for the crush of them.'

He began talking with Sadler about two globes of the world that he had ordered his agent to buy in Antwerp, one for himself and the other for a present to the King. Sadler answered that the price was very high; a thousand crowns or so, he had forgotten just how many. They had been twelve years in the making, but the agent had been afraid of the greatness of the expense.

Cromwell said:

'Tush; I must have the best of these Flemish furnishings.'

He signed to Viridus to send for Katharine Howard, and went on talking with Sadler about the furnishing of his house in the Austin Friars. He had his agents all over Flanders watching the noted masters of the crafts to see what notable pieces they might turn out; for he loved fine carvings, noble hangings, great worked chests and other signs of wealth, and the money was never thrown away, for the wood and the stuffs and the gold thread remained so long as you kept the moth and the woodlouse from them. To the King too he gave presents every day.

Katharine entered by a door from a corridor at which he had not expected her. She wore a great head-dress of net like the Queen's and her dress was in no disarray, neither were her cheeks flushed by anything more than apprehension. She said that she had been shown that way by a large gentleman with a great beard. She would not bring herself to mention the name of Throckmorton, so much she detested him.

Cromwell answered with a benevolent smile, 'Aye, Throckmorton had ever an eye for beauty. Otherwise you had come scurvily out of that wash.'

He twisted his mouth up as if he were mocking her, and asked her suddenly how the Lady Mary corresponded with her cousin the Emperor, for it was certain she had a means of writing to him?

Katharine flushed all over her face with relief and her heart stilled itself a little. Here at least there was no talk of the Tower at once for her, because she had written a letter to Bishop Gardiner. She answered that that day for the first time she had been in the Lady Mary's service.

He smiled benevolently still, and holding out a hand in a little warning gesture and with an air of pleasant reasonableness, said that she must earn her bread like other folks in his Highness' service.

'Why,' she answered, 'I have been marvellous ill, but I shall be more diligent in serving my mistress.'

He marked a distinction, pointing a fat finger at her heart-place. In the serving of her mistress she should do not enough work to pay for bodkins nor for sewing silk, since the Lady Mary asked nothing of her maids, neither their attendance, their converse, nor yet their needlework. Such a place asked nothing of one so fortunate as to fill it. To atone for it the service of the King demanded her labours.

'Why,' she said again, 'if I must spy in those parts it is a great pity that I ever came there as your woman; for who there shall open their hearts to me?'

He laughed at her comfortably still.

'You may put it about that you hate me,' he said. 'You may mix with them that love me not. In the end you may worm yourself into their secrets.'

Again a heavy flush covered Katharine's face from the chin to the brow. It was so difficult for her to keep from speaking her mind with her lips that she felt as if her whole face must be telling the truth to him. But he continued to shake his plump sides as if he were uttering inaudible, 'Ho—ho—ho's.'

'That is so easy,' he said. 'A child, I think, could compass it.' He put his hands behind his back and stretched his legs apart. She was very pleasant to look at with her flushings, and it amused him to toy with frightened women. 'It is in this way that you shall earn his Highness' bread.' It was known that Mary had this treasonable correspondence with the Emperor; in the devilish malignancy of her heart she desired that her sacred father should be cast down and slain, and continually she implored her cousin to invade her father's dominions, she sending him maps, plans of the new castles in building and the names of such as were malevolent within the realm. 'Therefore,' he finished, 'if you could discover her channels and those channels could then be stopped up, you would indeed both earn your bread and enter into high favour.'

He began again good-humouredly to give her careful directions as to how she should act; as for instance by offering to make for the printers a fair copy of the Lady Mary's Commentary upon Plautus. By pretending that certain words were obscure to her, she should find opportunities for coming suddenly into the room, and she should afford herself excuses for searching among his mistress's papers without awakening suspicions.

'Why, my face is too ingenuous,' Katharine said. 'I am not made for playing the spy.'

He laughed at her.

'That is so much the better,' he said. 'The best spies are those that have open countenances. It needs but a little schooling.'

'I should get me a hang-dog look very soon,' she answered. She paused for a minute and then spoke earnestly, holding out her hands. 'I would you would set me a nobler task. Very surely it is shameful that a daughter should so hate the father that begat her; and I know the angels weep to see her desire that the great and noble prince should be cast down and slain by his enemies. But, sir, it were the better task to seek to soften her mind. Such knowledge as I have of goodly writers should aid me rather to persuade her heart towards her father; for I know no texts that should make me skilful as a spy, but I can give you a dozen from Plautus alone that do inculcate a sweet and dutiful love from daughter to sire.'

He leered at her pleasantly.

'Why, you speak sweetly, by the book. If the Lady Mary were a man now...'

The hitherto silent men laid back their heads to laugh, and the Chancellor of the Augmentations suddenly rubbed his palms together, hissing like an ostler. But, seeing her look became angry and abashed, Cromwell stopped his sentence and once more held out a finger.

'Why, indeed,' he said, gravely, 'if you could do that you might be the first lady in the land, for neither the King nor I, nor yet all nor many have availed there.'

Katharine said:

'Surely there is a way to touch the heart of this noble lady, and by long seeking I may find.'

'Well, you have spoken many words,' Cromwell said. 'This is a great matter. If you shall achieve it, it shall be accounted to you both here and in heaven. But the other task I enjoin upon you.'

She was making sorrowfully to the door, and he called to her:

'I have found your cousin employment.'

The sudden mention made her stop as if she had been struck in the face, and she held her hand to her side. Her face was distorted with fear as she turned to answer:

'Aye. I knew. He hath told me. But I cannot thank you. I would not that my cousin should murder a prince of the Church.' She knew, from the feeling in her heart and the cruel sound of his voice that he had that knowledge already. If he wished to imprison her it could serve no turn to fence about that matter, and she steadied herself by catching hold of the tapestry with one hand behind her back. The faces of Cromwell's three assistants were upon her, hard, sardonic and grinning.

Viridus said, with an air of parade:

'I had told your lordship this lady had flaws in her loyalty.' And the Chancellor was raising his hands in horror, after the fashion of a Greek Chorus. Cromwell, however, grinned still at her.

'When the Queen Katharine died,' he said slowly, 'it was a great relief to this realm. When the late Arch Devil, Pope Clement, died, the King and I were mad with joy. But if all popes and all hostile queens and princes could be stricken with devils and dead to-morrow, his Highness would rather it were Reginald Pole.'

Katharine understood very well that he was setting before her the enormity of her offence: she stood still with her lips parted. He went on rehearsing the crimes of the cardinal: how he had been educated by the King's high bounty: how the King had offered him the Archbishopric of York: how he had the rather fled to the Bishop of Rome: how he had written a book, accusing the King of such crimes and heresies that all Christendom had cried out upon his Highness. Even then this Pole was in Paris with a bull from the Bishop of Rome calling upon the Emperor and the King of France to fall together upon their lord.

Katharine gasped:

'I would well he were dead. But not by my cousin. They should take my cousin and slay him.'

Cromwell had arranged this scene very carefully: for his power over the King fell away daily, and that day he had had to tell Baumbach, the Saxish ambassador, that there was no longer any hope of the King's allying himself with the Schmalkaldner league. Therefore he was the more hot to discover a new Papist treason. The suggestion of Viridus that Katharine might be made either to discover or to invent one had filled him with satisfaction. There was no one who could be more believed if she could be ground down into swearing away the life of her uncle or any other man of high station. And to grind her down thus needed only many threats. He infused gradually more terror into his narrow eyes, and spoke more gravely:

'Neither do I desire the death of this traitor so hotly as doth his Highness. For there be these foul lies— and have you not heard the ancient fool's prophecy that was made over thirty years ago: "That one with a Red Cap brought up from low degree should rule all the land under the King. (I trow ye know who that was.) And that after much mixing the land should by another Red Cap be reconciled or else brought to utter ruin"?'

'I am new to this place,' Katharine said; 'I never heard that saying. God help me, I wish this man were dead.'

His voice grew the more deep as he saw that she was the more daunted:

'Aye: and whether the land be reconciled to the Bishop of Rome, or be brought to utter ruin, the one and the other signify the downfall of his Highness.'

The Chancellor interrupted piously:

'God save us. Whither should we all flee then!'

'It is not,' Viridus commented dryly, 'that his Highness or my lord here do fear a fool prophecy made by a drunken man. But there being such a prophecy running up and down the land, and such a malignant and devilish Red Cap ranting up and down the world, the hearts of foolish subjects are made to turn.'

'Idiot wench,' the Chancellor suddenly yelped at her, 'ignorant, naughty harlot! You had better have died than have uttered those your pretty words.'

'Why,' Cromwell said gently, 'I am very sure that now you desire that your cousin should slay this traitor.' He paused, licked his lips and held out a hand. 'Upon your life,' he barked, 'tell no soul this secret.'

The faces of all the four men were again upon her, sardonic, leering and amused, and suddenly she felt that this was not the end of the matter: there was something untrue in this parade of threats. Cromwell was acting: they were all acting parts. Their speeches were all too long, too dryly spoken: they had been rehearsed! This was not the end of the matter—and neither her cousin nor Cardinal Pole was here the main point. She wondered for a wild moment if Cromwell, too, like Gardiner, thought that she had a voice with the King. But Cromwell knew as well as she that the King had seen her but once for a minute, and he was not a fool like Gardiner to run his nose into a mare's nest.

'There is no power upon earth could save you from your doom if through you this matter miscarried,' he said, softly: 'therefore, be you very careful: act as I would have you act: seek out that secret that I would know.'

It came irresistibly into Katharine's head:

'These men know already very well that I have written to Bishop Gardiner! This is to hold a halter continuously above my head!' Then, at least, they did not mean to do away with her instantly. She dropped her eyes upon the ground and stood submissively whilst Privy Seal's voice came cruel and level:

'You are a very fair wench, made for love and such stuff. You are an indifferent good Latinist who might offer good counsel. But be you very careful that you come not against me. You should not escape, but may burrow underground sooner than that. Your Aristotle should not help you, nor Lucretius, nor Lucan, nor Silius Italicus. Diodorus Siculus hath no maxim that should help you against me; but, like Diodorus the Dialectician, you should die of shame. Seneca shall help you if you but dally with that fool thought who sayeth: "Quaeris quo jaceas post obitum loco? Quo non nata jacent." Aye, thou shalt die and lie in an unknown grave as thou hadst never been born.'

She went, her knees trembling half with fear and half with rage, for it was impossible to imagine anything more threatening or more arrogant than his soft, cruel voice, that seemed to sound for long after in her ears, saying, 'I have you at my mercy; see you do as I have bidden you.'

Watching the door that closed upon her, Viridus said, with a negligent amusement:

'That fool Udal hath set it all about that your lordship designed her for the recreation of his Highness.'

'Why,' Cromwell answered, with his motionless smile of contempt for his fellow men, 'it is well to offer bribes to fools and threats to knaves.'

The Chancellor bleated, with amazed adulation, 'Marvel that your lordship should give so much care to such a worthless rag!'

'An I had never put my heart into trifles, I had never stood here,' Cromwell snarled at him. 'Would that my knaves would ever come to learn that!' He spoke again to Viridus: 'See that this wench come never near his Highness. I like not her complexion.'

'Well, we may clap her up at any moment,' his man answered.

VII

The King came to the revels at the Bishop of Winchester's, for these too were given in honour of the Queen, and he had altered in his mind to let the Emperor and Francis know that he was inclined to weaken in his new alliances. Besides, there was the newest suitor for the hand of the Lady Mary, the young Duke Philip of Wittelsbach, who must be shown how great were the resources of the land. Young, gay, dark, a famous warrior and a good Catholic, he sat behind the Queen and speaking German of a sort he made her smile at times. The play was the Menechmi of Plautus, and Duke Philip interpreted it to her. She seemed at times so nearly human that the King, glancing back over his shoulder to note whether she disgraced him, could settle down into his chair and rest both his back and his misgivings. Seeing the frown leave his brow all the courtiers grew glad behind him; Cromwell talked with animation to Baumbach, the ambassador from the Schmalkaldner league, since he had not seen the King so gay for many days, and Gardiner in his bishop's robes smiled with a black pleasure because his feast was so much more prosperous than Privy Seal's had been. There was no one there of the Lady Mary's household, because it was not seemly that she should be where her suitor was before he had been presented to her.

The large hall was lit with tapers at dusk and hung with ivy and with holly; dried woodruff, watermint and other sweet herbs were scattered about the floors to give an agreeable odour; the antlers of deer from the bishop's chase in Winchester were like a forest of dead boughs, branching from the walls, some gilded, some silvered, some supporting shields emblazoned with the arms of the See, of the bishop, of the King or of Cleves; an army of wood-pigeons and stock-doves with silver collars about their necks was at one time let fly into the hall, and the swish of their wings and afterwards their cooing among the golden rafters of the high ceiling made pleasing sound and mingled with the voices of sweet singing from the galleries at each end of the hall, near the roof. The players spoke their parts bravely, and, because this play was beloved among all others at the Court, there was a great and general contentment.

For the after scene they had a display of theology. There were three battles of men. In black with red hats, horns branching above them and in the centre a great devil with a triple tiara, who danced holding up an enormous key. These stood on the right. On the left were priests in fustian, holding enormous flagons of Rhenish wine and dancing in a drunken measure with their arms round more drunken doxies dressed like German women. In the centre stood grave and reverend men wearing horsehair beards and the long gowns of English bishops and priests. Before these there knelt an angel in flame-coloured robes with wings like the rainbow. The angel supported a great volume on the back of which might be read in letters of gold, 'Regis Nostri Sapientia.'

The great devil, dancing forward, brandishing his key, roared that these reverend men should kneel to him; he held out a cloven foot and bade them kiss it. But a venerable bishop cried out, 'You be Antichrist. I know you. You be the Arch Devil. But from this book I will confound you. Thank God that we have one that leads us aright.' Coming forward he read in Latin from the book of the King's Wisdom and the great devil fell back fainting into the arms of the men in red hats.

The King called out, 'By God, goodman Bishop, you have spoken well!' and the Court roared.

Then one from the other side danced out, holding his flagon and grasping his fat wife round the waist. He sang in a gross and German way, smacking his lips, that these reverend Englishmen should leave their godly ways and come down among the Lutherans. But the old bishop cried out, 'Ay, Dr Martinus, I know thee; thou despisest the Body of God; thou art a fornicator. God forbid that our English priests should go among women as ye do. Listen to wisdom. For, thank God, we have one to lead us aright!'

These words spread a sudden shiver into the hall, for no man there knew whether the King had commanded them to be uttered. The King sat back in his chair, half frowning; Anne blinked, Philip of Wittelsbach laughed aloud, the Catholic ambassadors, Chapuys and Marillac, who had fidgeted in their seats as if they would leave the hall, now leant forward.

'Aye,' the player bishop called out, 'our goodly Queen cometh from a Court that was never yet joined to your Schmalkaldners, nor to them that go by your name, Dr Martinus, thou lecher. Here in England you shall find no heresies but the pure and purged Word of God.'

Chapuys bent an aged white hand behind his ear to miss no word: his true and smiling face blinked benevolently. Cromwell smiled too, licking his lips dangerously; Baumbach, the Schmalkaldner, understanding nothing, rolled his German blue eyes in his great head like a pink baby's, and tried to catch the attention of Cromwell, who talked over his shoulder to one of his men. But the many Lutherans that there were in the hall scowled at the floor.

The player bishop was reading thunderous words of the King, written many years before, against married priests. Henry sat back in his round chair, grasping the arms with his enormous hands.

'Why, Master Bishop,' he called out. The player stopped his reading and looked at the King, his air of austerity never leaving him. Henry, however, waved his hand and said no more.

This dreadful incident caused a confusion in the players: they faltered: the player Lutheran slunk back to his place with his wife, and all of them stood with their hands hanging down. They consulted among themselves and at last filed out from the room, leaving the stage for some empty minutes bare and menacing. Men held their breath: the King was seen to be frowning. But a quick music was played from the galleries and a door opened behind. There came in many figures in white to symbolify the deities of ancient Greece and Rome, and, in black, with ashes upon her head, there was Ceres lamenting that Persephone had been carried into the realms of Pluto. No green thing should blow nor grow upon this earth, she wailed in a deep and full voice, until again her daughter trod there. The other deities covered their heads with their white skirts.

No one heeded this show very much in the hall, for the whispers over what had gone before never subsided again that day. Men turned their backs upon the stage in order to talk with others behind them, and it was generally agreed that if this refurbishing of old doctrines were no more than a bold stroke of Bishop Gardiner's, Henry at least had not scowled very harshly upon it. So that, for the most part, they thought that the Old Faith might come back again; whilst others suddenly remembered, much more clearly than before, that Cleves was a principality not truly Lutheran, and that the marriage with Anne had not tied them at all to the Schmalkaldner's league. Therefore this shadow of the old ways caused new uneasiness, for there was hardly any man there that had not some of the monastery lands.

The King was the man least moved in the hall: he listened to the lamentations of Mother Ceres and gazed at a number of naked boys who issued suddenly from the open door. They spread green herbs in a path from the door to the very feet of Anne, who blinked at them in amazement, and they paid no heed to Mother Ceres, who asked indignantly how any green thing could grow upon the earth that she had bidden lie barren till her daughter came again.

Persephone stood framed in the doorway: she was all in white, very slim and tall; in among her hair she had a wreath of green Egyptian stones called feridets, of which many remained in the treasuries of Winchester, because they were soft and of so little value that the visitors of the monasteries had left them there. And she had these green feridets, cut like leaves, worked into the white lawn, over her breasts. In her left arm there lay a cornucopia filled with gold coins, and in her right a silver coronet of olive leaves. She moved in a slow measure to the music, bending her knees to right and to left, and drawing her long dress into white lines and curves, until she stood in the centre of the green path. She smiled patiently and with a rapt expression as if she had come out of a dream. The wreath of olive leaves, she said, the gods sent to their most virtuous, most beauteous Queen, who had brought peace in England; the cornucopia filled with gold was the offering of Plutus to the noble and benevolent King of these parts. Her words could hardly be heard for the voices of the theologians in the hall before her.

Henry suddenly turned back, lifted his hand, and shouted:

'Be silent!'

Persephone's voice became very audible in the midst of the terrified hush of all these people, who feared their enormous King as if he were a wild beast that at one moment you could play with and the next struck you dead.

'—How happy is England among the nations!' The voice rang out clear and fluting like a boy's. 'Her people how free and bold! Her laws how gentle and beneficent, her nobles how courteous and sweet in their communings together for the public weal! How thrice happy that land when peace is upon the earth! Her women how virtuous, her husbandmen how satiated, her cattle how they let down their milk!'—She swayed round to the gods that were uncovering their heads behind her: 'Aye, my masters and fellow godheads: woe is me that we knew never this happy and contented country. Better it had been there to dwell than upon high Olympus: better than in the Cyclades: better than in the Islands of the Blest that hide amid the Bermoothean tempest. Woe is me!' Her expression grew more rapt; she paused as if she had lost the thread of the words and then spoke again, gazing far out over the hall as jugglers do in performing feats of balancing: 'For surely we had been more safe than reigning alone above the clouds had we lived here, the veriest hinds, beneath a King that is five times blessed, in that he is most wealthy and generous of rewards, most noble of courage, most eloquent, most learned in the law of men, and most high interpreter of the law of God!'

Seeing that the King smiled, as though he had received a just panegyric, a great clamour of applause went up in the hall, and swaying beneath the weight of the cornucopia she came to the King over the path of green herbs and boughs. Henry reached out his hands, himself, to take his present, smiling and genial; and that alone was a sign of great favour, for by rights she should have knelt with it, offered it and then receded, giving it into the arms of a serving man. She passed on, and would have crowned the Queen with the silver wreath; but the great hood that Anne wore stood in the way, therefore she laid it in the Queen's lap.

Henry caught at her hanging sleeve.

'That was a gay fine speech,' he said. 'I will have it printed.'

Little ripples of fear and coldness ran over her, for her dress was thin and her arms bared between the loops above. Her eyes roved round upon the people as if, tall and white, she were a Christian virgin in the agonies of martyrdom. She tried to pull her sleeve from between his great fingers, and she whispered in a sort of terror:

'You stay the masque!'

He lay back in his chair, laughing so that his grey beard shook.

'Why, thou art a pert baggage,' he said. 'I could stay their singing for good an I would.'

He looked her up and down, commanding and good-humouredly malicious. She put her hand to her throat as if it throbbed, and uttered with a calmness of desperation:

'That were great pity. They have practised much, and their breaths are passable sweet.'

The godheads with their beards of tow, their lyres and thunderbolts all gilt, stood in an awkward crescent, their music having stopped. Henry laughed at them.

'I know thy face,' he said. 'It would be less than a king to forget it.'

'I am Katharine Howard,' she faltered, stretching out her hands beseechingly. 'Let me go back to my place.'

'Oh, aye!' he answered. 'But thou'st shed thy rags since I saw thee on a mule.' He loosed her sleeve. 'Let the good men sing, 'a God's name.'

In her relief to be free she stumbled on the sweet herbs.

It was a dark night into which they went out from the bishop's palace. Cressets flared on his river steps, and there were torches down the long garden for those who went away by road. Because there would be a great crowd of embarkers at the bishop's landing place, so that there might be many hours to wait until their barge should come, Katharine, by the office of old Sir Nicholas, had made a compact with some of the maids of honour of the Lady Elizabeth; a barge was to wait for them at the Cross Keys, a common stage some ten minutes down the river. Katharine, laughing, gay with relief and gladdened with words of praise, held Margot's hand tight and kept her fingers on Sir Nicholas' sleeve. It was raining a fine drizzle, so that the air of the gardens smelt moist even against the odour of the torches. The old knight pulled the hood of his gown up over his head, for he was hoarse with a heavy cold. It was pitch black beyond the gate house; in the open fields before the wall torches here and there appeared to burn in mid-air, showing beneath them the heads and the hoods of their bearers hurrying home, and, where they turned to the right along a narrow lane, a torch showed far ahead above a crowd packed thick between dark house-fronts and gables. They glistened with wet and sent down from their gutters spouts of water that gleamed, catching the light of the torch, like threads of opal fire on the pallid dove colour of the towering house-fronts. The torch went round a corner, its light withdrew along the walls by long jumps as its bearer stepped into the distance ahead. Then it was all black. Walking was difficult over the immense cobbles of the roadway, but in the pack of the crowd it was impossible to fall, for people held one another. But it was also impossible to speak, and, muffling her face in her hood, Katharine walked smiling and squeezing Margot's hand out of pure pleasure with the world that was so fair in the midst of this blackness and this heavy cold.

There was a swishing repeated three times and three thuds and twists of white on heads and shoulders just before her. Undistinguishable yells of mockery dwindled down from high above, and a rush-light shone at an immense elevation illuminating a faint square of casement that might have been in the heavens. Three apprentices had thrown down paper bags of powdered chalk. The men who had been struck, and several others who had been maltreated on former nights, or who resented this continual 'prentice scandal, began a frightful outcry at the door of the house. More bags came bursting down and foul water; the yells and battlecries rolled, in the narrow space under the house-fronts that nearly kissed each other high overhead, and the crowd, brought to a standstill, swayed and pushed against the walls. Katharine lost her hold of the old knight's sleeve, and she could see no single thing. She felt round her in the blackness for his arm, but a heavy man stumbled against her. Suddenly his hand was under her arm, drawing her a little; his voice seemed to say: 'Down this gully is a way about.'

In the passage it was blacker than the mouth of hell, and her eyes still seemed to have in them the dazzle of light and triumph she had just left. There was a frightful stench of garbage; and it appeared to be a vault, because the outcry of the men besieging the door volleyed and echoed the more thunderously. There came the sharp click of a latch and Katharine found herself impelled to descend several steps into a blackness from which came up a breath of closer air and a smell of rotting straw. Fear suddenly seized upon her, and the conviction that another man had taken the place of the old knight during the scuffle. But a heavy pressure of an arm was suddenly round her waist, and she was forced forward. She caught a shriek from Margot; the girl's hand was torn from her own; a door slammed behind, and there was a deep silence in which the heavy breathing of a man became audible.

'If you cry out,' a soft voice said, 'I will let you go. But probably you will lose your life.'

She had not a breath at all in her, but she gasped:

'Will you do a rape?' and fumbled in her pocket for her crucifix. Her voice came back to her, muffled and close, so that she was in a very small cellar.

'When you have seen my face, you may love me,' came to her ears in an inane voice. 'I would you might, for you have a goodly mouth for kisses.'

She breathed heavily; the click of the beads on her cross filled the silence. She fitted the bar of the crucifix to her knuckles and felt her breath come calmer. For, if the man struck a light she could strike him in the face with the metal of her cross, held in the fist; she could blind him if she hit an eye. She stepped back a little and felt behind her the damp stone of a wall. The soft voice uttered more loudly:

'I offer you a present of great price; I can solve your perplexities.' Katharine breathed between her teeth and said nothing. 'But if you draw a knife,' the voice went on, 'I will set you loose; there are as good as Madam Howard.' On the door there came the sound of soft thuds. 'That is your maid, Margot Poins,' the voice said. 'You had better bid her begone. This is a very evil gully; she will be strangled.'

Katharine called:

'Go and fetch some one to break down this door.'

The voice commented:

'In the City she will find none to enter this gully; it is a sanctuary of outlaws.'

There was the faintest glimmer of a casement square, high up before Katharine; violence and carryings off were things familiar to her imagination. A hundred men might have desired her whilst she stood on high in the masque. She said hotly:

'If you will hold me here for a ransom, you will find none to pay it.'

She heard the soft hiss of a laugh, and the voice:

'I would myself pay more than other men, but I would have no man see us together.'

She shrank into herself, and held to the wall for comfort. She heard a click, and in the light of a shower of brilliant sparks was the phantom of a man's beard and dim walls; one tiny red glow remained in the tinder, like an illuminant in a black nothingness. He seemed to hold it about breast-high and to pause.

'You had best be rid of Margot Poins,' the musing voice came out of the thick air. 'Send her back to her mother's people: she gets you no friends.'

Katharine wondered if she might strike about eighteen inches above the tiny spark: or if in these impenetrable shadows there were a very tall man.

'Your Margot's folk miscall you in shameful terms. I would be your servant; but it is distasteful to a proper man to serve one that hath about her an atmosphere of lewdness.'

Katharine cursed at him to relieve the agony of her fear.

The voice answered composedly:

'One greater than the devil is my master. But it is good hearing that you are loyal to them that serve you: so you shall be loyal to me, for I will serve you well.'

The spark in the tinder moved upwards; the man began to blow on it; in the dim glimmer there appeared red lips, a hairy moustache, a straight nose, gleaming eyes that looked across the flame, a high narrow forehead, and the gleam of a jewel in a black cap. This glowing and dusky face appeared to hang in the air. Katharine shrank with despair and loathing: she had seen enough to know the man. She made a swift step towards it, her arm drawn back; but the glow of the box moved to one side, the ashes faded: there was already nothing before she could strike.

'You see I am Throckmorton: a goodly knight,' the voice said, laughing.

This man came from Lincolnshire, near her own home. He had been the brother of a gentleman who had a very small property, and he had had one sister. God alone knew for what crime his father had cursed Throckmorton and left his patrimony to the monks at Ely—but his sister had hanged herself. Throckmorton had disappeared.

In that black darkness she had seemed to feel his gloating over her helplessness, and his laughing over all the villainies of his hateful past. He was so loathsome to her that merely to be near him had made her tremble when, the day before, he had fawned over her and shown her the side door to Privy Seal's room. Now the sound of his breathing took away all her power to breathe. She panted:

'Infamous dog, I will have you shortened by the head for this rape.'

'It is true I am a fool to play cat and mouse,' he answered. 'But I was ever thus from a child: I have played silly pranks: listen to gravity. I bring you here because I would speak to you where no ear dare come to listen: this is a sanctuary of night robbers.' His voice took on fantastically and grotesquely the nasal tones of Doctors of Logic when they discuss abstract theses: 'I am a bold man to dare come here; but some of these are in my pay. Nevertheless I am a bold man, though indeed the step from life into death is so short and so easily passed that a man is a fool to fear it. Nevertheless some do fear it; therefore, as men go, I am bold; tho', since I set much store in the intervention of the saints on my behalf, may be I am not so bold. Yet I am a good man, or the saints would not protect me. On the other hand, I am fain to do their work for them: so may be, they would protect me whether I were virtuous or no. Maybe they would not, however: for it is a point still disputed as to whether a saint might use an evil tool to do good work. But, in short, I am here to tell you what Privy Seal would have of you.'

'God help the pair of you,' Katharine said. 'Have ye descended to cellar work now?'

'Madam Howard,' the voice came, 'for what manner of man do you take me? I am a very proper man that do love virtue. There are few such philosophers as I since I came out of Italy.'

It was certain to her now that Privy Seal, having seen her thick with the Bishop of Winchester, had delivered her into the hands of this vulture. 'If you have a knife,' she said, 'put it into me soon. God will look kindly on you and I would pardon you half the crime.' She closed her eyes and began to pray.

'Madam Howard,' he answered, in a lofty tone of aggrievement, 'the door is on the latch: the latch is at your hand to be found for a little fumbling: get you gone if you will not trust me.'

'Aye: you have cut-throats without,' Katharine said. She prayed in silence to Mary and the saints to take her into the kingdom of heaven with a short agony here below. Nevertheless, she could not believe that she was to die: for being still young, though death was always round her, she believed herself born to be immortal.

The sweat was cold upon her face; but Throckmorton was upbraiding her in a lofty nasal voice.

'I am an honourable knight,' he cried, in his affected and shocked tones. 'If I have undone men, it was for love of the republic. I have nipped many treasons in the bud. The land is safe for a true man, because of my work.'

'You are a werewolf,' she shuddered; 'you eat your brother.'

'Why, enough of this talk,' he answered. 'I offer you a service, will you take it? I am the son of a gentleman: I love wisdom for that she alone is good. Virtue I love for virtue's sake, and I serve my King. What more goeth to the making of a proper man? You cannot tell me.'

His voice changed suddenly:

'If you do hate a villain, now is the time to prove it. Would you have him down? Then tell your gossip Winchester that the time approaches to strike, and that I am ready to serve him. I have done some good work for the King's Highness through Privy Seal. But my nose is a good one. I begin to smell out that Privy Seal worketh treasonably.'

'You are a mad fool to think to trick me,' Katharine said. 'Neither you nor I, nor any man, believes that Privy Seal would work a treason. You would trick me into some foolish utterances. It needed not a cellar in a cut-throat's gully for that.'

'Madam Spitfire,' his voice answered, 'you are a true woman; I a true man. We may walk well together. Before the Most High God I wish you no ill.'

'Then let me go,' she cried. 'Tell me your lies some other where.'

'The latch is near your hand still,' he said. 'But I will speak to you no other where. It is only here in the abode of murder and evil men that in these evil times a man may speak his mind and fear no listener.'

She felt tremulously for the latch; it gave, and its rattling set her heart on the jump. When she pulled the door ajar she heard voices in the distant street. It rushed through her mind that he was set neither on murder nor unspeakable things. Or, indeed, he had cut-throats waiting to brain her on the top step. She said tremulously:

'Tell me what you will with me in haste!'

'Why, I have bidden your barge fellows wait for you,' he answered. 'Till cock-crow if need were. They shall not leave you. They fear me too much. Shut the door again, for you dread me no more.'

Her knees felt suddenly limp and she clung to the latch for support; she believed that Mary had turned the heart of this villain. He repeated that he smelt treason working in the mind of an evil man, and that he would have her tell the Bishop of Winchester.

'I did bring you here, for it is the quickest way. I came to you for I saw that you were neither craven nor fool: nor high placed so that it would be dangerous to be seen talking with you later, when you understood my good will. And I am drawn towards you since you come from near my home.'

Katharine said hurriedly, between her prayers:

'What will you of me? No man cometh to a woman without seeking something from her.'

'Why, I would have you look favourably upon me,' he answered. 'I am a goodly man.'

'I am meat for your masters,' she answered with bitter contempt. 'You have the blood of my kin on your hands.'

He sighed, half mockingly.

'If you will not give me your favours,' he said in a low, laughing voice, 'I would have you remember me according as my aid is of advantage to you.'

'God help you,' she said; 'I believe now that you have it in mind to betray your master.'

'I am a man that can be very helpful,' he answered, with his laughing assurance that had always in it the ring of a sneer. 'Tell Bishop Gardiner again, that the hour approaches to strike if these cowards will ever strike.'

Katharine felt her pulses beat more slowly.

'Sir,' she said, 'I tell you very plainly that I will not work for the advancement of the Bishop of Winchester. He turned me loose upon the street to-night after I had served him, with neither guard to my feet nor bit to my mouth. If my side goes up, he may go with it, but I love him not.'

'Why, then, devise with the Duke of Norfolk,' he answered after a pause. 'Gardiner is a black rogue and your uncle a yellow craven; but bid them join hands till the time comes for them to cut each other's throats.'

'You are a foul dog to talk thus of noblemen,' she said.

He answered:

'Oh, la! You have little to thank your uncle for. What do you want? Will you play for your own hand? Or will you partner those two against the other?'

'I will never partner with a spy and a villain,' she cried hotly.

He cried lightly:

'Ohé, Goosetherumfoodle! You will say differently before long. If you will fight in a fight you must have tools. Now you have none, and your situation is very parlous.'

'I stand on my legs, and no man can touch me,' she said hotly.

'But two men can hang you to-morrow,' he answered. 'One man you know; the other is the Sieur Gardiner. Cromwell hath contrived that you should write a treasonable letter; Gardiner holdeth that letter's self.'

Katharine braved her own sudden fears with:

'Men are not such villains.'

'They are as occasion makes them,' he answered, with his voice of a philosopher. 'What manner of men these times breed you should know if you be not a fool. It is very certain that Gardiner will hang you, with that letter, if you work not into his goodly hands. See how you stand in need of a counsellor. Now you wish you had done otherwise.'

She said hotly:

'Never. So I would act again to-morrow.'

'Oh fool madam,' he answered. 'Your cousin's province was never to come within a score miles of the cardinal. Being a drunkard and a boaster he was sent to Paris to get drunk and to boast.'

The horror of the blackness, the damp, the foul smell, and all this treachery made her voice faint. She stammered:

'Shew me a light, or let the door be opened. I am sick.'

'Neither,' he answered. 'I am as much as you in peril. With a light men may see in at the casement; with an open door they may come eavesdropping. When you have been in this world as long as I you will love black night as well.'

Her brain swam for a moment.

'My cousin was never in this plot against me,' she uttered faintly.

He answered lightly:

'You may keep your faith in that toppet. Where you are a fool is to have believed that Privy Seal, who is a wise man, or Viridus, who is a philosopher after my heart, would have sent such a sot and babbler on such a tickle errand.'

'He was sent!' protested Katharine.

'Aye, he was sent to blab about it in every tavern in Paris town. He was sent to frighten the Red Cap out of Paris town. He was suffered to blab to you that you might set your neck in a noose and be driven to be a spy.'

His soft chuckle came through the darkness like an obscene applause of a successful villainy; it was as if he were gloating over her folly and the rectitude of her mind.

'Red Cap was working mischief in Paris—but Red Cap is timorous. He will go post haste back to Rome, either because of your letter or because of your cousin's boasting. But there are real and secret murderers waiting for him in every town in Italy on the road to Rome. Some are at Brescia, some at Rimini: at Padua there is a man with his neck, like yours, in a noose. It is a goodly contrivance.'

'You are a vile pack,' Katharine said, and once more the smooth and unctuous sound came from his invisible throat.

'How shall you decide what is vileness, or where will you find a virtuous man?' he asked. 'Maybe you will find some among the bones of your old Romans. Yet your Seneca, in his day, did play the villain. Or maybe some at the Court of Mahound. I know not, for I was never there. But here is a goodly world, with prizes for them that can take them. Yet virtue may still flourish, for I have done middling well by serving my country. Now I am minded to retire into my lands, to cultivate good letters and to pursue virtue. For here about the Courts there are many distractions. The times are evil times. Yet will I do one good stroke more before I go.'

Katharine said hotly:

'If you go down into Lincolnshire, I will call upon every man there to fall upon you and hang you.'

'Why,' he said, 'that is why I did come to you, since you are from where my lands are. If I serve you, I would have you to smooth my path there. I ask no more, for now I crave rest and a private life. It is very assured that I should never find that here or in few parts of the land—so well I have served my King. Therefore, if I serve you, you and yours shall cast above my retired farms and my honourable leisure the shadow of your protection. I ask no more.' He chuckled almost inaudibly. 'I am set to watch you,' he said. 'Viridus will go to Paris to catch another traitor called Brancetor, for the world is full of traitors. Therefore, in a way, it rests with me to hang you.'

He seemed to be seated upon a cask, for there was a creaking of old wood, and he spoke very leisurely.

Katharine said, 'Good night, and God send you better thoughts.'

'Why, stay, and I will be brief,' he pleaded. 'I dally because it is sweet talking to a fair woman in a black place.'

'You are easily content, for all the sweet words you get from me,' she scorned him.

'See you,' he said earnestly. 'It is true that I am set to watch you. I love you because you are fair; I might bend you, since I hold you in the hollow of my hand. But I am a continent man, and there is here a greater stake to be had than any amorous satisfaction. I would save my country from a man who has been a friend, but is grown a villain. Listen.'

He appeared to pause to collect his words together.

'Baumbach, the Saxish ambassador, is here seeking to tack us to the Schmalkaldner heresies. Yesterday he was with Privy Seal, who loveth the Lutheran alliance. So Privy Seal takes him to his house, and shows him his marvellous armoury, which is such that no prince nor emperor hath elsewhere. So says Privy Seal to Baumbach: "I love your alliance; but his Highness will naught of it." And he fetched a heavy sigh.'

Katharine said:

'What is this hearsay to me?'

'He fetched a heavy sigh,' Throckmorton continued. 'And your uncle or Gardiner knew how heavy a sigh it was their hearts would be very glad.'

'This means that the King's Highness is very far from Privy Seal?' Katharine asked.

'His Highness hateth to do business with small princelings.' Throckmorton seemed to laugh at the King's name. 'His high and princely stomach loveth only to deal with his equals, who are great kings. I have seen the letters that have passed about this Cleves wedding. Not one of them is from his Highness' hand. It is Privy Seal alone that shall bear the weight of the blow when rupture cometh.'

'Well, she is a foul slut,' Katharine said, and her heart was full of sympathy for the heavy King.

'Nay, she is none such,' Throckmorton answered. 'If you look upon her with an unjaundiced eye, she will pass for a Christian to be kissed. It is not her body that his Highness hateth, but her fathering. This is a very old quarrel betwixt him and Privy Seal. His Highness hath been wont to see himself the arbiter of the Christian world. Now Privy Seal hath made of him an ally of German princelings. His Highness loveth the Old Faith and the old royal ways. Now Privy Seal doth seek to make him take up the faith of Schmalkaldners, who are a league of bakers and unfrocked monks. Madam Howard, I tell you that if there were but one man that could strike after the new Parliament is called together...'

Katharine cried:

'The very stones that Cromwell hath soaked with blood will rise to fall upon him when the King's feet no longer press them down.'

Throckmorton laughed almost inaudibly.

'Norfolk feareth Gardiner for a spy; Gardiner feareth the ambition of Norfolk; Bonner would sell them both to Privy Seal for the price of an archbishopric. The King himself is loth to strike, since no man in the land could get him together such another truckling Parliament as can Privy Seal.'

He stopped speaking and let his words soak into her in the darkness, and after a long pause her voice came back to her.

'It is true that I have heard no man speak as you do...I can see that his dear Highness must be hatefully inclined to this filthy alliance.'

'Why, you are minded to come into my hut with me,' he chuckled. 'There are few men so clear in the head as I am. So listen again to me. If you would strike at this man, it is of no avail to meddle with him at home. It shall in no way help you to clamour of good monks done to death, of honest men ruined, of virgins thrown on to dung-heaps. The King hath had the pence of these good monks, the lands of these honest men, and the golden neck-collars off these virgins.'

She called out, 'Keep thy tongue off this sacred King's name. I will listen to no more lewdness.'

A torch passing outside sent a moving square of light through the high grating across the floor of the cellar. The damp walls became dimly visible with shining snail-tracks on them, and his great form leaning negligently upon a cask, his hand arrested in the pulling of his long beard, his eyes gleaming upon her, sardonic and amused. The light twisted round abruptly and was gone.

'You are monstrous fair,' he said, and sighed. She shuddered.

'No,' his mocking voice came again, 'speak not to the King—not to whomsoever you shall elect to speak to the King—of this man's work at home. The King shall let him go very unwillingly, since no man can so pack a Parliament to do the King's pleasure. And he hath a nose for treasons that his Highness would give his own nose to possess.'

'Keep thy tongue off the King's name,' she said again.

He laughed, and continued pensively: 'A very pretty treason might be made up of his speech before his armoury to Baumbach. Mark again how it went. Says he: "Here are such weaponings as no king, nor prince, nor emperor hath in Christendom. And in this country of ours are twenty gentlemen, my friends, have armouries as great or greater." Then he sighs heavily, and saith: "But our King will never join with your Schmalkaldners. Yet I would give my head that he should."... Your madamship marks that this was said to the ambassador from the Lutheran league?'

'You cannot twist that into a treason,' Katharine whispered.

'No doubt,' he said reasonably, 'such words from a minister to an envoy are but a courtesy, as one would say, "I fain would help you, but my master wills it not."'

The voice suddenly grew crafty. 'But these words, spoken before an armoury and the matter of twenty gentlemen with armouries greater. Say that these twenty are creatures of my Lord Cromwell, implicitur, for the Lutheran cause. And again, the matter, "No king hath such an armoury."...No king, I would have you observe.'

'Why, this is monstrous foolish pettifogging,' Katharine said. 'No king would believe a treason in such words.'

'I call to mind Gilmaw of Hurstleas, near our homes,' the voice came, reflectively.

'I did know him,' said Katharine. 'You had his head.'

'You never heard how Privy Seal did that,' the voice came back mockingly. 'Goodman Gilmaw had many sheep died of the rot because it rained seven weeks on end. So, coming back from a market-day, with too much ale for prudence and too little for silence, he cried, "Curse on this rain! The weather was never good since knaves ruled about the King." So that came to the ears of Privy Seal, who made a treason of it, and had his sheep, and his house, and his lands, and his head. He was but one in ten thousand that have gone the same road home from market and made speeches as treasonable.'

'Thus poor Gilmaw died?' Katharine asked. 'What a foul world this is!'

'Time it was cleansed,' he answered.

He let his words rankle for a time, then he said softly: 'Privy Seal's words before his armoury were as treasonable as Gilmaw's on the market road.'

Again he paused.

'Privy Seal may call thee to account for such a treason,' he said afterwards. 'He holdeth thee in a hollow of his hand.'

She did not speak.

He said softly: 'It is a folly to be too proud to fight the world with the world's weapons.'

The heavy darkness seemed to thrill with her silence. He could tell neither whether she were pondering his words nor whether she still scorned him. He could not even hear her breathing.

'God help me!' he said at last, in an angry high note, 'I am not such a man as to be played with too long. People fear me.'

She kept silence still, and his voice grew high and shrill: 'Madam Howard, I can bend you to my will. I have the power to make such a report of you as will hang you to-morrow.'

Her voice came to him expressionlessly—without any inflexion. In few words, what would he have of her? She played his own darkness off against him, so that he could tell nothing new of her mood.

He answered swiftly: 'I will that you tell the men you know what I have told you. You are a very little thing; it were no more to me to cut you short than to drown a kitten. But my own neck I prize. What I have told you I would have come to the ears of my lord of Winchester. I may not be seen to speak with him myself. If you will not tell him, another will; but I would rather it were you.'

'Evil dreams make thy nights hideous!' she cried out so suddenly that his voice choked in his throat. 'Thou art such dirt as I would avoid to tread upon; and shall I take thee into my hand?' She was panting with disgust and scorn. 'I have listened to thee; listen thou to me. Thou art so filthy that if thou couldst make me a queen by the touch of a finger, I had rather be a goose-girl and eat grass. If by thy forged tales I could cast down Mahound, I had rather be his slave than thy accomplice! Could I lift my head if I had joined myself to thee? thou Judas to the Fiend. Junius Brutus, when he did lay siege to a town, had a citizen come to him that would play the traitor. He accepted his proffered help, and when the town was taken he did flay the betrayer. But thou art so filthy that thou shouldst make me do better than that noble Roman, for I would flay thee, disdaining to be aided by thee; and upon thy skin I would write a message to thy master saying that thou wouldst have betrayed him!'

His laugh rang out discordant and full of black mirth; for a long time his shoulders seemed to shake. He spoke at last quite calmly.

'You will have a very short course in this world,' he said.

A hoarse and hollow shouting reverberated from the gully; the glow of a torch grew bright in the window-space. Katharine had been upon the point of opening the door, but she paused, fearing to meet some night villains in the gully. Throckmorton was now silent, as if he utterly disdained her, and a frightful blow upon the wood of the door—so certain were they that the torch would pass on—made them spring some yards further into the cellar. The splintering blows were repeated; the sound of them was deafening. Glaring light entered suddenly through a great crack, and the smell of smoke. Then the door fell in half, one board of it across the steps, the other smashing back to the wall upon its hinges. Sparks dripped from the torch, smoke eddied down, and upon the cellar steps were the legs of a man who rested a great axe upon the ground and panted for breath.

'Up the steps!' he grunted. 'If you ever ran, now run. The guard will not enter here.'

Katharine sped up the steps. It was old Rochford's face that greeted hers beneath the torch. He grunted again, 'Run you; I am spent!' and suddenly dashed the torch to the ground.

At the entry of the tunnel some make of creature caught at her sleeve. She screamed and struck at a gleaming eye with the end of her crucifix. Then nothing held her, and she ran to where, at the mouth of the gully, there were a great many men with torches and swords peering into the darkness of the passage.

In the barge Margot made an outcry of joy and relief, and the other ladies uttered civil speeches. The old man, whose fur near the neck had been slashed by a knife-thrust as he came away, explained pleasantly that he was able to strike good blows still. But he shook his head nevertheless. It was evil, he said, to have such lovers as this new one. Her cousin was bad, but this rapscallion must be worse indeed to harbour her in such a place...Margot, who knew her London, had caught him at the barge, to which he had hurried.

'Aye,' he said, 'I thought you had played me a trick and gone off with some spark. But when I heard to what place, I fetched the guard along with me...Well for you that it was I, for they had not come for any other man, and then you had been stuck in the street. For, see you, whether you would have had me fetch you away or no it is ten to one that a gallant who would take you there would mean that you should never come away alive—and God help you whilst you lived in that place.'

Katharine said:

'Why, I pray God that you may die on the green grass yet, with time for a priest to shrive you. I was taken there against my will.' She told him no more of the truth, for it was not every man's matter, and already she had made up her mind that there was but one man to whom to speak...She went into the dark end of the barge and prayed until she came to Greenwich, for the fear of the things she had escaped still made her shudder, and in the company of Mary and the saints of Lincolnshire alone could she feel any calmness. She thought they whispered round her in the night amid the lapping of the water.

VIII

The stables were esteemed the most magnificent that the King had: three times they had been pulled down and again set up after designs by Holbein the painter. The buildings formed three sides of a square: the fourth gave into a great paddock, part of the park, in which the horses galloped or the mares ran with their foals. That morning there was a glint of sun in the opalescent clouds: horse-boys in grey with double roses worked on their chests were spreading sand in the great quadrangle, fenced in with white palings, between the buildings where the chargers were trained to the manage. Each wing of the buildings was a quarter of a mile long, of grey stone thatched with rushwork that came from the great beds all along the river and rose into curious peaks like bushes along each gable. On the right were the mares, the riding jennets for the women and their saddle rooms; on the left the pack animals, mules for priests and the places for their housings: in the centre, on each side of a vast barn that held the provender, were the stables of the coursers and stallions that the King himself rode or favoured; of these huge beasts there were two hundred: each in a cage within the houses—for many were savage tearers both of men and of each other. On the door of each cage there was written the name of the horse, as Sir Brian, Sir Bors, or Old Leo—and the sign of the constellation under which each was born, the months in which, in consequence, it was propitious or dangerous to ride them, and pentagons that should prevent witches, warlocks or evil spirits from casting spells upon the great beasts. Their housings and their stall armour, covered with grease to keep the rust from them, hung upon pulleys before each stall, and their polished neck armours branched out from the walls in a long file, waving over the gateways right into the distance, the face-pieces with the shining spikes in the foreheads hanging at the ends, the eyeholes carved out and the nostril places left vacant, so that they resembled an arcade of the skeletons of unicorns' heads.

It was quiet and warm in the long and light aisles: there was a faint smell of stable hartshorn and the sound of beans being munched leisurely. From time to time there came a thunder from distant boxes, as two untrained stallions that Privy Seal the day before had given the King kicked against the immense balks of the sliding doors in their cage-stalls.

The old knight was flustered because it was many days since the King had deigned to come in the morning, and there were many beasts to show him. In his steel armour, from which his old head stood out benign and silvery, he strutted stiffly from cage to cage, talking softly to his horses and cursing at the harnessers. Cicely Elliott sat on a high stool from which she could look out of window and gibed at him as he passed.

'Let me grease your potlids, goodly servant. You creak like a roasting-jack.' He smiled at her with an engrossed air, and hurried himself to pull tight the headstrap of a great barb that was fighting with four men.

A tucket of trumpets sounded, silvery and thin through the cold grey air: a page came running with his sallete-helmet.

'Why, I will lace it for him,' Cicely cried, and ran, pushing away the boy. She laced it under the chin and laughed. 'Now you may kiss my cheek so that I know what it is to be kissed by a man in potlids!'

He swung himself, grunting a little, into the high saddle and laughed at her with the air of a man very master of himself. The tucket thrilled again. Katharine Howard pushed the window open, craning out to see the King come: the horse, proud and mincing, appearing in its grey steel as great as an elephant, stepped yet so daintily that all its weight of iron made no more sound than the rhythmic jingling of a sabre, and man and horse passed like a flash of shadow out of the door.

Cicely hopped back on to the stool and shivered.

'We shall see these two old fellows very well without getting such a rheumatism as Lady Rochford's,' and she pulled the window to against Katharine's face and laughed at the vacant and far-away eyes that the girl turned upon her. 'You are thinking of the centaurs of the Isles of Greece,' she jeered, 'not of my knight and his old fashions of ironwork and horse dancing. Yet such another will never be again, so perfect in the old fashions.'

The old knight passed the window to the sound of trumpets towards his invisible master, swaying as easily to the gallop of his enormous steel beast as cupids that you may see in friezes ride upon dolphins down the sides of great billows; but Katharine's eyes were upon the ground.

The window showed only some yards of sand, of grey sky and of whitened railings; trumpet blew after trumpet, and behind her back horse after horse went out, its iron feet ringing on the bricks of the stable to die into thuds and silence once the door was passed.

Cicely Elliott plagued her, tickling her pink ears with a piece of straw and sending out shrieks of laughter, and Katharine, motionless as a flower in breathless sunlight, was inwardly trembling. She imagined that she must be pale and hollow-eyed enough to excite the compassion of the black-haired girl, for she had not slept at all for thinking, and her eyes ached and her hands felt weak, resting upon the brick of the window sill. Horses raced past, shaking the building, in pairs, in fours, in twelves. They curvetted together, pawed their way through intricate figures, arched their great necks, or, reined in suddenly at the gallop, cast up the sand in showers and great flakes of white foam.

The old knight came into view, motioning with his lance to invisible horsemen from the other side of the manage, and the top notes of his voice reached them thinly as he shouted the words of direction. But the King was still invisible.

Suddenly Cicely Elliott cried out:

'Why, the old boy hath dropped his lance! Quel malheur!'—and indeed the lance lay in the sand, the horse darting wildly aside at the thud of its fall. The old man shook his iron fist at the sky, and his face was full of rage and shame in the watery sunlight that penetrated into his open helmet. 'Poor old sinful man!' Cicely said with a note of concern deep in her throat. A knave in grey ran to pick up the lance, but the knight sat, his head hanging on his chest, like one mortally stricken riding from a battlefield.

Katharine's heart was in her mouth, and all her limbs were weak together; a great shoulder in heavy furs, the back of a great cap, came into the view of the window, an immense hand grasped the white balustrade of the manage rails. He was leaning over, a figure all squares, like that on a court-card, only that the embroidered bonnet raked abruptly to one side as if it had been thrown on to the square head. Henry was talking to the old knight across the sand. The sight went out of her eyes and her throat uttered indistinguishable words. She heard Cicely Elliott say:

'What will you do? My old knight is upon the point of tears,' and Katharine felt herself brushing along the wall of the corridor towards the open door.

The immense horse with his steel-plates spreading out like skirts from its haunches dropped its head motionlessly close to the rail, and the grey, wrinkling steel of the figure on its back caught the reflection of the low clouds in flakes of light and shadow.

The old knight muttered indistinguishable words of shame inside his helmet; the King said: 'Ay, God help us, we all grow old together!' and Katharine heard herself cry out:

'Last night you were about very late because evil men plotted against me. Any man might drop his lance in the morning...'

Henry moved his head leisurely over his shoulder; his eyelids went up, in haughty incredulity, so that the whites showed all round the dark pupils. He could not turn far enough to see her without moving his feet, and appearing to disdain so much trouble he addressed the old man heavily:

'Three times I dropped my pen, writing one letter yesterday,' he said; 'if you had my troubles you might groan of growing old.'

But the old man was too shaken with the disgrace to ride any more, and Henry added testily:

'I came here for distractions, and you have run me up against old cares because the sun shone in your eyes. If you will get tricking it with wenches over night you cannot be fresh in the morning. That is gospel for all of us. Get in and disarm. I have had enough of horses for the morning.'

As if he had dispatched that piece of business he turned, heavily and all of one piece, right round upon Katharine. He set his hands into his side and stood with his square feet wide apart:

'It is well that you remember how to kneel,' he laughed, ironically, motioning her to get up before she had reached her knees. 'You are the pertest baggage I have ever met.'

He had recognised her whilst the words were coming out of his great lips. 'Why, is it you the old fellow should marry? I heard he had found a young filly to frisk it with him.'

Katharine, her face pale and in consternation, stammered that Cicely Elliott was in the stables. He said:

'Bide there, I will go speak with her. The old fellow is very cast down; we must hearten him. It is true that he groweth old and has been a good servant.'

He pulled the dagger that hung from a thin gold chain on his neck into its proper place on his chest, squared his shoulders, and swayed majestically into the door of the stable. Katharine heard his voice raised to laugh and dropping into his gracious but still peremptory ardent tones. She remained alone upon the level square of smooth sand. Not a soul was in sight, for when the King came to seek distraction with his horses he brought no one that could tease him. She was filled with fears.

He beckoned her to him with his head, ducking it right down to his chest and back again, and the glances of his eyes seemed to strike her like hammer-blows when he came out from the door.

'It was you then that composed that fine speech about the Fortunate Isles?' he said. 'I had sent for you this morning. I will have it printed.'

She wanted to hang her head like a pupil before her master, but she needs must look him in the eyes, and her voice came strangely and unearthly to her own ears.

'I could not remember the speech the Bishop of Winchester set me to say. I warned him I have no memory for the Italian, and my fright muddled my wits.'

Internal laughter shook him, and once again he set his feet far apart, as if that aided him to look at her.

'Your fright!' he said.

'I am even now so frightened,' she uttered, 'that it is as if another spoke with my throat.'

His great mouth relaxed as if he accepted as his due a piece of skilful flattery. Suddenly she sank down upon her knees, her dress spreading out beneath her, her hands extended and her red lips parted as the beak of a bird opens with terror. He uttered lightly:

'Why, get up. You should kneel so only to your God,' and he touched his cap, with his habitual heavy gesture, at the sacred name.

'I have somewhat to ask,' she whispered.

He laughed again.

'They are always asking! But get up. I have left my stick in my room. Help me to my door.'

She felt the heavy weight of his arm upon her shoulder as soon as she stood beside him.

He asked her suddenly what she knew of the Fortunate Islands that she had talked of in her speech.

'They lie far in the Western Ocean; I had an Italian would have built me ships to reach them,' he said, and Katharine answered:

'I do take them to be a fable of the ancients, for they had no heaven to pray for.'

When his eyes were not upon her she was not afraid, and the heavy weight of his hand upon her shoulder made her feel firm to bear it. But she groaned inwardly because she had urgent words that must be said, and she imagined that nothing could be calmer in the Fortunate Islands themselves than this to walk and converse about their gracious image that shone down the ages. He said, with a heavy, dull voice:

'I would give no little to be there.'

Suddenly she heard herself say, her heart leaping in her chest:

'I do not like the errand they have sent my cousin upon.'

The blessed Utopia of the lost islands had stirred in the King all sorts of griefs that he would shake off, and all sorts of remembrances of youth, of open fields, and a wide world that shall be conquered—all the hopes and instincts of happiness, ineffable and indestructible, that never die in passionate men. He said dully, his thoughts far away:

'What errand have they sent him upon? Who is your goodly cousin?'

She answered:

'They put it about that he should murder Cardinal Pole,' and she shook so much that he was forced to take his hand from her shoulder.

He leaned upon the manage rail, and halted to rest his leg that pained him.

'It is a good errand enough,' he said.

She was panting like a bird that you hold in your hand, so that all her body shook, and she blurted out:

'I would not that my cousin should murder a Churchman!' and before his eyebrows could go up in an amazed and haughty stare: 'I am like to be hanged between Privy Seal and Winchester.'

He seemed to fall against the white bar of the rail for support, his eyes wide with incredulity.

He said: 'When were women hanged here?'

'Sir,' she said earnestly, 'you are the only one I can speak to. I am in great peril from these men.'

He shook his head at her.

'You have gone mad,' he said gravely. 'What is this fluster?'

'Give me your ear for a minute,' she pleaded. Her fear of him as a man seemed to have died down. As a king she had never feared him. 'These men do seek each other's lives, and many are like to be undone between them.'

His nostrils dilated like those of a high-mettled horse that starts back.

'What maggot is this?' he said imperiously. 'Here there is no disunion.'

He rolled his eyes angrily and breathed short, twisting his hands. It was part of his nature to insist that all the world should believe in the concord of his people. He had walked there to talk with a fair woman. He had imagined that she would pique him with pert speeches.

'Speak quickly,' he said in a peremptory voice, and his eyes wandered up the path between the rails and the stable walls. 'You are a pretty piece, but I have no time to waste in woeful nonsense.'

'Alas,' she said, 'this is the very truth of the truth. Privy Seal hath tricked me.'

He laughed heavily and incredulously, and he sat right down upon the rail. She began to tell him her whole story.

All through the night she had been thinking over the coil into which she had fallen. It was a matter of desperate haste, for she had imagined that Throckmorton would go at once or before dawn and make up a tale to Privy Seal so that she should be put out of the way. To her no counter-plotting was possible. Gardiner she regarded with a young disdain: he was a man who walked in plots. And she did not love him because he had treated her like a servant after she had walked in his masque. Her uncle Norfolk was a craven who had left her to sink or swim. Throckmorton, a werewolf who would defile her if she entered into any compact with him. He would inform against her, with the first light of the morning, and she had trembled in her room at every footstep that passed the door. She had imagined guards coming with their pikes down to take her. She had trembled in the very stables.

The King stood above these plots and counter-plots. She imagined him breathing a calmer air that alone was fit for her. To one of her house the King was no more than a man. At home she had regarded him very little. She had read too many chronicles. He was first among such men as her men-folk because her men-folk had so willed it: he was their leader, no more majestic than themselves, and less sacred than most priests. But in that black palace she felt that all men trembled before him. It gave her for him a respect: he was at least a man before whom all these cravens trembled. And she imagined herself such another being: strong, confident, unafraid.

Therefore to the King alone she could speak. She imagined him sympathising with her on account of the ignoble trick that Cromwell had played upon her, as if he too must recognise her such another as himself. Being young she felt that God and the saints alike fought on her side. She was accustomed to think of herself as so assured and so buoyant that she could bear alike the commands of such men as Cromwell, as Gardiner and as her cousin with a smile of wisdom. She could bide her time.

Throckmorton had shocked her, not because he was a villain who had laid hands upon her, but because he had fooled her so that unless she made haste those other men would prove too many for her. They would hang her.

Therefore she must speak to the King. Lying still, looking at the darkness, listening to the breathing of Margot Poins, who slept across the foot of her bed, she had felt no fear whatsoever of Henry. It was true she had trembled before him at the masque, but she swept that out of her mind. She could hardly believe that she had trembled and forgotten the Italian words that she should have spoken. Yet she had stood there transfixed, without a syllable in her mind. And she had managed to bring out any words at all only by desperately piecing together the idea of Ovid's poem and Aulus Gellius' Eulogy of Marcus Crassus, which was very familiar in her ears because she had always imagined for a hero such a man:

munificent, eloquent, noble and learned in the laws. The hall had seemed to blaze before her—it was only because she was so petrified with fright that she had not turned tail or fallen on her knees.

Therefore she must speak to him when he came to see his horses. She must bring him to her side before the tall spy with the eyes and the mouth that grinned as if at the thought of virtue could give Cromwell the signal to undo her.

She spoke vehemently to the King; she was indignant, because it seemed to her she was defiled by these foul men who had grasped at her.

'They have brought me down with a plot,' she said. She stretched out her hand and cried earnestly: 'Sir, believe that what I would have I ask for without any plotting.'

He leant back upon his rail. His round and boding eyes avoided her face.

'You have spoilt my morning betwixt you,' he muttered. First it was old Rochford who failed. Could a man not see his horses gallop without being put in mind of decay and death? Had he need of that? 'Why, I asked you for pleasant converse,' he finished.

She pleaded: 'Sir, I knew not that Pole was a traitor. Before God, I would now that he were caught up. But assuredly a way could be found with the Bishop of Rome...'

'This is a parcel of nonsense,' he shouted suddenly, dismissing her whole story. Would she have him believe it thinkable that a spy should swear away a woman's life? She had far better spend her time composing of fine speeches.

'Sir,' she cried, 'before the Most High God...'

He lifted his hand.

'I am tired of perpetual tears,' he muttered, and looked up the perspective of stable walls and white rails as if he would hurry away.

She said desperately: 'You will meet with tears perpetual so long as this man...'

He lifted his hand, clenched right over his head.

'By God,' he bayed, 'may I never rest from cat and dog quarrels? I will not hear you. It is to drive a man mad when most he needs solace.'

He jerked himself down from the rail and shot over his shoulder:

'You will break your head if you run against a wall; I will have you in gaol ere night fall.' And he seemed to push her backward with his great hand stretched out.

'Why, sometimes,' Throckmorton said, 'a very perfect folly is like a very perfect wisdom.' He sat upon her table. 'So it is in this case, he did send for me. No happening could have been more fortunate.'

He had sent away the man from her door and had entered without any leave, laughing ironically in his immense fan-shaped beard.

'Your ladyship thought to have stolen a march upon me,' he said. 'You could have done me no better service.'

She was utterly overcome with weariness. She sat motionless in her chair and listened to him.

He folded his arms and crossed his legs.

'So he did send for me,' he said. 'You would have had him belabour me with great words. But his Highness is a politician like some others. He beat about the bush. And be sure I left him openings to come in to my tidings.'

Katharine hung her head and thought bitterly that she had had the boldness; this other man reaped the spoils. He leaned forward and sighed. Then he laughed.

'You might wonder that I love you,' he said. 'But it is in the nature of profound politicians to love women that be simple, as it is the nature of sinners to love them that be virtuous. Do not believe that an evil man loveth evil. He contemns it. Do not believe that a politician loveth guile. He makes use of it to carry him into such a security that he may declare his true nature. Moreover, there is no evil man, since no man believeth himself to be evil. I love you.'

Katharine closed her eyes and let her head fall back in her chair. The dusk was falling slowly, and she shivered.

'You have no warrant to take me away?' she asked, expressionlessly.

He laughed again.

'Thus,' he said, 'devious men love women that be simple. And, for a profound, devious and guileful politician you shall find none to match his Highness.'

He looked at Katharine with scrutinising and malicious eyes. She never moved.

'I would have you listen,' he said.

She had had no one to talk to all that day. There was no single creature with whom she could discuss. She might have asked counsel of old Rochford. But apart from the disorder of his mind he had another trouble. He had a horse for sale, and he had given the refusal of it to a man called Stey who lived in Warwickshire. In the meanwhile two Frenchmen had made him a greater offer, and no answer came from Warwickshire. He was in a fume. Cicely Elliott was watching him and thinking of nothing else, Margot Poins was weeping all day, because the magister had been bidden to go to Paris to turn into Latin the letters of Sir Thomas Wyatt. There was no one around Katharine that was not engrossed in his own affairs. In that beehive of a place she had been utterly alone with horror in her soul. Thus she could hardly piece together Throckmorton's meanings. She thought he had come to gibe at her.

'Why should I listen?' she said.

'Because,' he answered sardonically, 'you have a great journey indicated for you, and I would instruct you as to certain peaks that you may climb.'

She had been using her rosary, and she moved it in her lap.

'Any poor hedge priest would be a better guide on such a journey,' she answered listlessly.

'Why, God help us all,' he laughed, 'that were to carry simplicity into a throne-room. In a stable-yard it served. But you will not always find a king among horse-straws.'

'God send I find the King of Peace on a prison pallet,' she answered.

'Why, we are at cross purposes,' he said lightly. He laughed still more loudly when he heard that the King had threatened her with a gaol.

'Do you not see,' he asked, 'how that implies a great favour towards you?'

'Oh, mock on,' she answered.

He leaned forward and spoke tenderly.

'Why, poor child,' he said. 'If a man be moved because you moved him, it was you who moved him. Now, if you can move such a heavy man that is a certain proof that he is not indifferent to you.'

'He threatened me with a gaol,' Katharine said bitterly.

'Aye,' Throckmorton answered, 'for you were in fault to him. That is ever the weakness of your simple natures. They will go brutally to work upon a man.'

'Tell me, then, in three words, what his Highness will do with me,' she said.

'There you go brutally to work again,' he said. 'I am a poor man that do love you. You ask what another man will do with you that affects you.'

He stood up to his full height, dressed all in black velvet.

'Let us, then, be calm,' he said, though his voice trembled and he paused as if he had forgotten the thread of his argument. 'Why, even so, you were in grievous fault to his Highness that is a prince much troubled. As thus: You were certain of the rightness of your cause.'

'It is that of the dear saints,' Katharine said...He touched his bonnet with three fingers.

'You are certain,' he repeated. 'Nevertheless, here is a man whose fury is like an agony to him. He looks favourably upon you. But, if a man be formed to fight he must fight, and call the wrong side good.'

'God help you,' Katharine said. 'What can be good that is set in array against the elect of God?'

'These be brave words,' he answered, 'but the days of the Crusades be over. Here is a King that fights with a world that is part good, part evil. In part he fights for the dear saints; in part they that fight against him fight for the elect of God. Then he must call all things well upon his side, if he is not to fail where he is right as well as where he is wrong.'

'I do not take you well,' Katharine said. 'When the Lacedæmonians strove with the Great King...'

'Why, dear heart,' he said, 'those were the days of a black and white world; now we are all grey or piebald.'

'Then tell me what the King will do with me,' she answered.

He made a grimace.

'All your learning will not make of you but a very woman. It is: What will he do? It is: A truce to words. It is: Get to the point. But the point is this...'

'In the name of heaven,' she said, 'shall I go to gaol or no?'

'Then in the name of heaven,' he said, 'you shall—this next month, or next year, or in ten years' time. That is very certain, since you goad a King to fury.'

She opened her mouth, but he silenced her with his hand.

'No, you shall not go to gaol upon this quarrel!' She sank back into her chair. He surveyed her with a sardonic malice.

'But it is very certain,' he said, 'that had there been there ready a clerk with a warrant and a pen, you had not again seen the light of day until you came to a worse place on a hill.'

Katharine shivered.

'Why, get you gone, and leave me to pray,' she said.

He stretched out towards her a quivering hand.

'Aye, there you be again, simple and brutal!' His jaws grinned beneath his beard. 'I love the air you breathe. I go about to tell a tale in a long way that shall take a long time, so that I may stay with you. You cry: "For pity, for pity, come to the point." I have pity. So you cry, having obtained your desire, "Get ye gone, and let me pray!"'

She said wearily:

'I have had too many men besiege me with their suits.'

He shrugged his great shoulders and cried:

'Yet you never had friend better than I, who bring you comfort hoping for none in return.'

'Why,' she answered, 'it is a passing bitter thing that my sole friend must be a man accounted so evil.'

He moved backwards again to the table; set his white hands upon it behind him, and balancing himself upon them swung one of his legs slowly.

'It is a good doctrine of the Holy Church,' he said, 'to call no man evil until he be dead.' He looked down at the ground, and then, suddenly, he seemed to mock at her and at himself. 'Doubtless, had such a white soul as yours led me from my first day, you to-day had counted me as white. It is evident that I was not born with a nature that warped towards sin. For, let us put it that Good is that thing that you wish.' He looked up at her maliciously. 'Let that be Good. Then, very certainly, since I am enlisted heart and soul in the desire that you may have what you wish, you have worked a conversion in me.'

'I will no longer bear with your mocking,' she said. She began to feel herself strong enough to command for him.

'Why,' he answered, 'hear me you shall. And I must mock, since to mock and to desire are my nature. You pay too little heed to men's natures, therefore the day will come to shed tears. That is very certain, for you will knock against the whole world.'

'Why, yes,' she answered. 'I am as God made me.'

'So are all Christians,' he retorted. 'But some of us strive to improve on the pattern.' She made an impatient movement with her hands, and he seemed to force himself to come to a point. 'It may be that you will never hear me speak again,' he said quickly. 'Both for you and for me these times are full of danger. Let me then leave you this legacy of advice...Here is a picture of the King's Highness.'

'I shall never go near his Highness again,' Katharine said.

'Aye, but you will,' he answered, 'for 'tis your nature to meddle; or 'tis your nature to work for the blessed saints. Put it which way you will. But his Highness meditateth to come near you.'

'Why, you are mad,' Katharine said wearily. 'This is that maggot of Magister Udal's.'

He lifted one finger in an affected, philosophic gesture.

'Oh, nay,' he laughed. 'That his Highness meditateth more speech with you I am assured. For he did ask me where you usually resorted.'

'He would know if I be a traitor.'

'Aye, but from your own word of mouth he would know it.' He grinned once more at her. 'Do you think that I would forbear to court you if I were not afraid of another than you?'

She shrugged her shoulders up to her ears, and he sniggered, stroking his beard.

'You may take that as a proof very certain,' he said. 'None of your hatred should have prevented me, for I am a very likewaorthy man. Ladies that have hated afore now, I have won to love me. With you, too, I would essay the adventure. You are most fair, most virtuous, most simple—aye, and most lovable. But for the moment I am afraid. From now on, for many months, I shall not be seen to frequent you. For I have known such matters of old. A great net is cast: many fish—smaller than I be, who am a proper man—are taken up.'

'It is good hearing that you will no more frequent me,' Katharine said.

He nodded his great head.

'Why, I speak of what is in my mind,' he answered. 'Think upon it, and it will grow clear when it is too late. But here I will draw you a picture of the King.'

'I have seen his Highness with mine own eyes,' she caught him up.

'But your eyes are so clear,' he sighed. 'They see the black and the white of a man. The grey they miss. And you are slow to learn. Nevertheless, already you have learned that here we have no yea-nay world of evil and good...'

'No,' she said, 'that I have not learned, nor never shall.'

'Oh, aye,' he mocked at her. 'You have learned that the Bishop of Winchester, who is on the side of your hosts of heaven, is a knave and a fool. You have learned that I, whom you have accounted a villain, am for you, and a very wise man. You have learned that Privy Seal, for whose fall you have prayed these ten years, is, his deeds apart, the only good man in this quaking place.'

'His acts are most hateful,' Katharine said stoutly.

'But these are not the days of Plutarch,' he answered. 'And I doubt the days of Plutarch never were. For already you have learned that a man may act most evilly, even as Privy Seal, and yet be the best man in the world. And...' he ducked his great head sardonically at her, 'you have learned that a man may be most evil and yet act passing well for your good. So I will draw the picture of the King for you...'

Something seductive in his voice, and the good humour with which he called himself villain, made Katharine say no more than:

'Why, you are an incorrigible babbler!'

Whilst he had talked she had grown assured that the King meditated no imprisoning of her. The conviction had come so gradually that it had merely changed her terrified weariness into a soft languor. She lay back in her chair and felt a comfortable limpness in all her limbs.

'His Highness,' Throckmorton said, 'God preserve him and send him good fortune—is a great and formidable club. His Highness is a most great and most majestic bull. He is a thunderbolt and a glorious light; he is a storm of hail and a beneficent sun. There are few men more certain than he when he is certain. There is no one so full of doubts when he doubteth. There is no wind so mighty as he when he is inspired to blow; but God alone, who directeth the wind in its flight, knoweth when he will storm through the world. His Highness is a balance of a pair of scales. Now he is up, now down. Those who have ruled him have taken account of this. If you had known the Sieur Cromwell as I have, you would have known this very well. The excellent the Privy Seal hath been beknaved by the hour, and hath borne it with a great composure. For, well he knew that the King, standing in midst of a world of doubts, would, in the next hour, the next week, or the next month, come in the midst of doubts to be of Privy Seal's mind. Then Privy Seal hath pushed him to action. Now his Highness is a good lover, and being himself a great doubter, he loveth a simple and convinced nature. Therefore he hath loved Privy Seal...'

'In the name of the saints,' Katharine laughed, 'call you Privy Seal's a simple nature?'

He answered imperturbably:

'Call you Cato's a complex one? He who for days and days and years and years said always one thing alone: "Carthage must be destroyed!"'

'But this man is no noble Roman,' Katharine cried indignantly.

'There was never a nature more Roman,' Throckmorton mocked at her. 'For if Cato cried for years: Delenda est Carthago, Cromwell hath contrived for years: Floreat rex meus. Cato stuck at no means. Privy Seal hath stuck at none. Madam Howard: Privy Seal wrote to the King in his first letter, when he was but a simple servant of the Cardinal, "I, Thomas Cromwell, if you will give ear to me, will make your Grace the richest and most puissant king ever there was." So he wrote ten years agone; so he hath said and written daily for all those years. This it is to have a simple nature...'

'But the vile deeds!' Katharine said.

'Madam Howard,' Throckmorton laughed, 'I would ask you how many broken treaties, how many deeds of treachery, went to the making of the Roman state, since Sinon a traitor brought about the fall of Troy, since Aeneas betrayed Queen Dido and brought the Romans into Italy, until Sylla played false with Marius, Cæsar with the friends of Sylla, Brutus with Cæsar, Antony with Brutus, Octavius with Antony— aye, and until the Blessed Constantine played false to Rome herself.'

'Foul man, ye blaspheme,' Katharine cried.

'God keep me from that sin,' he answered gravely.

'—And of all these traitors,' she continued, 'not one but fell.'

'Aye, by another traitor,' he caught her up. 'It was then as now. Men fell, but treachery prospered—aye, and Rome prospered. So may this realm of England prosper exceedingly. For it is very certain that Cromwell hath brought it to a great pitch, yet Cromwell made himself by betraying the great Cardinal.'

Katharine protested too ardently to let him continue. The land was brought to a low and vile estate. And it was known that Cromwell had been, before all things, and to his own peril, faithful to the great Cardinal's cause.

Throckmorton shrugged his shoulders.

'Without doubt you know these histories better than I,' he answered. 'But judge them how you will, it is very certain that the King, who loveth simple natures, loveth Privy Seal.'

'Yet you have said that he lay under a great shadow,' Katharine convicted him.

'Well,' he said composedly, 'the balance is down against him. This league with Cleves hath brought him into disfavour. But well he knoweth that, and it will be but a short time ere he will work again, and many years shall pass ere again he shall misjudge. Such mistakes hath he made before this. But there hath never been one to strike at him in the right way and at the right time. Here then is an opening.'

Katharine regarded him with a curiosity that was friendly and awakened: he caught her expression and laughed.

'Why, you begin to learn,' he said.

'When you speak clearly I can take your meaning,' she answered.

'Then believe me,' he said earnestly. 'Tell all with whom you may come together. And you may come to your uncle very easily. Tell him that if he may find France and Spain embroiled within this five months, Privy Seal and Cleves may fall together. But, if he delay till Privy Seal hath shaken him clear of Cleves, Cromwell shall be our over-king for twenty years.'

He paused and then continued:

'Believe me again. Every word that is spoken against Privy Seal shall tell its tale—until he hath shaken himself clear of this Cleves coil. His Highness shall rave, but the words will rankle. His Highness shall threaten you—but he shall not strike—for he will doubt. It is by his doubts that you may take him.'

'God help me,' Katharine said. 'What is this of "you" to me?'

He did not heed her, but continued:

'You may speak what you will against Privy Seal—but speak never a word against the glory of the land. It is when you do call this realm the Fortunate Land that at once you make his Highness incline towards you—and doubt. "Island of the Blest," say you. This his Highness rejoices, saying to himself: "My governing appeareth Fortunate to the World." But his Highness knoweth full well the flaws that be in his Fortunate Island. And specially will he set himself to redress wrongs, assuage tears, set up chantries, and make his peace with God. But if you come to him saying: "This land is torn with dissent. Here heresies breed and despair stalks abroad"; if you say all is not well, his Highness getteth enraged. "All is well," he will swear. "All is well, for I made it"—and he would throw his cap into the face of Almighty God rather than change one jot of his work. In short, if you will praise him you make him humble, for at bottom the man is humble; if you will blame him you will render him rigid as steel and more proud than the lightning. For, before the world's eyes, this man must be proud, else he would die.'

Katharine had her hand upon her cheek. She said musingly:

'His Highness did threaten me with a gaol. But you say he will not strike. If I should pray him to restore the Church of God, would he not strike then?'

'Child,' Throckmorton answered, 'it will lie with the way you ask it. If you say: "This land is heathen, your Grace hath so made it," his Highness will be more than terrible. But if you say: "This land prospereth exceedingly and is beloved of the Mother of God," his Highness will begin to doubt that he hath done little to pleasure God's Mother—or to pleasure you who love that Heavenly Rose. Say how all good people rejoice that his Highness hath given them a faith pure and acceptable. And very shortly his Highness will begin to wonder of his Faith.'

'But that were an ignoble flattery,' Katharine said.

He answered quietly:

'No! no! For indeed his Highness hath given all he could give. It is the hard world that hath pushed him against you and against his good will. Believe me, his Highness loveth good doctrine better than you, I, or the Bishop of Rome. So that...'

He paused, and concluded:

'This Lord Cromwell moves in the shadow of a little thing that casts hardly any shadow. You have seen it?'

She shook her head negligently, and he laughed:

'Why, you will see it yet. A small, square thing upon a green hill. The noblest of our land kneel before it, by his Highness' orders. Yet the worship of idols is contemned now.' He let his malicious eyes wander over her relaxed, utterly resting figure.

'I would ye would suffer me to kiss you on the mouth,' he sighed.

'Why, get you gone,' she said, without anger.

'Oh, aye,' he said, with some feeling. 'It is pleasant to be desired as I desire you. But it is true that ye be meat for my masters.'

'I will take help from none of your lies.' She returned to her main position.

He removed his bonnet, and bowed so low to her that his great and shining beard hung far away from his chest.

'Madam Howard,' he mocked, 'my lies will help you well when the time comes.'

PART THREE

I

March was a month of great storms of rain in that year, and the river-walls of the Thames were much weakened. April opened fine enough for men to get about the land, so that, on a day towards the middle of the month, there was a meeting of seven Protestant men from Kent and Essex, of two German servants of the Count of Oberstein, and of two other German men in the living-room of Badge, the printer, in Austin Friars. It happened that the tide was high at four in the afternoon, and, after a morning of glints of sun, great rain fell. Thus, when the Lord Oberstein's men set out into the weather, they must needs turn back, because the water was all out between Austin Friars and the river. They came again into the house, not very unwillingly, to resume their arguments about Justification by Faith, about the estate of the Queen Anne, about the King's mind towards her, and about the price of wool in Flanders.

The printer himself was gloomy and abstracted; arguments about Justification interested him little, and when the talk fell upon the price of wool, he remained standing, absolutely lost in gloomy dreams. It grew a little dark in the room, the sky being so overcast, and suddenly, all the voices having fallen, there was a gurgle of water by the threshold, and a little flood, coming in between sill and floor, reached as it were, a tiny finger of witness towards his great feet. He looked down at it uninterestedly, and said:

'Talk how you will, I can measure this thing by words and by print. Here hath this Queen been with us a matter of four months. Now in my chronicle the pageants that have been made in her honour fill but five pages.' Whereas the chronicling of the jousts, pageants, merry-nights, masques and hawkings that had been given in the first four months of the Queen Jane had occupied sixteen pages, and for the Queen Anne Boleyn sixty and four. 'What sort of honour is it, then, that the King's Highness showeth the Queen?' He shook his head gloomily.

'Why, goodman,' a woolstapler from the Tower Hamlets cried at him, 'when they shot off the great guns against her coming to Westminster in February all my windows were broken by the shrinking of the earth. Such ordnance was never yet shot off in a Queen's honour.'

The printer remained gloomily silent for a minute; the wind howled in the chimney-place, and the embers of the fire spat and rustled.

'Even as ye are held here by the storm, so is the faith of God in these lands,' he said. 'This is the rainy season.' More water came in beneath the door, and he added, 'Pray God we be not all drowned in our holes.'

A motionless German, who had no English, shifted his feet from the wet floor to the cross-bar of his chair. Gloom, dispiritude, and dampness brooded in the low, dark room. But a young man from Kent, who, being used to ill weather, was not to be cast down by gloomy skies, cried out in his own dialect that they had arms to use and leaders to lead them.

'Aye, and we have racks to be stretched on and hang-men to stretch them,' the printer answered. 'Is it with the sound of ordnance that a Queen is best welcomed? When she came to Westminster, what welcome had she? Sirs, I tell you the Mayor of London brought only barges and pennons and targets to her honour. The King's Highness ordered no better state; therefore the King's Highness honoureth not this Queen.'

A scrivener who had copied chronicles for another printer answered him:

'Master Printer John Badge, ye are too much in love with velvet; ye are too avid of gold. Earlier records of this realm told of blows struck, of ships setting sail, of godly ways of life and of towns in France taken by storm. But in your books of the new reign we read all day of cloths of estate, of cloth of gold, of blue silk full of eyes of gold, of garlands of laurels set with brims of gold, of gilt bars, of crystal corals, of black velvet set with stones, and of how the King and his men do shift their suits six times in one day. The fifth Harry never shifted his harness for fourteen days in the field.'

The printer shrugged his enormous shoulders.

'Oh, ignorant!' he said. 'A hundred years ago kings made war with blows. Now it is done with black velvets or the lack of black velvets. And I love laurel with brims of gold if such garlands crown a Queen of our faith. And I lament their lack if by it the King's Highness maketh war upon our faith. And Privy Seal shall dine with the Bishop of Winchester, and righteousness kiss with the whoredom of abomination.'

'An my Lord Cromwell knew how many armed men he had to his beck he had never made peace with Winchester,' the man from Kent cried. He rose from his bench and went to stand near the fire.

A door-latch clicked, and in the dark corner of the room appeared something pale and shining—the face of old Badge, who held open the stair-door and grinned at the assembly, leaning down from a high step.

'Weather-bound all,' he quavered maliciously. 'I will tell you why.'

He slipped down the step, pulling behind him the large figure of his grandchild Margot.

'Get you gone back,' the printer snarled at her.

'That will I not,' her gruff voice came. 'See where my back is wet with the drippings through the roof.'

She and her grandfather had been sitting on a bed in the upper room, but the rain was trickling now through the thatch. The printer made a nervous stride to his printing stick, and, brandishing it in the air, poured out these words:

'Whores and harlots shall not stand in the sight of the godly.'

Margot shrank back upon the stair-place and remained there, holding the bolt of the door in her hand, ready to shut off access to the upper house.

'I will take no beating, uncle,' she panted; 'this is my grandfather's abode and dwelling.'

The old man was sniggering towards the window. He had gathered up his gown about his knees and picked his way between the pools of water on the floor and the Lutherans on their chairs towards the window. He mounted upon an oak chest that stood beneath the casement and, peering out, chuckled at what he saw.

'A mill race and a dam,' he muttered. 'This floor will be a duck pond in an hour.'

'Harlot and servant of a harlot,' the printer called to his niece. The Lutherans, who came from houses where father quarrelled with son and mother with daughter, hardly troubled more than to echo the printer's words of abuse. But one of them, a grizzled man in a blue cloak, who had been an ancient friend of the household, broke out:

'Naughty wench, thou wast at the ordeal of Dr Barnes.'

Margot, drawing her knees up to her chin where she sat on the stairs, answered nothing. Had she not feared her uncle's stick, she was minded to have taken a mop to the floor and to have put a clout in the doorway.

'Abominable naughty wench,' the grizzled man went on. 'How had ye the heart to aid in that grim scene? Knew ye no duty to your elders?'

Margot closed the skirts round her ankles to keep away the upward draught and answered reasonably:

'Why, Neighbour Ned, my mistress made me go with her to see a heretic swinged. And, so dull is it in our service, that I would go to a puppet show far less fine and thank thee for the chance.'

The printer spat upon the floor when she mentioned her mistress.

'I will catechize,' he muttered. 'Answer me as I charge thee.'

The old man, standing on the chest, tapped one of the Germans on the shoulder.

'See you that wall, friend?' he laughed. 'Is it not a noble dam to stay the flood back into our house? Now the Lord Cromwell...'

The Lanzknecht rolled his eyes round, because he understood no English. The old man went on talking, but no one there, not even Margot Poins, heeded him. She looked at her uncle reasonably, and said:

'Why, an thou wilt set down thy stick I will even consider thee, uncle.' He threw the stick into the corner and immediately she went to fetch a mop from the cooking closet, where there lived a mumbling old housekeeper. The printer followed her with gloomy eyes.

'Is not thy mistress a naughty woman?' he asked, as a judge talks to a prisoner condemned.

She answered, 'Nay,' as if she had hardly attended to him.

'Is she not a Papist?'

She answered, 'Aye,' in the same tone and mopped the floor beneath a man's chair.

Her grandfather, standing high on the oak chest, so that his bonnet brushed the beams of the dark ceiling, quavered at her:

'Would she not bring down this Crummock, whose wall hath formed a dam so that my land-space is now a stream and my house-floor a frog pond?'

She answered, 'Aye, grandfer,' and went on with her mopping.

'Did she not go with a man to a cellar of the Rogues' Sanctuary after Winchester's feast?' Neighbour Ned barked at her. 'Such are they that would bring down our Lord!'

'Did she not even so with her cousin before he went to Calais?' her uncle asked.

Margot answered seriously:

'Nay, uncle, no night but what she hath slept in these arms of mine that you see.'

'Aye, you are her creature,' Neighbour Ned groaned.

'Foul thing,' the printer shouted. 'Eyes are upon thee and upon her. It was the worst day's work that ever she did when she took thee to her arms. For I swear to God that her name shall be accursed in the land. I swear to God...'

He choked in his throat. His companions muttered Harlot; Strumpet; Spouse of the Fiend. And suddenly the printer shouted:

'See you; Udal is her go-between with the King, and he shall receive thee as his price. He conveyeth her to his Highness, she hath paid him with thy virtue. Foul wench, be these words not true?'

She leaned upon her mop handle and said:

'Why, uncle, it is a foul bird that 'files his own nest.'

He shook his immense fist in her face.

'Shame shall out in the communion of the godly, be it whose kin it will.'

'Why, I wish the communion of the godly joy in its hot tales,' she answered. 'As for me, speak you with the magister when he comes from France. As for my mistress, three times she hath seen the King since Winchester's feast was three months agone. She in no wise affected his Highness till she had heard his Highness confute the errors of Dr Barnes in the small closet. When she came away therefrom she said that his Highness was like a god for his knowledge of God's law. If you want better tales than that go to a wench from the stairs to make them for you.'

'Aye,' said their neighbour, 'three times hath she been with the King. And the price of the first time was the warrant that took thee to pay Udal for his connivance. And the price of the second was that the King's Highness should confute our sacred Barnes in the conclave. And the price of the third was that the Lord Cromwell should dine with the Bishop of Winchester and righteousness sit with its head in ashes.'

'Why, have it as thou wilt, Neighbour Ned,' she answered. 'In my life of twenty years thou hast brought me twenty sugar cates. God forbid that I should stay thy willing lips over a sweet morsel.'

In the gloomy and spiritless silence that fell upon them all—since no man there much believed the things that were alleged, but all very thoroughly believed that evil days were stored up against them—the bursting open of the door made so great a sound that the speechless German tilted backward with his chair and lay on the ground, before any of them knew what was the cause. The black figure of a boy shut out the grey light and the torrents of rain. His head was bare, his frieze clothes dripped and sagged upon his skin: he waved his clenched fist half at the sky and half at Margot's face and screamed:

'I ha' carried letters for thee, 'twixt thy mistress and the King! I ha' carried letters. I...ha'...been gaoled for it.'

'O fool,' Margot's deep voice uttered, unmoved, 'the letters went not between those two. And thou art free; come in from the rain.'

He staggered across the prostrate German.

'I ha' lost my advancement,' he sobbed. 'Where shall I go? Twenty hours I have hidden in the reeds by the riverside. I shall be taken again.'

'There is no hot pursuit for thee then,' Margot said, 'for in all the twenty hours no man hath sought thee here.' She had the heavy immobility of an elemental force. No fright could move her till she saw the cause for fright. 'I will fetch thee a dram of strong waters.'

He passed his hand across his wet forehead.

'Thy mistress is taken,' he cried. 'I saw Privy Seal's pikes go to her doorway.'

'Now God be praised,' the printer cried out, and caught at the boy's wrist. 'Tell your tale!' and he shook him on his legs.

'Me, too, Privy Seal had taken—but I 'scaped free,' he gasped. 'These twain had promised me advancement for braving their screeds. And I ha' lost it.'

'Gossips all,' the Neighbour Ned barked out, 'to your feet and let us sing: "A fortress fast is God the Lord." The harlot of the world is down.'

II

During the time that had ensued between January and that month of March, it had been proved to Katharine Howard how well Throckmorton, the spy, voiced the men folk of their day. He had left her alone, but she seemed to feel his presence in all the air. He passed her in corridors, and she knew from his very silence that he was carrying on a fumbling game with her uncle Norfolk, and with Gardiner of Winchester. He had not induced her to play his game—but he seemed to have made her see that every man else in the world was playing a game like his. It was not, precisely, any more a world of black and white that she saw, but a world of men who did one thing in order that something very different might happen a long time afterwards.

The main Court had moved from Greenwich to Hampton towards the end of January, but the Lady Mary, with her ladies, came to a manor house at Isleworth; and shut in as she was with a grim mistress—who assuredly was all white or black—Katharine found herself like one with ears strained to catch sounds from a distance, listening for the smallest rumours that could come from the other great house up stream.

The other ladies each had their men, as Cicely Elliott had the old knight. One of them had even six, who one day fought a mêlée for her favours on an eyot before the manor windows. These men came by barge in the evenings, or rode over the flats with a spare horse to take their mistresses a-hawking after the herons in the swampy places. So that each of them had her channel by which true gossip might reach her. But Katharine had none. Till the opening of March the magister came to whisper with Margot Poins—then he was sent again to Paris to set his pen at the service of Sir Thomas Wyatt, who had so many letters to write. Thus she heard much women's tattle, but knew nothing of what passed. Only it seemed certain that Gardiner of Winchester was seeing fit—God knows why—to be hot in favour of the Old Faith. It was certain, from six several accounts, that at Paul's Cross he had preached a sermon full of a very violent and acceptable doctrine. She wondered what move in the game this was: it was assuredly not for the love of God. No doubt it was part of Throckmorton's plan. The Lutherans were to be stirred to outrages in order to prove to the King how insolent were they upon whom Privy Seal relied.

It gratified her to see how acute her prescience had been when Dr Barnes made his furious reply to the bishop. For Dr Barnes was one of Privy Seal's most noted men: an insolent fool whom he had taken out of the gutter to send ambassador to the Schmalkaldners. And it was on the day when Gardiner made his complaint to the King about Dr Barnes, that her uncle Norfolk sent to her to come to him at Hampton.

He awaited her, grim and jaundiced, in the centre of a great, empty room, where, shivering with cold, he did not let his voice exceed a croaking whisper though there was panelling and no arras on the dim walls. But, to his queries, she answered clearly:

'Nay, I serve the Lady Mary with her Latin. I hear no tales and I bear none to any man.' And again:

'Three times I have spoken with the King's Highness, the Lady Mary being by. And once it was of the Islands of the Blest, and once of the Latin books I read, and once of indifferent matters—such as of how apple trees may be planted against a wall in Lincolnshire.'

Her uncle gazed at her: his dark eyes were motionless and malignant by habit; he opened his lips to speak; closed them again without a word spoken. He looked at a rose, carved in a far corner of the ceiling, looked at her again, and muttered:

'The French are making great works at Ardres.'

'Oh, aye,' she answered, 'my cousin Tom wrote me as much. He is commanded to stay at Calais.'

'Tell me,' he said, 'will they go against Calais town in good earnest?'

'If I knew that,' she answered, 'I should have had it in private words from my lady whom I serve. And, if I had it in private words I would tell it neither to you nor to any man.'

He scowled patiently and muttered:

'Then tell in private words back again this: That if the French King or the Emperor do war upon us now Privy Seal will sit upon the King's back for ever.'

'Ah, I know who hath talked with you,' she answered. 'Uncle, give me your hand to kiss, for I must back to my mistress.'

He put his thin hand grimly behind his back.

'Ye spy, then, for others,' he said. 'Go kiss their feet.'

She laughed in a nettled voice:

'If the others get no more from me than your Grace of Norfolk...'

He frowned ominously, pivoted stiffly round on his heels, and said over his shoulder:

'Then I will have thy cousin clapped up the first time he is found in a drunken brawl at Calais.'

She was after him beseechingly, with her hands held out:

'Oh no, uncle,' and 'Oh, dear uncle. Let poor fool Tom be drunken when drunken brawls work no manner of ill.'

'Then get you sent to the King of France, through the channel that you wot of, the message I have given you to convey.' He kept his back to her and spoke as if to the distant door.

'Why must I mull in these matters?' she asked him piteously, 'or why must poor Tom? God help him, he found me bread when you had left me to starve.' It came to her as pitiful that her cousin, swaggering and unconscious, at a great distance, should be undone because these men quarrelled near her. He moved stiffly round again—he was so bolstered over with clothes against the cold.

'It is not you that must meddle here,' he said. 'It is your mistress. Only she will be believed by those you wot of.'

'Speak you yourself,' she said.

He scowled hatefully.

'Who of the French would believe me,' he snarled. He had been so made a tool of by Privy Seal in times past that he had lost all hope of credence.

'If I may come to it, I will do it,' she said suddenly.

After all, it seemed to her, this action might bring about the downfall of Privy Seal—and she desired his downfall. It would be a folly to refuse her aid merely because her uncle was a craven man or Throckmorton a knave. It was a true thing that she was to ask the Lady Mary to say—that if France and Spain should molest England together the Cleves alliance must stand for good—and with it Privy Seal.

'But, a' God's name, let poor Tom be,' she added.

He stood perfectly motionless for a moment, shrugged his shoulders straight up and down, stood motionless for another moment, and then held out his hand. She touched it with her lips.

There was a certain cate, or small cake, made of a paste sweetened with honey and flavoured with cinnamon, that Katharine Howard very much loved. She had never tasted them till one day the King had come to visit his daughter, bearing with his own hands a great box of them. He had had the receipt from Thomas Cromwell, who had had it of a Jew in Italy. Mary so much disaffected her father that, taking them from his hands with one knee nearly upon the ground, she had said that her birth ill-fitted her to eat these princely viands, and she had placed them on a ledge of her writing-pulpit. Heaving a heavy sigh, he glanced at her book and said that he would not have her spoil her eyes with too much of study; let her bid Lady Katharine to read and write for her.

'She will have greater need of her eyes than ever I of mine,' Mary answered with her passionless voice.

'I will not have you spoil your eyes,' he said heavily, and she gave him back the reply:

'My eyes are your Highness'.'

He made with his shoulders a slow movement of exasperation, and, turning to Katharine Howard, he began once more to talk of the Islands of the Blest. He was dressed all in black furs that day, so that his face appeared less pallid than when he had worn scarlet, and it seemed to her suddenly that he was a very pitiful man—a man who could do nothing; and one who, as Throckmorton had said, was nothing but a doubt. There beside him, between the two of them, stood his daughter—pale, straight, silent, her hands clasped before her. And her father had come to placate her. He had brought her cates to eat, or he would have beaten her into loving him. Yet Mary of England stood as rigid as a knife-blade; you could move her neither by love nor by threats. This man had sinned against this daughter; here he was brought up against an implacability. He was omnipotent in everything else; this was his Pillars of Hercules. So she exerted herself to be pleasant with him, and at one moment of the afternoon he stretched out a great hand to the cinnamon cakes and placed one in his own mouth. He sat still, and, his great jaws moving slowly, he said that he scarcely doubted that, if he himself could set sail with a great armada and many men, he should find a calm region of tranquil husbandry and a pure faith.

'It might be found,' he said; then he sighed heavily, and, looking earnestly at her, brushed the crumbs from the furs about his neck.

'One day, doubtless, your Highness shall find them,' Katharine answered, 'if your Highness shall apply yourself to the task.' She was impatient with him for his sighs. Let him, if he would, abandon his kingdom and his daughter to set out upon a quest, or let him stay where he was and set to work at any other task.

'But whether your Highness shall find them beyond the Western Isles or hidden in this realm of England...'

He shrugged his great shoulders right up till the furs on them were brushed by the feathers that fell from his bonnet.

'God, wench!' he said gloomily, 'that is a question you are main happy to have time to dally with. I have wife and child, and kith and kin, and a plaguey basket of rotten apples to make cider from.'

He pulled himself out of his chair with both hands on the arms, stretched his legs as if they were cramped, and rolled towards the door.

'Why, read of this matter in old books,' he said, 'and if you find the place you shall take me there.' Then he spoke bitterly to the Lady Mary, who had never moved.

'Since your eyes are mine, I bid you not spoil them,' he said. 'Let this lady aid you. She has ten times more of learning than you have.' But, taking his jewelled walking-stick from beside the door, he added, 'God, wench! you are my child. I have read your commentary, and I, a man who have as much of good letters as any man in Christendom, am well content to father you.'

'Did your Highness mark—this book being my child—which side of the paper it was written on?' his daughter asked.

Katharine Howard sighed, for it was the Lady Mary's bitter jest that she wrote on the rough side of the paper, having been born on the wrong side of the blanket.

'Madam Howard,' she said to Katharine with a cold sneer, as of a very aged woman, 'my father, who has taken many things from me to give to other women, takes now my commentary to give to you. Pray you finish it, and I will save mine eyes.'

As the King closed the door behind him she moved across to the chair and sat herself down to gaze at the coals. Katharine knelt at her feet and stretched out her hands. She was, she said, her mistress's woman. But the Lady Mary turned obdurately the side of her face to her suppliant; only her fingers picked at her black dress.

'I am your woman,' Katharine said. 'Before God and St Anthony, the King is naught to me! Before God and the Mother of God, no man is aught to me! I swear that I am your woman. I swear that I will speak as you bid me speak, or be silent. May God do so to me if in aught I act other than may be of service to you!'

'Then you may sit motionless till the green mould is over your cheeks,' Mary answered.

But two days later, in the afternoon, Katharine Howard came upon her mistress with her jaws moving voraciously. Half of the cinnamon cates were eaten from the box on the writing-pulpit. A convulsion of rage passed over the girl's dark figure; her eyes dilated and appeared to blaze with a hot and threatening fury.

'If I could have thy head, before God I would shorten thee by the neck!' she said. 'Stay now; go not. Take thy hand from the door-latch.'

Sudden sobs shook her, and tears dropped down her furrowed and pallid cheeks. She was tormented always by a gnawing and terrible hunger that no meat and no bread might satisfy, so that, being alone with the cates in the cold spring afternoon, she had, in spite of the donor, been forced always nearer and nearer to them.

'God help me!' she said at last. 'Udal is gone, and the scullion that supplied me in secret has the small-pox. How may I get me things to eat?'

'To have stayed to ask me!' Katharine cried. 'What a folly was here!' For, as a daughter of the King, the Lady Mary was little more than herself; but because she was daughter to a queen that was at once a saint and martyr, Katharine was ready to spend her life in her service.

'I would stay to ask a service of any man or woman,' Mary answered, 'save only that I have this great hunger.' She clutched angrily at her skirt, and so calmed herself.

'How may you help me?' she asked grimly. 'There are many that would put poison in my food. My mother was poisoned.'

'I would eat myself of all the food that I bring you,' said Katharine.

'And if thou wast poisoned, I must get me another, and yet another after that. You know who it is that would have me away.'

At that hint of the presence of Cromwell, Katharine grew more serious.

'I will save of my own food,' she answered simply.

'Till your bones stick through your skin!' Mary sneered. 'See you, do you know one man you could trust?'

The shadow fell the more deeply upon Katharine, because her cousin—as she remembered every day—the one man that she could trust, was in Calais town.

'I know of two women,' she said; 'my maid Margot and Cicely Elliott.'

Mary of England reflected for a long time. Her eyes sunk deep in her head, grey and baleful, had the look of her father's.

'Cicely Elliott is too well known for my woman,' she said. 'Thy maid Margot is a great lump, too. Hath she no lover?'

The magister was in Paris.

'But a brother she hath,' Katharine said; 'one set upon advancement.'

Mary said moodily:

'Advancement, then, may be in this. God knoweth his own good time. But you might tell him; or it were better you should bid her tell him... In short words, and fur...wait.'

She had a certain snake-like eagerness and vehemence in her motions. She opened swiftly an aumbry in which there stood a tankard of milk. She took a clean pen, and then turned upon Katharine.

'Before thou goest upon this errand,' she said, 'I would have thee know that, for thee, there may be a traitor's death in this—and some glory in Heaven.'

'You write to the Empress,' Katharine cried.

'I write to a man,' the Lady Mary said. 'Might you speak with clear eyes to my father if you knew more than that?'

'I do not believe that you would bring your father down,' Katharine said.

'Why, you have a very comfortable habit of belief,' Mary sneered at her. 'In two words! Will you carry this treasonable letter or no?'

'God help me,' Katharine cried.

'Well, God help you,' her mistress jeered. 'Two nights agone you swore to be my woman and no other man's. Here you are in a taking. Think upon it.'

She dipped her white pen in the milk and began to write upon a great sheet of paper, holding her head aslant to see the shine of the fluid.

Katharine fought a battle within herself. Here was treason to the King—but that was a little thing to her. Yet the King was a father whom she would bring back to this daughter, and the traitor was a daughter whom she was sworn to serve and pledged to bring back to this father. If then she conveyed this letter...

'Tell me,' she asked of the intent figure above the paper, 'when, if ever, this plot shall burst?'

'Madam Howard,' the other answered, 'I heard thee not.'

'I say I will convey your Highness' letter if the plot shall not burst for many days. If it be to come soon I will forswear myself and be no longer your woman.'

'Why, what a pax is here?' her mistress faced round on her. 'What muddles thy clear head? I doubt, knowing the craven kings that are of my party, no plot shall burst for ten years. And so?'

'Before then thou mayest be brought back to thy father,' Katharine said.

Mary of England burst into a hoarse laughter.

'As God's my life,' she cried, 'that may well be. And you may find a chaste whore before either.'

Whilst she was finishing her letter, Katharine Howard prayed that Mary the Mother of Mercy might soften the hatred of this daughter, even as, of old times, she had turned the heart of Lucius the Syracusan. Then there should be an end to plotting and this letter might work no ill.

Having waved the sheet of paper in the air to dry it, Mary crumpled it into a ball.

'See you,' she said, 'if this miscarry I run a scant risk. For, if this be a treason, this treason is well enough known already to them you wot of. They might have had my head this six years on one shift or another had they so dared. So to me it matters little.—But for thee—and for thy maid Margot and this maid's brother and his house and his father and his leman—death may fall on ye all if this ball of paper miscarry.'

Katharine made no answer and her mistress spoke on.

'Take now this paper ball, give it to thy maid Margot, bid thy maid Margot bear it to her brother Ned.' Her brother Ned should place it in his sleeve and walk with it to Herring Lane at Hampton. There, over against the house of the Sieur Chapuys, who was the Emperor's ambassador to this Christian nation— over against that house there was a cookshop to which resorted the servants of the ambassador. Passing it by, Katharine's maid's brother should thrust his hand in at the door and cry 'a pox on all stinking Kaiserliks and Papists,'—and he should cast the paper at that cook's head. Then out would come master cook to his door and claim reparation. And for reparation Margot's brother Ned should buy such viands as the cook should offer him. These viands he was to bring, as a good brother should, to his hungry sister, and these viands his sister should take to her room—which was Katharine's room. 'And, of an evening,' she finished, 'I shall come to thy room to commune with thee of the writers that be dead and yet beloved. Hast thou the lesson by heart? I will say it again.'

III

It was in that way, however sorely against her liking, that Katharine Howard came into a plot. It subdued her, it seemed to age her, it was as if she had parted with some virtue. When again she spoke with the King, who came to loll in his daughter's armed chair one day out of every week, it troubled her to find that she could speak to him with her old tranquillity. She was ashamed at feeling no shame, since all the while these letters were passing behind his back. Once even he had been talking to her of how they nailed pear trees against the walls in her Lincolnshire home.

'Our garden man would say...' she began a sentence. Her eye fell upon one of these very crumpled balls of paper. It lay upon the table and it confused her to think that it appeared like an apple. 'Would say...would say...' she faltered.

He looked at her with enquiring eyes, round in his great head.

'It is too late,' she finished.

'Even too late for what?' he asked.

'Too late in the year to set the trees back,' she answered and her fit of nervousness had passed. 'For there is a fluid in trees that runneth upward in the spring of the year to greet the blessed sun.'

'Why, what a wise lady is this!' he said, half earnest. 'I would I had such an adviser as thou hast,' he continued to his daughter.

He frowned for a moment, remembering that, being who he was, he should stand in need of no advice.

'See you,' he said to Katharine. 'You have spoken of many things and wisely, after a woman's fashion of book-learning. Now I am minded that you should hear me speak upon the Word of God which is a man's matter and a King's. This day sennight I am to have brought to my closet a heretic, Dr Barnes. If ye will ye may hear me confound him with goodly doctrines.'

He raised both his eyebrows heavily and looked first at the Lady Mary.

'You, I am minded, shall hear a word of true doctrine.'

And to Katharine, 'I would hear how you think that I can manage a disputation. For the fellow is the sturdiest rogue with a yard of tongue to wag.'

Katharine maintained a duteous silence; the Lady Mary stood with her hands clasped before her. Upon Katharine he smiled suddenly and heavily.

'I grow too old to be a match for thee in the learning of this world. Thy tongue has outstripped me since I am become stale...But hear me in the other make of talk.'

'I ask no better,' Katharine said.

'Therefore,' he finished, 'I am minded that you, Mog, and your ladies all, do move your residences from here to my house at Hampton. This is an old and dark place; there you shall be better honoured.'

He lay back in his chair and was pleased with the care that he took of his daughter. Katharine glided intently across the smooth bare floor and took the ball of paper in her hand. His eyes followed her and he moved his head round after her movements, heavily, and without any motion of his great body. He was in a comfortable mood, having slept well the night before, and having conversed agreeably in the bosom of a family where pleasant conversation was a rare thing. For the Lady Mary had forborne to utter biting speeches, since her eyes too had been upon that ball of paper. The King did not stay for many minutes after Katharine had gone.

She was excited, troubled and amused—and, indeed, the passing of those letters held her thoughts in those few days. Thus it was easy to give the paper to her maid Margot, and easy to give Margot the directions. But she knew very well by what shift Margot persuaded her scarlet-clothed springald of a brother to take the ball and to throw it into the cookshop. For the young Poins was set upon advancement, and Margot, buxom, substantial and honest-faced, stood before him and said: 'Here is your chance for advancement made...' if he could carry these missives very secretly.

'For, brother Poins,' she said, 'thou knowest these great folks reward greatly—and these things pass between folks very great. If I tell thee no names it is because thou canst see more through a stone wall than common folk.'

So the young Poins cocked his bonnet more jauntily, and, setting out up river to Hampton, changed his scarlet clothes for a grey coat and puritan hose, and in the dark did his errand very well. He carried a large poke in which he put the larded capons and the round loaves that the cook sold to him. Later, following a reed path along the river, he came swiftly down to Isleworth with his bag on a cord and, in the darkness from beneath the walls, he slung bag and cord in at Katharine Howard's open window. For several times this happened before the Lady Mary's court was moved to Hampton. At first, Katharine had her tremors to put up with—and it was only when, each evening, with a thump and swish, the bag, sweeping out of the darkness, sped across her floor—it was only then that Katharine's heart ceased from pulsing with a flutter. All the while the letters were out of her own hands she moved on tiptoe, as if she were a hunter intent on surprising a coy quarry. Nevertheless, it was impossible for her to believe that this was a dangerous game; it was impossible to believe that the heavy, unsuspicious and benevolent man who tried clumsily to gain his daughter's love with bribes of cakes and kerchiefs—that this man could be roused to order her to her death because she conveyed from one place to another a ball of paper. It was more like a game of passing a ring from hand to hand behind the players' backs, for kisses for forfeits if the ring were caught. Nevertheless, this was treason-felony; yet it was furthering the dear cause of the saints.

It was on the day on which her uncle Norfolk had sent for her that the King had his interview with the heretical Dr Barnes—nicknamed Antoninus Anglicanus.

The Lady Mary and Katharine Howard and her maid, Margot, were set in a tiny closet in which there was, in a hole in the wall, a niche for the King's confessor. The King's own chamber was empty when they passed through, and they left the door between ajar. There came a burst of voices, and swiftly the Bishop of Winchester himself entered their closet. He lifted his black eyebrows at sight of them, and rubbed his thin hands with satisfaction.

'Now we shall hear one of Crummock's henchmen swinged,' he whispered. He raised a finger for them to lend ear and gazed through the crack of the door. They heard a harsh voice, like a dog's bay, utter clearly:

'Now goodly goodman Doctor, thou hast spoken certain words at Paul's Cross. They touched on Justification; thou shalt justify them to me now.' There came a sound of a man who cleared his throat—and then again the heavy voice:

'Why, be not cast down; we spoke as doctor to doctor. Without a doubt thou art learned. Show then thy learning. Wast brave at Paul's Cross. Justify now!'

Gardiner, turning from gazing through the door-crack, grinned at the three women.

'He rated me at Paul's Cross!' he said. 'He thumped me as I had been a thrashing floor.' They missed the Doctor's voice—but the King's came again:

'Why, this is a folly. I am Supreme Head, but I bid thee to speak.'

There was a long pause till they caught the words.

'Your Highness, I do surrender my learning to your Highness'.' Then, indeed, there was a great roar:

'Unworthy knave; surrender thyself to none but God. He is above me as above thee. To none but God.'

There was another long silence, and then the King's voice again:

'Why, get thee gone. Shalt to gaol for a craven...' And then came a hissing sound of vexation, a dull thud, and other noises.

The King's bonnet lay on the floor, and the King himself alone was padding down the room when they opened their door. His face was red with rage.

'Why, what a clever fiend is this Cromwell!' the Lady Mary said; but the Bishop of Winchester was laughing. He pushed Margot Poins from the closet, but caught Katharine Howard tightly by the arm.

'Thou shalt write what thy uncle asked of thee!' he commanded in a low voice, 'an thou do it not, thy cousin shall to gaol! I have a letter thou didst write me.'

A black despair settled for a moment upon Katharine, but the King was standing before her. He had walked with inaudible swiftness up from the other end of the room.

'Didst not hear me argue!' he said, with the vexation of a great child. 'That poxy knave out-marched me!'

'Why,' the Lady Mary sniggered at him, 'thy brewer's son is too many for your Highness.'

Henry snarled round at her; but she folded her hands before her and uttered:

'The brewer's son made your Highness Supreme Head of the Church. Therefore, the brewer's son hath tied your Highness' tongue. For who may argue with your Highness?'

He looked at her for a moment with a bemused face.

'Very well,' he said.

'The brewer's son should have made your Highness the lowest suppliant at the Church doors. Then, if, for the astounding of certain beholders, your Highness were minded to argue, your Highness should find adversaries.'

The bitter irony of her words made Katharine Howard angry. This poor, heavy man had other matters for misgiving than to be badgered by a woman. But the irony was lost upon the King. He said very simply:

'Why, that is true. If I be the Head, the Tail shall fear to bandy words with me.' He addressed himself again to Katharine: 'I am sorry that you did not hear me argue. I am main good at these arguments.' He looked reflectively at Gardiner and said: 'Friend Winchester, one day I will cast a main at arguments with thee, and Kat Howard shall hear. But I doubt thou art little skilled with thy tongue.'

'Why, I will make a better shift with my tongue than Privy Seal's men dare,' the bishop said. He glanced under his brows at Henry, as if he were measuring the ground for a leap.

'The Lady Mary is in the right,' he ventured.

The King, who was thinking out a speech to Katharine, said, 'Anan?' and Gardiner ventured further:

'I hold it for true that this man held his peace, because Cromwell so commanded it. He is Cromwell's creature, and Cromwell is minded to escape from the business with a whole skin.'

The King bent him an attentive ear.

'It is to me, in the end, that Privy Seal owes amends,' Gardiner said rancorously. 'Since it was at me that this man, by Cromwell's orders, did hurl his foul words at Paul's Cross.'

The King said:

'Why, it is true that thou art more sound in doctrine than is Privy Seal. What wouldst thou have?'

Gardiner made an immense gesture, as if he would have embraced the whole world.

Katharine Howard trembled. Here they were, all the three of them Cromwell's enemies. They were all alone with the King in a favouring mood, and she was on the point of crying out:

'Give us Privy Seal's head.'

But, in this very moment of his opportunity, Gardiner faltered. Even the blackness of his hatred could not make him bold.

'That he should make me amends in public for the foul words that knave uttered. That they should both sue to me for pardon: that it should be showed to the world what manner of man it is that they have dared to flout.'

'Why, goodman Bishop, it shall be done,' the King said, and Katharine groaned aloud. A clock with two quarter boys beside the large fireplace chimed the hour of four.

'Aye!' the King commented to Katharine. 'I thought to have had a pleasanter hour of it. Now you see what manner of life is mine: I must go to a plaguing council!'

'An I were your Highness,' Katharine cried, 'I would be avenged on them that marred my pleasures.'

He touched her benevolently upon the cheek.

'Sweetheart,' he said, 'an thou wert me thou'dst do great things.' He rolled towards the door, heavy and mountainous: with the latch in his hand, he cried over his shoulder: 'But thou shalt yet hear me argue!'

'What a morning you have made of this!' Katharine threw at the bishop. The Lady Mary shrugged her shoulders to her ears and turned away. Gardiner said:

'Anan?'

'Oh, well your Holiness knows,' Katharine said. 'You might have come within an ace of having Cromwell down.'

His eyes flashed, and he swallowed with a bitter delight.

'I have him at my feet,' he said. 'He shall do public reparation to me. You have heard the King say so.'

There were tears of vexation in Katharine's eyes.

'Well I know how it is that this brewer's son has king'd it so long!' she said. 'An I had been a man it had been his head or mine.'

Gardiner shook himself like a dog that is newly out of the water.

'Madam Howard,' he said, 'you are mighty high. I have observed how the King spoke all his words for your ear. His passions are beyond words and beyond shame.'

The Lady Mary was almost out of the room, and he came close enough to speak in Katharine's ears.

'But be you certain that his Highness' passions are not beyond the reverse of passion, which is jealousy. You have a cousin at Calais...'

Katharine moved away from him.

'Why, God help you, priest,' she said. 'Do you think you are the only man that knows that?'

He laughed melodiously, with a great anger.

'But I am the man that knoweth best how to use my knowledge. Therefore you shall do my will.'

Katharine Howard laughed back at him:

'Where your lordship's will marches with mine I will do it,' she said. 'But I am main weary of your lordship's threats. You know the words of Artemidorus?'

Gardiner contained his rage.

'You will write the letter we have asked you to write?'

She laughed again, and faced him, radiant, fair and flushed in the cheeks.

'In so far as you beg me to write a letter praying the King of France and the Emperor to abstain from war upon this land, I will write the letter. But, in so far as that helps forward the plotting of you and a knave called Throckmorton, I am main sorry that I must write it.'

The bishop drew back, and uttered:

'Madam Howard, ye are forward.'

'Why, God help your lordship,' she said. 'Where I see little course for respect I show little. You see I am friends with the King—therefore leave you my cousin be. Because I am friends with the King, who is a man among wolves, I will pray my mistress to indite a letter that shall save this King some troubles. But, if you threaten me with my cousin, or my cousin with me, I will use my friendship with the King as well against you as against any other.'

Gardiner swallowed in his throat, winked his eyes, and muttered:

'Why, so you do what we will, it matters little in what spirit you shall do it.'

'So you and my uncle and Throckmorton keep your feet from my paths, you may have my leavings,' she said. 'And they will be the larger part, since I ask little for myself.'

He gave her his episcopal blessing as she followed the Lady Mary to her rooms.

Her mind was made up—and she knew that it had been made up hastily, but she was never one to give much time to doubting. She wished these men to leave her out of their plots—but four men are stronger than one woman. Yet, as her philosophy had it, you may make a woman your tool, but she will bend in your hand and strike where she will, for all that. Therefore she must plot, but not with them.

As soon as she could she found the Lady Mary alone, and, setting her valour up against the other's dark and rigid figure, she spoke rapidly:

She would have her lady write to her friends across the sea that, if Cromwell were ever to fall, they must now stay their hands against the King: they must diminish their bands, discontinue their fortifyings and feign even to quarrel amongst themselves. Otherwise the King must rest firm in his alliance with Cleves, to counterbalance them.

The Lady Mary raised her eyebrows with a show of insolent astonishment that was for all the world like the King's.

'You affect my father!' she said. 'Is it not a dainty plan?'

Katharine brushed past her words with:

'It matters little who affects what thing. The main is that Privy Seal must be cast down.'

'Carthage must be destroyed, O Cato,' the Lady Mary sneered. 'Ye are peremptory.'

'I am as God made me,' Katharine answered. 'I am for God's Church...' She had a sharp spasm of impatience. 'Here is a thing to do, and the one and the other snarl like dogs, each for his separate ends.'

'Oh, la, la,' the Lady Mary laughed.

'A Howard is as good as any man,' Katharine said. Her ingenuous face flushed, and she moved her hand to her throat. 'God help me: it is true that I swore to be your woman. But it is the true province of your woman to lead you to work for justice and the truth.'

A black malignancy settled upon the face of the princess.

'I have been called bastard,' she said. 'My mother was done to death.'

'No true man believes you misbegotten,' Katharine answered hotly.

'Well, it is proclaimed treason, to speak thus,' the Lady Mary sneered.

'Neither can you give your sainted mother her life again.' Katharine ignored her words. 'But these actions were not your father's. It was an ill man forced him to them. The saints be good to you; is it not time to forgive a sad man that would make amends? I would have you to write this letter.'

The Lady Mary's lips moved into the curves of a tormenting smile.

'You plead your lover's cause main well,' she uttered.

Katharine had another motion of impatience.

'Your cause I plead main better,' she said. 'It is certain that, this man once down, your bastardy should be reversed.'

'I do not ask it,' the Lady Mary said.

'But I ask that you give us peace here, so that the King may make amends to many that he hath sorely wronged. Do you not see that the King inclineth to the Church of God? Do you not see...'

'I see very plainly that I needs must thank you for better housing,' Mary answered. 'It is certain that my father had never brought me from that well at Isleworth, had it not been that he desireth converse with thee at his ease.'

Katharine's lips parted with a hot anger, but before she could speak the bitter girl said calmly:

'Oh, I have not said thou art his leman. I know my father. His blood is not hot—but his ears crave tickling. Tickle them whilst thou mayest. Have I stayed thee? Have I sent thee from my room when he did come?'

Katharine cast back the purple hood from over her forehead, she brushed her hand across her brow, and made herself calm.

'This is a trifling folly,' she said. 'In two words: will your Highness write me this letter?'

'Then, in four words,' Mary answered, 'my Highness cares not.'

The mobile brows above Katharine's blue eyes made a hard straight line.

'An you will not,' she brought out, 'I will leave your Highness' service. I will get me away to Calais, where my father is.'

'Why, you will never do that,' the Lady Mary said; 'you have tasted blood here.'

Katharine hung her head and meditated for a space.

'No, before God,' she said earnestly, 'I think you judge me wrong. I think I am not as you think me. I think that I do seek no ends of my own.'

The Lady Mary raised her eyebrows and snickered ironically.

'But of this I am very certain,' Katharine said. She spoke more earnestly, seeming to plead: 'If I thought that I were grown a self-seeker, by Mars who changed Alectryon to a cock, and by Pallas Athene who changed Arachne to a spider—if I were so changed, I would get me gone from this place. But here is a thing that I may do. If you will aid me to do it I will stay. If you will not I will get me gone.'

'Good wench,' Mary answered, 'let us say for the sake of peace that thou art honest...Yet I have sworn by other gods than thine that never will I do aught that shall be of aid, comfort or succour to my father's cause.'

'Take back your oaths!' Katharine cried.

'For thee!' Mary said. 'Wench, thou hast brought me food: thou hast served me in the matter of letters. I might only with great trouble get another so to serve me. But, by Mars and Pallas and all the constellation of the deities, thou mightest get thee to Hell's flames or ever I would take back an oath.'

'Oh, madness,' Katharine cried out. 'Oh, mad frenzy of one whom the gods would destroy.' Three times before she had reined in her anger: now she stretched out her hands with her habitual gesture of pitiful despair. Her eyes looked straight before her, and, as she inclined her knees, the folds of her grey dress bent round her on the floor.

'Here I have pleaded with you, and you have gibed me with the love of the King. Here I have been earnest with you, and you have mocked. God help me!' she sobbed, with a catch in her throat. 'Here is rest, peace and the blessing of God offered to this land. Here is a province that is offered back to the Mother of God and the dear hosts of heaven. Here might we bring an erring King back to the right way, a sinful man back unto his God. But you, for a parcel of wrongs of your own...'

'Now hold thy peace,' Mary said, between anger and irony. 'Here is a matter of a farthing or two. Be the letter written, and kiss upon it.'

Katharine stayed herself in the tremor of her emotions, and the Lady Mary said drily:

'Be the letter written. But thou shalt write it. I have sworn that I will do nothing to give this King ease.'

'But my writing...' Katharine began.

'Thou shalt write,' Mary interrupted her harshly. 'If thou wilt have this King at peace for a space that Cromwell may fall, why I am at one with thee. For this King is such a palterer that without this knave at his back I might have had him down ten years ago. Therefore, thou shalt write, and I will countersign the words.'

'That were to write thyself,' Katharine said.

'Good wench,' the Lady Mary said. 'I am thy slave: but take what thou canst get.'

Towards six of the next day young Poins clambered in at Katharine Howard's window and stood, pale, dripping with rain and his teeth chattering, between Cicely Elliott and her old knight.

'The letter,' he said. 'They have taken thy letter. My advancement is at an end!' And he fell upon the floor.

Going jauntily along the Hampton Street, he had been filled, that afternoon, with visions of advancement. Drifts of rain hid the osiers across the river and made the mud ooze in over the laces of his shoes. The tall white and black house, where the Emperor's ambassador had his lodgings, leaned in all its newness over the path, and the water from its gutters fell right into the river, making a bridge above a passer's head. The little cookshop, with its feet, as it were, in the water, made a small hut nestling down beneath the shadow of the great house. It was much used by Chapuys' grooms, trencher boys and javelin men, because the cook was a Fleming, and had a comfortable hand in stewing eels.

Ned Poins must pass the ambassador's house in his walk, but in under the dark archway there stood four men sheltering, in grey cloaks that reached to their feet. Stepping gingerly on the brick causeway that led down to the barge-steps, they came and stood before the young man, three being in a line together and one a little to the side. He hardly looked at them because he was thinking: 'This afternoon I will say to my sister Margot: "Fifteen letters I have carried for thy great persons. I have carried them with secrecy and speed. Now, by Cock, I will be advanced to ancient."' He had imagined his sister pleading with him to be patient, and himself stamping with his foot and swearing that he would be advanced instantly.

The solitary one of the four men barred his way, and said:

'No further! You go back with us!'

Poins swung his cape back and touched his sword-hilt.

'You will have your neck stretched if you stay me,' he said.

The other loosened his cloak which had covered him up to the nose. He showed a mocking mouth, a long red beard that blew aside in a wild gust of the weather, and displayed on his breast the lion badge of the Lord Privy Seal.

'An you will not come you shall be carried!' he said.

'Nick Throckmorton,' Poins answered, 'I will slit thy weazand! I am on a greater errand than thine.'

It was strong in his mind that he was bearing a letter for the King's Highness. The other three laid hands swiftly upon him, and a wet cloak flapped over his head. They had his elbows bound together behind his back before his eyes again had the river and the muddy path to look upon. Throckmorton grinned sardonically, and they forced him along in the mud. The rain fell down; his cloak was gone. And then a great dread entered into his simple mind. It kept running through his head:

'I was carrying a letter for the King—I was carrying a letter for the King!' but his addled brains would bear his thoughts no further until he was cast loose in the very room of Privy Seal himself. They had used him very roughly, and he staggered back against the wall, gasping for breath and weeping with rage and fear.

Privy Seal stood before the fire; his eyes lifted a little but he said nothing at all. Throckmorton took a dagger from the chain round his neck, and cut the bag from the boy's girdle. Still smiling sardonically, he placed it in Privy Seal's fat hands.

'Here is the great secret,' he said. 'I took it even in the gates of Chapuys.'

Privy Seal started a little and cried, 'Ah!' The boy would have spoken, but he feared even to cry out; his eyes were starting from his head, and his breath came in great gusts that shook him. Privy Seal sat down in a large chair by the fire and considered for a moment. Then he slowly drew out the crumpled ball of paper. Here at last he held the Lady Mary utterly in his power; here at last, at the eleventh hour, he had a new opportunity to show to the King his vigilance, his power, and how necessary he was to the safety of the realm. He had been beginning to despair; Winchester was to confess the King that night. Now he held them...

'I have been diligent,' Throckmorton said. 'I had had the Lady Mary set in the room that has a spy-hole beside a rose in the ceiling. So I saw the writing of this letter.'

Cromwell said, 'Ah!' He had pulled the paper apart, smoothed it across his knee, and looked at it attentively. Then he held it close to the fire, for no blank paper could trouble the Privy Seal. This was a child's trick at best.

In the warmth faint lines became visible on the paper; they darkened and darkened beneath his intent eyes. Behind his back Throckmorton, with his immense beard and sardonic eyes, rubbed his hands and smiled. Privy Seal's fingers trembled, but he gave no further sign.

Suddenly he cried, 'What!' and then, 'Both women! both...'

He fell back in the chair, and the sudden quaver of his face, the deep breath that he drew, showed his immense joy.

'God of my heart! Both women!' he said again.

The rain hurled itself with a great rustling against the casement. Though it was so early, it was already nearly dark. Cromwell sat up suddenly and pointed at the boy.

'Take that rat away!' he said. 'Set him in irons, and come back here.'

Throckmorton caught the quivering boy by the ear and led him out at the door. He took him down a small stair that opened behind a curtain. At the stair-foot he pulled open a small, heavy door. He still held his dagger, and he cut the ropes that tied Poins' elbows. With a sudden alacrity and a grin of malice he kicked him violently.

'Get you gone to your mistress,' he said.

Poins stood for a moment, wavering on his feet. He slipped miserably in the mud of the park, and suddenly he ran. His grey, straining form disappeared round the end of the dark buildings, and then Throckmorton waved a hand at the grey sky and laughed noiselessly. Thomas Cromwell was making notes in his tablets when his spy re-entered the room, with the rain-drops glistening in his beard.

'Here are some notes for you,' Cromwell said. He rose to his feet with a swift and intense energy. 'I have given you five farms. Now I go to the King.'

Throckmorton spoke gently.

'You are over-eager,' he said. 'It is early to go to the King's Highness. We may find much more yet.'

'It is already late,' Cromwell said.

'Sir,' Throckmorton urged, 'consider that the King is much affected to this lady. Consider that this letter contains nothing that is treasonable; rather it urges peace upon the King's enemies.'

'Aye,' said Cromwell; 'but it is written covertly to the King's enemies.'

'That, it is true, is a treason,' Throckmorton said; 'but it is very certain that the Lady Mary hath written letters very much more hateful. By questioning this boy that we have in gaol, by gaoling this Lady Katharine—why, we shall put her to the thumbscrews!—by gaol and by thumbscrew, we shall gar her to set her hand to another make of confession. Then you may go to the King's Highness.'

'Nick Throckmorton,' Cromwell said, 'Winchester hath to-night the King's ear...'

'Sir,' Throckmorton answered, and a tremble in his calm voice showed his eagerness, 'I beseech you to give my words your thoughts. Winchester hath the King's ear for the moment; but I will get you letters wherein these ladies shall reveal Winchester for the traitor that we know him to be. Listen to me...' He paused and let his crafty eyes run over his master's face. 'Let this matter be for an hour. See you, you shall make a warrant to take this Lady Katharine.'

He paused and appeared to reflect.

'In an hour she shall be here. Give me leave to use my thumbscrews...'

'Aye, but Winchester,' Cromwell said.

'Why,' Throckmorton answered confidently, 'in an hour, too, Winchester shall be with the King in the King's Privy Chapel. There will be a make of prayers; ten minutes to that. There shall be Gardiner talking to the King against your lordship; ten minutes to that. And, Winchester being craven, it shall cost him twice ten minutes to come to begging your lordship's head of the King, if ever he dare to beg it. But he never shall.'

Cromwell said, 'Well, well!'

'There we have forty minutes,' Throckmorton said. He licked his lips and held his long beard in his hand carefully, as if it had been a bird. 'But give me ten minutes to do my will upon this lady's body, and ten to write down what she shall confess. Then, if it take your lordship ten minutes to dress yourself finely, you shall have still ten in which you shall show the King how his Winchester is traitor to him.'

Cromwell considered for a minute; his lips twitched cautiously the one above the other.

'This is a great matter,' he said. He paused again. 'If this lady should not confess! And it is very certain that the King affects her.'

'Give me ten minutes of her company,' the spy answered.

Cromwell considered again.

'You are very certain,' he said; and then:

'Wilt thou stake thy head upon it?'

Throckmorton wagged his beard slowly up and down.

'Thy head and beard!' Cromwell repeated. He struck his hands briskly together. 'It is thine own asking. God help thee if thou failest!'

'I will lay nothing to your lordship's door,' Throckmorton said eagerly.

'God knows!' Cromwell said. 'No man that hath served me have I deserted. So it is that no one hath betrayed me. But thou shalt take this lady without warrant from my hand.'

Throckmorton nodded.

'If thou shalt wring avowal from her thou shalt be the wealthiest commoner of England,' Cromwell said. 'But I will not be here. Nay, thou shalt take her to thine own rooms. I will not be seen in this matter. And if thou fail...'

'Sir, I stand more sure of my succeeding than ever your lordship stood,' Throckmorton answered him.

'It is not I that shall betray thee if thou fail,' Cromwell answered. 'Get thee gone swiftly...' He took the jewelled badge from his cap that lay on the table. 'Thou hast served me well,' he said; 'take this in case I never see thy face again.'

'Oh, you shall see my triumph!' Throckmorton answered.

He bent himself nearly double as he passed through the door.

Cromwell sat down in his great chair, and his eyes gazed at nothing through the tapestry of his room.

IV

In Katharine Howard's room they had the form of the boy, wet, grey, and mud-draggled, lying on the ground between them. Cicely Elliott rose in her chair: it was not any part of her nature to succour fainting knaves, and she let him stay where he was. Old Rochford raised his hands, and cried out to Katharine:

'You have been sending letters again!'

Katharine stood absolutely still. They had taken her letters!

She neither spoke nor stirred. Slowly, as she remembered that this was indeed a treason, that here without doubt was death, that she was outwitted, that she was now the chattel of whosoever held her letters—as point after point came into her mind, the blood fled from her face. Cicely Elliott sat down in her chair again, and whilst the two sat watching her in the falling dusk they seemed to withdraw themselves from her world of friendship and to become spectators. Ten minutes before she would have laughed at this nightmare: it had seemed to her impossible that her letters could have been taken. So many had got in safety to their bourne. Now...

'Who has my letter?' she cried.

How did she know what was to arise: who was to strike the blow: whence it would come: what could she still do to palliate its effects? The boy lay motionless upon the floor, his face sideways upon the boards.

'Who? Who? Who?' she cried. She wrung her hands, and kneeling, with a swift violence shook him by the coat near his neck. His head struck the boards and he fell back, motionless still, and like a dead man.

Cicely Elliott looked around her in the darkening room: beside the ambry there hung a brush of feathers such as they used for the dusting of their indoor clothes. She glided and hopped to the brush and back to the hearth: thrust the feathers into the coals and stood again, the brush hissing and spluttering, before Katharine on her knees.

'Dust the springald's face,' she tittered.

At the touch of the hot feathers and the acrid perfume in his nostrils, the boy sneezed, stirred and opened his eyes.

'Who has my letter?' Katharine cried.

The lids opened wide in amazement, he saw her face and suddenly closed his eyes, and lay down with his face to the floor. A spasm of despair brought his knees up to his chin, his cropped yellow head went backwards and forwards upon the boards.

'I have lost my advancement,' he sobbed. 'I have lost my advancement.' A smell of strong liquors diffused itself from him.

'Oh beast,' Katharine cried from her knees, 'who hath my letter?'

'I have lost my advancement,' he moaned.

She sprang from her feet to the fireplace and caught the iron tongs with which they were wont to place pieces of wood upon the fire. She struck him a hard blow upon the arm between the shoulder and elbow.

'Sot!' she cried. 'Tell me! Tell me!'

He rose to his seat and held his arms to protect his head and eyes. When he stuttered:

'Nick Throckmorton had it!' her hand fell powerless to her side; but when he added: 'He gave it to Privy Seal!' she cast the tongs into the brands to save herself from cleaving open his head.

'God!' she said drily, 'you have lost your advancement. And I mine!... And I mine.'

She wavered to her chair by the hearth-place, and covered her face with her white hands.

The boy got to his knees, then to his feet; he staggered backwards into the arras beside the door.

'God's curse on you!' he said. 'Where is Margot? That I may beat her! That I may beat her as you have beaten me.' He waved his hand with a tipsy ferocity and staggered through the door.

'Was it for this I did play the — for thee?' he menaced her. 'By Cock! I will swinge that harlot!'

The old knight got to his feet. He laid his hand heavily upon Cicely Elliott's shoulder.

'Best begone from here,' he said, 'this is no quarrel of mine or thine.'

'Why, get thee gone, old boy,' she laughed over her shoulder. 'Seven of my men have been done to death in such like marlocks. I would not have thee die as they did.'

'Come with me,' he said in her ear. 'I have dropped my lance. Never shall I ride to horse again. I would not lose thee; art all I have.'

'Why, get thee gone for a brave old boy,' she said. 'I will come ere the last pynot has chattered its last chatter.'

'It is no light matter,' he answered. 'I am Rochford of Bosworth Hedge. But I have lost lance and horse and manhood. I will not lose my dandery thing too.'

Katharine Howard sat, a dark figure in the twilight, with the fire shining upon her hands that covered her face. Cicely Elliott looked at her and stirred.

'Why,' she said, 'I have lost father and mother and men-folk and sister. But my itch to know I will not lose, if I pay my head for the price. I would give a silken gown to know this tale.'

Katharine Howard uncovered her face; it shewed white even in the rays of the fire. One finger raised itself to a level with her temple.

'Listen!' she uttered. They heard through the closed door a dull thud, metallic and hard—and another after four great beats of their hearts.

'Pikestaves!' the old knight groaned. His mouth fell open. Katharine Howard shrieked; she sprang to the clothes press, to the window—and then to the shadows beside the fireplace where she cowered and sobbed. The door swung back: a great man stood in the half light and cried out:

'The Lady Katharine Howard.'

The old knight raised his hands above his head—but Cicely Elliott turned her back to the fire.

'What would you with me?' she asked. Her face was all in shadows.

'I have a warrant to take the Lady Katharine.'

Cicely Elliott screamed out:

'Me! Me! Ah God! ah God!'

She shrank back; she waved her hands, then suddenly she caught at the coif above her head and pulled forward the tail of her hood till, like a veil, it covered her face.

'Let me not be seen!' she uttered hoarsely.

The old knight's impatient desires burst through his terror.

'Nick Throckmorton,' he bleated, 'yon mad wench of mine...'

But the large man cut in on his words with a harsh and peremptory vehemence.

'It is very dark. You cannot see who I be. Thank your God I cannot see whether you be a man who fought by a hedge or no. There shall be reports written of this. Hold your peace.'

Nevertheless the old man made a spluttering noise of one about to speak.

'Hold your peace,' Throckmorton said roughly, again, 'I cannot see your face. Can you walk, madam, and very fast?'

He caught her roughly by the wrist and they passed out, twin blots of darkness, at the doorway. The clank of the pike-staves sounded on the boards without, and old Rochford was tearing at his white hairs in the little light from the fire.

Katharine Howard ran swiftly from the shadow of the fireplace.

'Give me time, till they have passed the stairhead,' she whispered. 'For pity! for pity.'

'For pity,' he muttered. 'This is to stake one's last years upon woman.' He turned upon her, and his white face and pale blue eyes glinted at her hatefully.

'What pity had Cicely Elliott upon me then?'

'Till they are out of the gate,' she pleaded, 'that I may get me gone.'

At her back she was cut off from the night and the rain by a black range of corridors. She had never been through them because they led to rooms of men that she did not know. But, down the passage and down the stairway was the only exit to the rest of the palace and the air. She threw open her press so that the hinges cracked. She caught her cloak and she caught her hood. She had nowhither to run—but there she was at the end of a large trap. Their footsteps as they receded echoed and whispered up the stairway from below.

'For pity!' she pleaded. 'For pity! I will go miles away before it is morning.'

He had been wavering on his feet, torn backwards and forwards literally and visibly, between desire and fear, but at the sound of her voice he shook with rage.

'Curses on you that ever you came here,' he said. 'If you go free I shall lose my dandling thing.'

He made as if to catch her by the wrist; but changing his purpose, ran from the room, shouting:

'Ho la!...Throck...morton...That...is not...' His voice was lost in reverberations and echoes.

In the darkness she stood desolately still. She thought of how Romans would have awaited their captors: the ideal of a still and worthy surrender was part of her blood. Here was the end of her cord; she must fold her hands. She folded her hands. After all, she thought, what was death?

'It is to pass from the hardly known to the hardly unknown.' She quoted Lucretius. It was very dark all around her: the noises of distant outcries reached her dimly.

'Vix ignotum,' she repeated mechanically, and then the words: 'Surely it were better to pass from the world of unjust judges to sit with the mighty...'

A great burst of sound roamed, vivid and alive, from the distant stairhead. She started and cried out. Then there came the sound of feet hastily stepping the stair treads, coming upwards. A man was coming to lay hands upon her!

Then, suddenly she was running, breathing hard, filled with the fear of a man's touch. At last, in front of her was a pale, leaded window; she turned to the right; she was in a long corridor; she ran; it seemed that she ran for miles. She was gasping, 'For pity! for pity!' to the saints of heaven. She stayed to listen; there was a silence, then a voice in the distance. She listened and listened. The feet began to run again, the sole of one shoe struck the ground hard, the other scarcely sounded. She could not tell whether they came towards her or no. Then she began to run again, for it was certain now that they came towards her. As if at the sound of her own feet the footfalls came faster. Desperately, she lifted one foot and tore her shoe off, then the other. She half overbalanced, and catching at the arras to save herself, it fell with a rustling sound. She craved for darkness; when she ran there was a pale shimmer of night—but the aperture of an arch tempted her. She ran and sprang, upwards, in a very black, narrow stairway.

At the top there was—light! and the passage ended in a window. A great way off, a pine torch was stuck in a wall, a knave in armour sat on the floor beneath it—the heavy breathing was coming up the stairway. She crept on tiptoe across the passage to the curtains beside the casement.

Then a man was within touch of her hand, panting hard, and he stood still as if he were out of breath. His voice called in gasps to the knave at the end of the gallery:

'Ho...There...Simon!...Peter!...Hath one passed that way?'

The voice came back:

'No one! The King comes!'

He moved a step down the corridor and, as he was lifting the arras a little way away, she moved to peep through a crack in the curtain.

It was Throckmorton! The distant light glinted along his beard. At the slight movement she made he was agog to listen, so that his ears appeared to be pricked up. He moved swiftly back to cover the stairhead. In the distance, beneath the light, the groom was laying cards upon the floor between his parted legs.

Throckmorton whispered suddenly:

'I can hear thee breathe. Art near! Listen!'

She leant back against the wall and trembled.

'This seems like a treachery,' he whispered. 'It is none. Listen? There is little time! Do you hear me?'

She kept her peace.

'Do you hear me?' he asked. 'Before God, I am true to you.'

When still she did not speak he hissed with vexation and raised one hand above his head. He sank his forehead in swift meditation.

'Listen,' he said again. 'To take you I have only to tear down this arras. Do you hear?'

He bared his head once more and said aloud to himself,

'But perhaps she is even in the chapel.'

He stepped across the corridor, lifted a latch and looked in at double doors that were just beside her. Then, swiftly, he moved back once more to cover the stairhead.

'God! God! God!' she heard him mutter between his teeth.

'Listen!' he said again. 'Listen! listen! listen!' The words seemed to form part of an eager, hissed refrain. He was trembling with haste.

He began to press the arras, along the wall towards her, with his finger tips. Her breast sank with a sickening fall. Then, suddenly, he started back again; she could not understand why he did not come further—then she noticed that he was afraid, still, to leave the stairhead.

But why did he not call his men to him? He had a whole army at his back.

He was peering into the shadows—and something familiar in the poise of his head, his intent gaze, the line of his shoulders, as you may see a cat's outlined against a lighted doorway, filled her with an intense lust for revenge. This man had wormed himself into her presence: he was a traitor over and over again. And he had fooled her! He had made her believe that he was lover to her. He had made her believe, and he had fooled her. He had shown her letter to Privy Seal.

After the night in the cellar she had had the end of her crucifix sharpened till it was needle-pointed. She trembled with eagerness. This foul carrion beast had fooled her that he might get her more utterly in his power. For this he had brought her down. He would have her to himself—in some dungeon of Privy Seal's. Her fair hopes ended in this filth...

He was muttering:

'Listen if you be there! Before God, Katharine Howard, I am true to you. Listen! Listen!'

His hand shivered, turned against the light. He was hearkening to some distant sound. He was looking away.

She tore the arras aside and sprang at him with her hand on high. But, at the sharp sound of the tearing cloth, he started to one side and the needle point that should have pierced his face struck softly in at his shoulder or thereabouts. He gave a sharp hiss of pain...

She was wrestling with him then. One of his hands was hot across her mouth, the other held her throat.

'Oh fool!' his voice sounded. 'Bide you still.' He snorted with fury and held her to him. The embroidery on his chest scraped her knuckles as she tried to strike upwards at his face. Her crucifix had fallen. He strove to muffle her with his elbows, but with a blind rage of struggle she freed her wrists and, in the darkness, struck where she thought his mouth would be.

Then his hand over her mouth loosened and set free her great scream. It rang down the corridor and seemed to petrify his grasp upon her. His fingers loosened—and again she was running, bent forward, crying out, in a vast thirst for mere flight.

As she ran, a red patch before her eyes, distant and clear beneath the torch, took the form of the King. Her cries were still loud, but they died in her throat...

He was standing still with his fingers in his ears.

'Dear God,' she cried, 'they have laid hands upon me. They have laid hands upon me.' And she pressed her fingers hard across her throat as if to wipe away the stain of Throckmorton's touch.

The King lifted his fingers from his ears.

'Bones of Jago,' he cried, 'what new whimsy is this?'

'They have laid hands upon me,' she cried and fell upon her knees.

'Why,' he said, 'here is a day nightmare. I know all your tale of a letter. Come now, pretty one. Up, pretty soul.' He bent over benevolently and stroked her hand.

'These dark passages are frightening to maids. Up now, pretty. I was thinking of thee.

'Who the devil shall harm thee?' he muttered again. 'This is mine own house. Come, pray with me. Prayer is a very soothing thing. I was bound to pray. I pray ever at nightfall. Up now. Come—pray, pray, pray!'

His heavy benevolence for a moment shed a calmness upon the place. She rose, and pressing back the hair from her forehead, saw the long, still corridor, the guard beneath the torch, the doors of the chapel.

She said to herself pitifully: 'What comes next?' She was too wearied to move again.

Suddenly the King said:

'Child, you did well to come to me, when you came in the stables.'

She leaned against the tapestry upon the wall to listen to him.

'It is true,' he admitted, 'that you have men that hate you and your house. The Bishop of Winchester did show me a letter you wrote. I do pardon it in you. It was well written.'

'Ah,' she uttered wearily, 'so you say now. But you shall change your mind ere morning.'

'Body of God, no,' he answered. 'My mind is made up concerning you. Let us call a truce to these things. It is my hour for prayer. Let us go to pray.'

Knowing how this King's mind would change from hour to hour, she had little hope in his words. Nevertheless slowly it came into her mind that if she were ever to act, now that he was in the mood was the very hour. But she knew nothing of the coil in which she now was. Yet without the King she could do nothing; she was in the hands of other men: of Throckmorton, of Privy Seal, of God knew whom.

'Sir,' she said, 'at the end of this passage stood a man.'

The King looked past her into the gloom.

'He stands there still,' he said. 'He is tying his arm with a kerchief. He looks like one Throckmorton.'

'Then, if he have not run,' she said. 'Call him here. He has had my knife in his arm. He holds a letter of mine.'

His neck stiffened suddenly.

'You have been writing amorous epistles?' he muttered.

'God knows there was naught of love,' she answered. 'Do you bid him unpouch it.' She closed her eyes; she was done with this matter.

Henry called:

'Ho, you, approach!' and as through the shadows Throckmorton's shoes clattered on the boards he held out a thickly gloved hand. Throckmorton made no motion to put anything into it, and the King needs must speak.

'This lady's letter,' he muttered.

Throckmorton bowed his head.

'Privy Seal holdeth it,' he answered.

'You are all of a make,' the King said gloomily. 'Can no woman write a letter but what you will be of it?'

'Sir,' Throckmorton said, 'this lady would have Privy Seal down.'

'Well, she shall have him down,' the King threatened him. 'And thee! and all of thy train!'

'I do lose much blood,' Throckmorton answered. 'Pray you let me finish the binding of my arm.'

He took between his teeth one end of his kerchief and the other in his right hand, and pulled and knotted with his head bent.

'Make haste!' the King grumbled. 'Here! Lend room.' And himself he took one end of the knot and pulled it tight, breathing heavily.

'Now speak,' he said. 'I am not one made for the healing of cripples.'

Throckmorton brushed the black blood from the furs on his sleeve, using his gloves.

'Sir,' he said, 'I am in pain and my knees tremble, because I have lost much blood. I were more minded to take to my pallet. Nevertheless, I am a man that do bear no grudge, being rather a very proper man, and one intent to do well to my country and its Lord.'

'Sir,' the King said, 'if you are minded to speak ill of this lady you had best had no mouth.'

Throckmorton fell upon one knee.

'Grant me the boon to be her advocate,' he said. 'And let me speak swiftly, for Privy Seal shall come soon and the Bishop of Winchester.'

'Ass that you are,' the King said, 'fetch me a stool from the chapel, that I may not stand all the day.'

Throckmorton ran swiftly to the folding doors.

'—Winchester comes,' he said hurriedly, when he returned.

The King sat himself gingerly down upon the three-legged stool, balancing himself with his legs wide apart. A dark face peered from the folding doors: a priest's shape came out from them.

'Cousin of Winchester,' the King called, 'bide where you be.'

He had the air of a man hardly intent on what the spy could say. He had already made up his mind as to what he himself was to say to Katharine.

'Sir,' Throckmorton said, 'this lady loves you well, and most well she loveth your Highness' daughter. Most well, therefore, doth she hate Privy Seal. I, as your Highness knoweth, have for long well loved Privy Seal. Now I love others better—the common weal and your great and beneficent Highness. As I have told your Highness, this Lady Katharine hath laboured very heartily to bring the Lady Mary to love you. But that might not be. Now, your Highness being minded to give to these your happy realms a lasting peace, was intent that the Lady Mary should write a letter, very urgently, to your Highness' foes urging them to make a truce with this realm, so that your Highness might cast out certain evil men and then better purge this realm of certain false doctrines.'

Amazement, that was almost a horror, made Katharine open wide the two hands that hung at her side.

'You!' she cried to the King. 'You would have that letter written?'

He looked at her with a heavy astonishment.

'Wherefore not?' he asked.

'My God! my God!' she said. 'And I have suffered!'

Her first feeling of horror at this endless plot hardly gave way to relief. She had been used as a tool; she had done the work. But she had been betrayed.

'Aye, would I have the letter written,' the King said. 'What could better serve my turn? Would I not have mine enemies stay their arming against me?'

'Then I have written your letter,' she said bitterly. 'That is why I should be gaoled.'

The King's look of heavy astonishment did not leave him.

'Why, sweetheart, shalt be made a countess,' he said. 'Y' have done more in this than I or any man could do with my daughter.'

'Wherefore, then, should this man have gaoled me?' Katharine asked.

The King turned his heavy gaze upon Throckmorton. The big man's eyes had a sunny and devious smile.

'Sir,' he said, 'this is a subtle conceit of mine, since I am a subtle man. If I am set a task I do it ever in mine own way. Here there was a task...

'Pray you let me sit upon the floor!' he craved. 'My legs begin to fail.'

The King made a small motion with his hand, and the great man, letting himself down by one hand against the arras, leaned back his head and stretched his long legs half across the corridor.

'In ten minutes Privy Seal shall be here with the letter,' he said. 'My head swims, but I will be brief.'

He closed his eyes and passed his hand across his forehead.

'I do a task ever in mine own way,' he began again. 'Here am I. Here is Privy Seal. Your Highness is minded to know what passes in the mind of Privy Seal. Well: I am Privy Seal's servant. Now, if I am to come at the mind of Privy Seal, I must serve him well. In this thing I might seem to serve him main well. Listen...'

He cleared his throat and then spoke again.

'Your Highness would have this letter written by the Lady Mary. That, with the help of this fair dame, was a thing passing easy. But neither your Highness nor Privy Seal knew the channel through which these letters passed. Yet I discovered it. Now, think I to myself: here is a secret for which Privy Seal would give his head. Therefore, how better may I ingratiate myself with Privy Seal than by telling him this same fine secret?'

'Oh, devil!' Katharine Howard called out. 'Who was Judas to thee?'

Throckmorton raised his head, and winked upwards at her.

'It was a fine device?' he asked. 'Why, I am a subtle man...Do you not see?' he said. 'The King's Highness would have me keep the confidence of Privy Seal that I may learn out his secrets. How better should I keep that confidence than by seeming to betray your secret to Privy Seal?

'It was very certain,' he added, 'that Privy Seal should give a warrant to gaol your la'ship. But it was still more certain that the King's Highness should pardon you. Therefore no bones should have been broken. And I did come myself to take you to a safe place, and to enlighten you as to the comedy.'

'Oh, Judas, Judas,' she cried.

'Could you but have trusted me,' he said reproachfully, 'you had spared yourself a mad canter and me a maimed arm.'

'Why, you have done well,' the King said heavily. 'But you speak this lady too saucily.'

He was in a high and ponderous good humour, but he stayed to reflect for a moment, with his head on one side, to see what he had gained.

'This letter is written,' he said. 'But Cromwell holdeth it. How, then, has it profited me?'

'Why,' Throckmorton said, 'Privy Seal shall come to bring the letter to your Highness; your Highness shall deliver it to me; I to the cook; the cook to the ambassador; the ambassador to the kings. And so the kings shall be prayed, by your daughter, whom they heed, to stay all unfriendly hands against your Highness.'

'You are a shrewd fellow,' the King said.

'I have a shrewd ache in the head,' the spy answered. 'If you would give me a boon, let me begone.'

The King got stiffly up from his stool, and, bracing his feet firmly, gave the spy one hand. The tall man shook upon his legs.

'Why, I have done well!' he said, smiling. 'Now Privy Seal shall take me for his very bedfellow, until it shall please your Highness to deal with him for good and all.'

He went, waveringly, along the corridor, brushing the hangings with his shoulder.

Katharine stood out before the King.

'Now I will get me gone,' she said. 'This is no place for me.'

He surveyed her amiably, resting his hands on his red-clothed thighs as he sat his legs akimbo on his stool.

'Why, it is main cold here,' he said. 'But bide a short space.'

'I am not made for courts,' she answered.

'We will go pray anon,' he quieted her, with his hand stretched out. 'Give me a space for meditation, I am not yet in the mood for prayer.'

She pleaded, 'Let me begone.'

'Body of God,' he said good-humouredly. 'It is fitting that at this time that you do pray. You have escaped a great peril. But I am wont to drive away earthly passions ere I come before the Throne of grace.'

'Sir,' she pleaded more urgently, 'the night draws near. Before morning I would be upon my road to Calais.'

He looked at her interestedly, and questioned in a peremptory voice:

'Upon what errand? I have heard of no journeying of yours.'

'I am not made for courts,' she repeated.

He said: 'Anan?' with a sudden, half-comprehending anger, and she quailed.

'I will get me gone to Calais,' she uttered. 'And then to a nunnery. I am not for this world.'

He uttered a tremendous: 'Body of God,' and repeated it four times.

He sprang to his feet and she shrank against the wall. His eyes rolled in his great head, and suddenly he shouted:

'Ungrateful child. Ungrateful!' Then he lost words; his swollen brow moved up and down. She was afraid to speak again.

Then, suddenly, with a light and brushing step, the Lord Privy Seal was coming towards them. His sagacious eyes looked from one to the other, his lips moved with their sideways motion.

'Fiend,' the King uttered. 'Give me the letter and get thee out of earshot.' And whilst Cromwell was bending before his person, he continued: 'I have pardoned this lady. I would have you both clasp hands.'

Cromwell's mouth fell open for a minute.

'Your Highness knoweth the contents?' he asked. And by then he appeared as calm as when he asked a question about the price of chalk at Calais.

'My Highness knoweth!' Henry said friendlily. He crumpled the letter in his hand, and then, remembering its use, moved to put it in his own pouch. 'This lady has done very well to speak to me who am the fountainhead of power.'

'Get thee out of earshot,' he repeated. 'I have things as to which I would admonish this lady.'

'Your Highness knoweth...' Privy Seal began again, then his eye fell upon Winchester, who still stayed by the chapel door at the far end of the corridor. He threw up his hands.

'Sir,' he said. 'Traitors have come to you!'

Gardiner, indeed, was gliding towards them, drawn, in spite of all prudence, by his invincible hatred.

The King watched the pair of them with his crafty eyes, deep seated in his head.

'It is certain that no traitors have come to me,' he uttered gently; and to Cromwell: 'You have a nose for them.'

He appeared placable and was very quiet.

Winchester, his black eyes glaring with desire, was almost upon them in the shadows.

'Here is enough of wrangling,' Henry said. He appeared to meditate, and then uttered: 'As well here as elsewhere.'

'Sir,' Gardiner said, 'if Privy Seal misleads me, I have somewhat to say of Privy Seal.'

'Cousin of Winchester,' Henry answered. 'Stretch out your hand, I would have you end your tulzies in this place.'

Winchester, bringing out his words with a snake's coldness, seemed to whisper:

'Your Highness did promise that Privy Seal should make me amends.'

'Why, Privy Seal shall make amends,' the King answered. 'It was his man that did miscall thee. Therefore, Privy Seal shall come to dine with thee, and shall, in the presence of all men, hold out to thee his hand.'

'Let him come, then, with great state,' the bishop stuck to his note.

'Aye, with a great state,' the King answered. 'I will have an end to these quarrels.'

He set his hand cordially upon Privy Seal's shoulder.

'For thee,' he said, 'I would have thee think between now and the assembling of the Parliaments of what title thou wilt have to an earldom.'

Cromwell fell upon one knee, and, in Latin, made three words of a speech of thanks.

'Why, good man,' the King said, 'art a man very valuable to me.' His eyes rested upon Katharine for a moment. 'I am well watched for by one and the other of you,' he went on. 'Each of you by now has brought me a letter of this lady's.'

Katharine cried out at Gardiner:

'You too!'

His eyes sought the ground, and then looked defiantly into hers.

'You did threaten me!' he said doggedly. 'I was minded to be betimes.'

'Why, end it all, now and here,' the King said. 'Here is a folly with a silly wench in it.'

'Here was a treason that I would show your Highness,' the Bishop said doggedly.

'Sirs,' the King said. He touched his bonnet: 'God in His great mercy has seen fit much to trouble me. But here are troubles that I may end. Now I have ended them all. If this lady would not have her cousin to murder a cardinal, God, she would not. There are a plenty others to do that work.'

He pressed one hand on Cromwell's chest and pushed him backwards gently.

'Get thee gone, now,' he said, 'out of earshot. I shall speak with thee soon.—And you!' he added to Winchester.

'Body of God, Body of God,' he muttered beneath his breath, as they went, 'very soon now I can rid me of these knaves,' and then, suddenly, he blared upon Katharine:

'Thou seest how I am plagued and would'st leave me. Before the Most High God, I swear thou shalt not.'

She fell upon her knees.

'With each that speaks, I find a new traitor to me,' she said. 'Let me begone.'

He threatened her with one hand.

'Wench,' he said, 'I have had better converse with thee than with man or child this several years. Thinkest thou I will let thee go?'

She began to sob:

'What rest may I have? What rest?'

He mocked her:

'What rest may I have? What rest? My nights are full of evil dreams! God help me. Have I offered thee foul usage? Have I pursued thee with amorous suits?'

She said pitifully:

'You had better have done that than set me amongst these plotters.'

'I have never seen a woman so goodly to look upon as thou art,' he answered.

She covered her face with her hands, but he pulled them apart and gazed at it.

'Child,' he said, 'I will cherish thee as I would a young lamb. Shalt have Cromwell's head; shalt have Winchester in what gaol thou wilt when I have used them.'

She put her fingers in her ears.

'For pity,' she whispered. 'Let me begone.'

'Why,' he reasoned with her, 'I cannot let thee have Cromwell down before he has called this Parliament. There is no man like him for calling of truckling Parliaments. And, rest assured,' he uttered solemnly, 'that that man dies that comes between thee and me from this day on.'

'Let me begone,' she said wearily. 'Let me begone. I am afraid to look upon these happenings.'

'Look then upon nothing,' he answered. 'Stay you by my daughter's side. Even yet you shall win for me her obedience. If you shall earn the love of the dear saints, I will much honour you and set you on high before all the land.'

She said:

'For pity, for pity. Here is a too great danger for my soul.'

'Never, never,' he answered. 'You shall live closed in. No man shall speak with you but only I. You shall be as you were in a cloister. An you will, you shall have great wealth. Your house shall be advanced; your father close his eyes in honour and estate. None shall walk before you in the land.'

She said: 'No. No.'

'See you,' he said. 'This world goes very wearily with me. I am upon a make of husbandry that bringeth little joy. I have no rest, no music, no corner to hide in save in thy converse and the regard of thy countenance.'

He paused to search her face with his narrow eyes.

'God knows that the Queen there is is no wife of mine,' he said slowly. 'If thou wilt wait till the accomplished time...'

She said:

'No, no!' and her voice had an urgent sharpness.

She stretched out both her hands, being still upon her knees. Her fair face worked convulsively, her lips moved, and her hood, falling away from her brows, showed her hair that had golden glints.

'For pity let me go,' she moaned. 'For pity.'

He answered:

'When I renounce my kingdom and my life!'

From opposite ends of the gallery Winchester and Cromwell watched them with intent and winking eyes.

'Let us go pray,' the King said. 'For now I am in the mood.'

She got upon her legs wearily, and, for a moment, took his hand to steady herself.

Ford Madox Ford was born Ford Hermann Hueffer on 17th December 1873 in Wimbledon, London, England, to Catherine Madox Brown and Francis Hueffer. He was the eldest of three. His father, who became the music critic for The Times, was German and his mother English. He was named after his maternal grandfather, the Pre-Raphaelite painter Ford Madox Brown.

In 1889, after the death of his father, Ford and his brother, Oliver, went to live with their grandfather in London.

Ford later graduated from the University College School in London, but never went on to attend university.

In 1894, Ford eloped with his girlfriend from school Elsie Martindale. The couple were married in Gloucester and moved to Bonnington. By 1901, they had moved on to Winchelsea with their two daughters, Christina (1897) and Katharine (1900). Ford's neighbors in Winchelsea included the authors Henry James and H.G. Wells.

Ford collaborated with Joseph Conrad on three novels; The Inheritors (1901), Romance (1903) and The Nature of a Crime (published in 1924 but written much earlier). Ford would later complain that with Conrad, and indeed all his collaborators, his contribution was overshadowed by theirs.

In 1904, Ford suffered an agoraphobic breakdown due to increasing financial and marital problems. He travelled to Germany to spend time with family there and undergo treatment.

Among Ford's classic works are The Fifth Queen trilogy (1906–1908). These were historical novels based on the life of Catherine Howard, which Conrad, at the time, called 'the swan song of historical romance.'

In 1908, Ford founded The English Review. Within its pages he published works by and promoted the careers of Thomas Hardy, H. G. Wells, Joseph Conrad, Henry James, May Sinclair, John Galsworthy and William Butler Yeats; and debuted works by Ezra Pound, Wyndham Lewis, D. H. Lawrence and Norman Douglas.

Ford also wrote some outstanding poetry during his career. In the early decades of the century Ezra Pound and other Modernist poets in London valued his poetry for its treatment of modern subjects in contemporary diction as they sought to gain traction for their ideas.

Perhaps his most well-known work is The Good Soldier which was published in 1915. The story is set just before the carnage of WWI and narrates the tragic expatriate lives of both a British and an American couple using intricate flashbacks.

Ford was involved in British war propaganda as World War I ferociously unfolded across Europe. Among his colleagues were Arnold Bennett, G. K. Chesterton, John Galsworthy, Hilaire Belloc and Gilbert Murray. In his time there he wrote two propaganda books; When Blood is Their Argument: An Analysis of Prussian Culture (1915), with the help of Richard Aldington, and Between St Dennis and St George: A Sketch of Three Civilizations (1915).

Shortly after finishing the books he decided to enlist for the front line. He was 41 but accepted into the Welch Regiment on 30th July 1915.

Ford's poem Antwerp (1915) was praised by T.S. Eliot as "the only good poem I have met with on the subject of the war".

Ford's experiences both on the front line in France and his previous propaganda activities provided rich seams of experience for his later four volume work Parade's End, set before, during and after World War I in England and the Front line.

Ford had used the name of Ford Madox Hueffer, but, after World War I, thinking it sounded too Germanic and a probable hinderance to his career, changed it to Ford Madox Ford in 1919.

Romantic complications for Ford were something of a speciality and during his life he embarked on several affairs. Between 1918 and 1927 he lived with Stella Bowen, an Australian artist twenty years his junior. In 1920 they had a daughter together, Julia Madox Ford.

In 1924, he founded The Transatlantic Review, a journal with great influence on modern literature. Staying with the artistic community in the Latin Quarter of Paris, Ford befriended James Joyce, Ernest Hemingway, Gertrude Stein, Ezra Pound and Jean Rhys, all of whom he would publish.

Jean Rhys was initially of interest to Ford because, as she was born in the West Indies, she had, he declared, 'a terrifying insight and ... passion for stating the case of the underdog, she has let her pen loose on the Left Banks of the Old World'. It was also Ford who said she should change her name from Ella Williams to Jean Rhys.

At the time her husband was in jail for what Rhys described as 'currency irregularities' and so it seemed perfectly reasonable that she move in with Ford and Stella. In such close proximity they began an affair which would later end acrimoniously.

In Hemingway's Parisian memoir A Moveable Feast he describes a meeting with Ford at a café in the early 1920s. His description of Ford; 'as upright as an ambulatory, well clothed, up-ended hogshead.'

In reviewing his collaboration with Joseph Conrad, Ford said 'he disowns me now that he has become better known than I am. I helped Joseph Conrad, I helped Hemingway. I helped a dozen, a score of writers, and many of them have beaten me. I'm now an old man and I'll die without making a name like Hemingway.' At this Ford began to sob. Then he began to cry.

In the summer of 1927, Ford had moved to Avignon in France to convert a mill into both a home and a workshop. He called it 'Le Vieux Moulin'.

In 1929, he published The English Novel: From the Earliest Days to the Death of Joseph Conrad, a brisk and accessible overview of the history of English novels.

Ford spent the last years of his life teaching at Olivet College in Olivet, Michigan.

During his career Ford wrote dozens of novels as well as essays, poetry, memoirs and literary criticism. But as he himself said his works were overshadowed by those who found fame an easier friend. Today he is well-regarded but known only for a few works rather than the grand arc of his career.

Ford Madox Ford died on 26th June 1939 at Deauville, France at the age of 65.

The Shifting of the Fire, as H. Ford Hueffer (1892)
The Brown Owl, as H. Ford Hueffer (1892)
The Queen Who Flew: A Fairy Tale (1894)
The Cinque Ports (1900)
The Inheritors: An Extravagant Story, Joseph Conrad and Ford M. Hueffer (1901)
Rossetti (1902)
Romance, Joseph Conrad and Ford M. (1903)
The Benefactor (1905)
The Soul of London (1905)
The Heart of the Country (1906)
The Fifth Queen (Part One of The Fifth Queen trilogy) (1906)
Privy Seal (Part Two of The Fifth Queen trilogy) (1907)
An English Girl (1907)
The Fifth Queen Crowned (Part Three of The Fifth Queen trilogy) (1908)
Mr Apollo (1908)
The Half Moon (1909)
A Call (1910)
The Portrait (1910)
The Critical Attitude, as Ford Madox Hueffer (1911)
The Simple Life Limited, as Daniel Chaucer (1911)
Ladies Whose Bright Eyes (1911) (extensively revised in 1935)
The Panel (1912)
The New Humpty Dumpty, as Daniel Chaucer (1912)
Henry James (1913)
Mr Fleight (1913)
The Young Lovell (1913)
Antwerp (eight-page poem) (1915)
Henry James, A Critical Study (1915).
Between St Dennis and St George (1915)
The Good Soldier (1915)
Zeppelin Nights, with Violet Hunt (1915)
The Marsden Case (1923)
Women and Men (1923)
Mr Bosphorous (1923)
The Nature of a Crime, with Joseph Conrad (1924)
Joseph Conrad, A Personal Remembrance (1924)
Some Do Not . . . (1924)
No More Parades (1925)
A Man Could Stand Up (1926)
A Mirror To France (1926)
New York is Not America (1927)
New York Essays, Rudge (1927)
New Poems (1927)

Last Post (1928)
A Little Less Than Gods (1928)
No Enemy (1929)
The English Novel: From the Earliest Days to the Death of Joseph Conrad (One Hour Series) (1929)
The English Novel (1930)
Return to Yesterday (1932)
When the Wicked Man (1932)
The Rash Act (1933)
It Was the Nightingale (1933)
Henry for Hugh (1934)
Provence, Unwin, 1935.
Ladies Whose Bright Eyes (revised version) (1935)
Portraits from Life: Memories and Criticism of Henry James, Joseph Conrad, Thomas Hardy, H.G. Wells, Stephen Crane, D.H. Lawrence, John Galsworthy, Ivan Turgenev, W.H. Hudson, Theodore Dreiser, A.C. Swinburne (1937)
Great Trade Route (1937)
Vive Le Roy (1937)
The March of Literature (1938)

www.ingramcontent.com/pod-product-compliance
Lightning Source LLC
Chambersburg PA
CBHW071945170626
46813CB00005B/1830